MW00414792

THE MARSHAL'S PROMISE

A CRIMSON ROSE NOVEL BOOK 1

CATHRYN CHANDLER

FIVE SISTERS PUBLISHING

Cover Art: carrie@cheekycovers.com

Proofreading Service: Heather Belleguelle of Behest Indie Novelist
Services

❀ Created with Vellum

BOOKS BY CATHRYN CHANDLER

The Circle of Friends Series:

Believing in Dreams (Maggie & Ian)

Believing in Love (Beth & John)

Believing in Promises (Abby & Cade)

Only One Dream (Lillian & Charles)

Only One Love (Rayne & Tremain)

Only One Promise (Shannon & Luke)

Only One Beginning (Dina & Cook)

Box Sets:

The Believing In Series

The Only One Series

The Crimson Rose Novels:

The Marshal's Promise (Dorrie & Jules)

The Rancher's Dream (Coming in June, 2018)

Loving Amelia (Coming in August, 2018)

Be the first to receive notification of new releases. Subscribe to the mailing list here:

http://eepurl.com/bLBOtX

1

U S Marshal Jules McKenzie turned in his saddle and looked over at the heavily bearded deputy trailing along behind him.

"You're sure this is the place?"

"That's what the conductor said, Marshal. He saw them rolling in the grass when he looked out the window."

The marshal's deep-blue eyes narrowed as he studied the train track and the sharp curve it took to go around the deep gully that ran along to their left. He gauged the bend in the tracks before turning to study the trees growing in a group just a quarter-mile off. His thick dark hair stirred under a gentle breeze as he sat on top of the large stallion and considered the area around them.

"It's a good spot," he finally said. "It would have to slow down for the curve." He raised a gloved hand and pointed at the trees in the distance. "And has some cover."

The deputy, who was a good decade older than Jules twenty-nine years, pulled his horse to a stop and twisted his body around to see where the marshal was pointing.

"Cover for what?"

"Unless you think they walked away, those two men had help." Jules made another visual sweep of the ground. It was the perfect place to jump off a train, taking the Wells Fargo cash box with them, and leaving behind one dead bank guard.

The conductor hadn't thought to check the baggage car until after the train had pulled into San Francisco, which is where the city sheriff had contacted one of the two US Marshals in town. Jules was one, and his older brother, Cade, was the other.

Since Cade was off on official business with a federal judge, Jules had drawn the task of investigating what had happened to the bank's money. And their guard.

Jules swung a long leg over the back of his tall stallion, using a single stirrup to step to the ground. He glanced over at the deputy.

"Let's have a look, Frank."

The two men spent the next twenty minutes quartering the area around the tracks. About halfway around the curve, Jules found what he was looking for. There were deep gouges in the earth, along with a swath of flattened grass. He followed it out and away from the tracks until he saw two pairs of boot prints in the soft ground.

"Over here," he called out, his gaze glued to the ground as he tracked the men for another twenty yards. There he stopped and squatted down, grunting when Frank came up beside him. He pointed to the patch of churned-up dirt in front of him. "Here. The boot prints disappear but there're three sets of hooves here."

Frank knelt beside him and put his nose close to the ground. "Sure looks like it. One of those horses has two crooked shoes."

Jules leaned over to get a better look at what Frank was

pointing at. *There's a mistake*, Jules thought as he studied the tracks. Now all he had to do was find a horse with two crooked shoes, and he'd have his robber-turned-killer.

Frank stood. "It's getting dark, Marshal."

The younger man looked up at the sky then nodded. "We'll make camp over near that tree line and head back at first light."

The two men found a dry level spot, and with an efficiency born from many hours of practice, had camp set up and their supper consumed in less than an hour. By the time they'd finished, night had descended on the open country, its inky darkness only broken by the light from their small campfire. Since Frank had volunteered to take the first watch, Jules rolled out his blanket, using his saddle for a pillow. He settled onto his hard makeshift bed and stacked his hands behind his head as he gazed up at the stars. The three men had robbed the train and killed a guard for a few hundred dollars. It wasn't a small sum of money, but it wasn't worth taking a man's life over either. Jules shook his head at the stupidity of it.

Knowing his turn to stand watch would come soon enough, Jules tipped his hat down over his face. As always, a pair of deep-brown eyes which always shone with a quiet warmth, floated into his mind. He used to banish them the minute they appeared, but he'd given up on that a couple of years ago. He'd finally decided that as long as he kept it to himself, it hurt no one to see her in his dreams.

And she helped him sleep.

2

"It's good to see you, Ethan."

Jules gave the tall dark-haired man a hard slap on the back before he pulled him into a one-armed hug. He laughed when his childhood friend shoved him back.

"Good to see you too, Jules. But from more of a distance."

After he got in another back slap, both for good measure and because he enjoyed annoying his visitor, Jules inclined his head toward the other man standing next to Ethan and grinned.

"I guess all that roaming about in the Northwest Territory hasn't changed his disposition much."

"Fancy word for saying a man's not too friendly." Robbie Smith shrugged when Ethan pinned him with an unblinking stare. "See what I mean?"

"He used to be friendly enough." Jules' blue eyes gleamed as he stepped back and gave Ethan the once-over. The two men were just over the same six-foot height, that went with their long legs and rugged builds. Since Jules' hair had grown darker as he'd gotten older, he was now within a couple of shades of the same dark sable color as Ethan's, although Jules still had his blue eyes while Ethan's were a deep-brown. "I wonder what he's done that's made him so prickly? Maybe I should arrest him."

Robbie grinned. "It isn't what he's done so much as what he hasn't done." He danced back a quick step when the tall, solidly built Ethan's eyes narrowed even more.

Knowing that Robbie tended to poke bears even though it was never a good idea, Jules decided that was all the teasing Ethan would stand for, no matter how good-natured, or well-intentioned, his friends were.

"Let's go into my study and enjoy a cigar and drink." Jules led the way down the hall to a cozy-sized room located at the far end. The wood used for the bookcases and desk gleamed with a rich and dark color, while the two chairs clustered together were covered in leather with just enough stuffing to keep a man comfortable. It was clearly a refuge from the quiet pastels that were prominent in the rest of the home he shared with his brother, sister-in-law, and their two children.

"A drink, anyway. Abby's made it clear to all of us that she isn't too fond of anyone smoking in her house." Robbie walked over to one of the chairs placed in front of the desk and plopped into it. He set his hat on the floor beside him and ran a hand through his thick blond hair. Tall and lean, he looked like the rancher he was as he stretched his legs out in front of him and propped one booted ankle over the other.

Ethan's mouth twitched. "You'd seem all grown up if it weren't for that pretty face of yours."

Robbie frowned. He still had the boyish good looks that had carried him through most of his childhood pranks with little more than a scolding. "Better than that prickly face you're so fond of. Won't attract many women with that brush you're wearing."

Ethan's hand rubbed across a bearded cheek. "I'm not looking to attract a woman. But I'm getting the idea that you're looking hard for one." He gave the rancher a knowing smile. "In the mood to take a wife?"

Robbie's hand instantly shot out as if he were warding off an attack. "Whoa. No. Not a wife. I'm looking for a cook. The men need more variety than Shue's meals."

His current cook had been a long-time friend and resident on the ranch Ethan's sister, Shannon, and her husband, Luke, owned that was a two-day ride from Robbie's new spread.

"Shue told you she'd keep you in plain hot food. Nothing more and nothing less, as I recall."

"That she did, Ethan. And the fact is, it's good enough. But she's not too keen on doing so much of it. She says it doesn't leave her enough time to hunt, or pan the streams for gold, though lord knows why she thinks she'd find any so far from the mountains."

Jules leaned back in his chair behind his desk and enjoyed listening to the banter between two of the best friends a man could have. It made him smile to have the three of them here together in his house again. With Robbie busy on the ranch he managed for Lillian, who was another of their honorary aunts, and Ethan always tracking down men for John's investigation business, or delivering horses from his sister's ranch, they'd rarely been together at the same time and in the same place. At least not for the last five years or so. That's when Ethan had started taking long trips away from home, and Robbie had settled in at the old ranch that Lillian had originally built as a haven for orphans.

The three men had a whole passel of honorary aunts, uncles, and cousins they all considered family, although only a few of them were blood relations. They were a family by choice, started by two remarkable women, Lillian and Maggie, who'd become fast friends during the gold rush days twenty years ago. Jules and his older brother, Cade, had joined the family when his brother had married Dr. Abagail Metler, Lillian's cousin who'd come out to San Francisco to practice medicine.

Jules grinned. His sister-in-law had been disappointed when he'd chosen to follow his brother's footsteps and become a US Marshal, rather than a doctor. But maybe she'd have better luck with her own son and daughter.

"What's so funny?" Robbie demanded. "You're grinning like you think Ethan's insults aren't fighting words."

"They're more truth than insult," Jules said calmly. "And you don't fight unless you're backed into a corner." He glanced over at Ethan. "If you're through taking your shots at Robbie, care to tell us what brings you into town?"

"John asked me to stop by to see Charles every few weeks if I was around."

Charles Jamison was Lillian's husband. A gambler who'd come to make his fortune at the tables in the rowdy gold-fueled town of twenty years ago. His gambling hall, The Crimson Rose, was still one of the most frequented spots in the city. But now it was being fed by the silver found in the mountains to the east, rather than gold.

Robbie leaned forward in his chair. "Why?"

"I don't know. But John came out to the ranch a couple of weeks ago. He spent a long time talking to my sister and brother-in-law, but all he told me was that he hoped I'd stick around for a while, and to stop in and see Charles. He said he'd be sending a message through the telegraph office to Charles when he had a job he needed done."

Now Jules leaned forward too. "He said *when* he had a job, not *if* he had one?"

Ethan nodded. "And he seemed worried, too."

Robbie and Jules exchanged a glance. Very little disturbed John. Although he'd been born into a wealthy shipping family on the East Coast, he'd always claimed he'd never liked sailing, and had started his own investigation business. At first he'd only been dealing with thefts from his family's company, but had quickly taken on other clients until it had grown into a thriving concern. Davis Investigations now boasted many kinds of customers. Including the kind who needed a dangerous job done. Which were generally the ones that Ethan took on.

Jules worried about that, and his friend who was doing them. But since being a marshal wasn't the safest occupation to take up either, he didn't have a lot of room to question Ethan's choice of jobs.

"If John is worried, it must be something bad." Robbie frowned. "Did you ask him about it?"

"Sure did. He said it was an old problem, and he needed to go look into it."

"That's it? Just an old problem?"

"Robbie, I asked. That's all he said. There wasn't much else I could do about that." Ethan blew out a breath. "I tried prying it out of Shannon, but my sister was as close-mouthed as John. So was Luke."

Jules scratched his chin. "Well, whatever it is, we won't hear about it until they're good and ready to let us know." He relaxed back into his chair. "Not that I'm unhappy to see you, Ethan, but are you going to get around to telling us what brought you into town?"

"Your business." When Jules raised an eyebrow, Ethan nodded. "Have you heard of that Green Gang who's been robbing federal payrolls up in the Northwest?"

The question surprised Jules. He hadn't seen Ethan in months. How did his friend happen to know about the pack of outlaws he'd not only just heard of, but suspected he'd run up against for the first time a few weeks ago?

"I have. Did you pick up word on them when you were up north?"

"Delivered some horses to Fort Gaston. The captain there told me about them. It seems their payroll was late because the paymaster was on his way to the fort when he was robbed and left for dead."

Jules listened intently. He'd received word of that, but at least that paymaster had survived. The guard on the new train service from Sacramento hadn't been so lucky.

"Did the captain have anything else to say?"

Ethan smiled. "The paymaster did. He said there were three men. Their voices were muffled by the bandannas across their faces, but he remembered that they weren't too big, and at least a couple of them had green eyes. He could see that much."

"Is that a fact." Jules mulled that over for a moment.

"I went out to take a look around the place where he said it happened. That's why I'm here talking with you." Ethan's brown eyes went flat. "Found it easily enough. Four sets of tracks at the ambush site. But only three sets heading out to the south. One of those horses has two crooked shoes. Left front hoof and the right back one."

"That's kind of begging to be caught, isn't it?" Robbie shifted in his chair. "I won't ask if you followed them, since that would be a stupid question for a tracker. Did they go inland or turn for the coast?"

Jules didn't consider either prospect a good one. Robbie's ranch was nearer the coast, while Ethan's family was located more inland.

"Inland." Ethan rested his elbows on his knees. "They were in a hurry or I would have caught up with them. But it looked like they were headed for the gold fields."

"Or the train out of Sacramento."

Both Ethan and Robbie stared at the man sitting behind the desk. He nodded back at them. "I've been looking for three men since a guard was discovered dead in the baggage car of a train a couple of weeks ago. The cash box was missing. Wasn't much in it, but it was enough to keep them in supplies for a while." He leaned back in his chair and heaved a long breath. "When I questioned the passengers, several of them mentioned that two men had left their car and never returned. I figured those two killed the guard and jumped the train where a third man had the horses."

"Was the cash box going to an army camp?" Ethan asked.

"No. It was a Wells Fargo shipment." Jules saw the question in his friend's eyes. "I know this gang has only been robbing the military, but now I'm thinking they've widened their reach. Took a man out to where the train conductor said he saw them, and the train would have been moving the slowest." He sent a pointed look to Ethan. "Saw the gouges where they likely threw the cash box and then jumped off the train themselves. There was a set of horse tracks nearby. Ground was soft. It was easy to spot the two crooked shoes."

"If they're changing their targets, they could easily attack a ranch during the day when most of the hands are out looking after the stock." Robbie's jaw hardened as he clenched his teeth.

Ethan nodded. "Which is why I stopped at Tremain's place on the way here. He and Rayne are the most isolated on that horse ranch of theirs, and too close to those tracks I was following for my peace of mind."

"Those fancy horses they raise are worth a lot of money," Robbie observed, his frown an exact match to Ethan's.

"But hard to conceal if you stole one. They aren't the type of animals you can parade around town and hope no one notices." Jules pushed back from his desk. "I'll get the men together and have a look around outside the city. Maybe they've holed up in a camp somewhere."

"Big place to search." Ethan straightened up and got to his feet.

"Like looking for a particular pebble in a stream," Jules agreed. "But I'm hoping word will get to them about the search. They might decide to head out."

"Then they'd just become someone else's problem," Robbie said. "It would be better to catch them, so they aren't anyone's problem."

Jules couldn't argue with that, but it was a lot easier said than done.

"If you have any ideas on how I can do that, I'd be happy to listen to them."

Robbie glanced over at Ethan. "You've got the best tracker in the country standing right there."

"Who's going to be leaving again soon. Luke needs more horses delivered." Ethan sent Jules a brief smile. "But I can help until then."

"I'd appreciate that." Jules grinned when his cousin Dina appeared in the doorway. Short, with graying hair and a beaming smile, Dina had more than twenty years on him, and he'd always considered her more a mother than a cousin. She'd also been running the household for as long as he could remember. She still came to the house every day even though she'd married Cook, who was famous all over the city for the sumptuous meals he prepared at The Crimson Rose.

"You have a visitor, Jules. And for once, I'm happy to say it's a very pleasant one." She switched her gaze over to Ethan. "Well look who the wind blew in." She quickly crossed the room and enveloped him in a warm hug. "Everyone will be so glad to see you." She leaned over to one side so she could grab one of Robbie's hands and give it a squeeze. "You too."

Releasing them both, she stepped back and took in the three tall, strong men standing in front of her. "Oh my. It's been so long since you all ran through this house together." A slight mist shone in her eyes. "I do miss that. And of course, Ammie was always in the middle."

"For some of us, she still is." Robbie slanted a look at Ethan who ducked his head.

"I insist that you stay for supper. You should spend time with the family." After both men nodded their agreement, Dina clapped her hands together. "I wish Ammie could be here, but I know she has another engagement tonight." Everyone pretended not to see Ethan tense up.

"And we can't forget Dorrie either." She smiled at Jules. "Who, by the way, is your visitor. She's waiting for you in the parlor. Make sure you invite her for supper too."

"Dorrie?" Jules looked toward the open doorway. Dorrie was Maggie's oldest daughter and was three years younger than him. She was as outspoken as her mother, who'd landed in San Francisco from Ireland two decades ago, tagging along with her father and brothers who'd come to find gold in the mountains to the east. But since Dorrie was adopted, and didn't appear to be a bit Irish, Jules often wondered where that speak-your-mind trait of hers had come from. And when she hadn't been helping with her younger sister or at Maggie's dress shop, she'd also tended to get into as much mischief as Ammie had. The two of them still did, even though both women were grown and should know better.

He ran a hand through his hair. "She's in the parlor?"

Robbie grinned at him. "I do believe that's what Dina just said." He looked at Jules' feet and then back up at the marshal's face as he pointed at the door. "I also believe the parlor is that way, but your boots still seem to be planted in here."

"Oh you boys, leave him alone now." Dina smiled at her much younger cousin who she'd helped raise when his mother had died giving birth. "I would have brought her back to the kitchen, but she said she had some official business to discuss. Which means she should wait in the parlor."

"Official business?"

"Something wrong with your hearing? You keep repeating what Dina says." Ethan joined Robbie in grinning at their friend.

"Just took me by surprise. The family doesn't usually drop in to talk business with me. Most of the time they're looking for Doctor Abby."

"Wonder what she wants?" Robbie lifted his shoulders. "Could be anything."

"I don't know." Jules took another glance through the open doorway to the empty hall that led to the parlor.

"Are you intending to find out, or are you just going to stand here?" Robbie quickly crossed the room. "*I'd* like to see Dorrie. She's grown easy on the eyes over the last few years. And maybe she can cook?"

Jules' eyebrows snapped together. "What? She's not going out to your ranch and doing your cooking."

Robbie simply waved a hand in the air as he disappeared into the hallway. Annoyed, Jules skirted around the edge of the desk and went after him, while a silent Ethan trailed behind.

3

B y the time Jules reached the parlor, Robbie was already standing next to Dorrie, her hand held firmly in one of his. Irritated that the rancher would take liberties with any woman when she was in his house, even if she was a relative of sorts, Jules made sure his boot steps were heavy when he walked into the room. Apparently undeterred by the threat in the stomping sound behind him, Robbie turned his head and grinned at his friend.

"Guess what? Dorrie likes to cook. She says she's even taken a few lessons from Dina and Cook himself."

Since Dina's husband was known for his cooking abilities, it was a high recommendation, and put a niggle of worry into the back of Jules' mind.

"I doubt if Dorrie came here looking for a job, Robbie." The marshal clapped a firm hand on his friend's shoulder and pulled him back and out of the way, forcing Robbie to let go of Dorrie's hand. Jules' gaze narrowed into a warning before he turned a smile on his visitor.

Dorrie Dolan was slender without looking as if she'd

blow over in a puff of wind. Her caramel-colored hair, with lighter streaks of brown running through it, was pulled back and tied at the nape of her neck with a wide bow. Its sky-blue color matched her dress. Deep-brown eyes, fringed with a thick ring of lashes, gazed back at him, and her skin was tinted to a light bronze by the perpetual California sun. She was more than pretty, but not classically beautiful, with a face that tended to haunt a man at the oddest times.

He should know.

Reminding himself that Dorrie was here on official business, Jules hooked his thumbs into his wide leather belt and dipped his head into a quick bow. "It's good to see you, Dorrie."

She peeked around him. "I didn't know that all of you were here." She smiled, showing a dimple in one cheek. "I wasn't expecting that, or I'd have come a little later on."

"Why?" Robbie stuck out his lip in an exaggerated imitation of an unhappy toddler. "Don't you want to see us?" He grinned when Dorrie looked up at the ceiling and shook her head.

"You're a tease, Robbie Smith, and always were. Even when we were little." She smiled at Ethan. "Although I don't remember you as a little one. You were always the oldest, biggest, and strongest."

Ethan laughed. "That's only because I didn't join the family until I was almost grown. You'll have to take my word for it that I was once a kid."

"You were only fourteen when Shannon took you in as her brother, so hardly grown up," Jules interjected. He waited until Dorrie's gaze came back to him. "Dina said you had something you wanted to talk to me about? Did Ian send you?"

"No. Da doesn't know I'm here." She darted a quick look at the other two men.

They picked up on it and immediately made their excuses of having to get around to dropping in on the rest of the family, promising Jules they'd be back later for supper since they'd promised Dina they'd be there. After they'd made their noisy exit, with Robbie managing to give Dorrie a hug in spite of the hard stare from Jules, silence settled over the room.

As a US Marshal, Jules had long experience on waiting out stubborn witnesses. He kept his gaze on Dorrie as he shifted into a comfortable stance.

"They both look good." Dorrie inclined her head at Jules. "So do you. This is the first time I've seen you in the last month, even though we live in the same place."

"San Francisco's pretty big, Dorrie."

She shrugged. "I guess. But it seems you've been making yourself scarce." She looked past him at the parlor doors. "And so have those two. I don't suppose they'll be including Ammie and her Aunt Charlotte on their visiting list while they're in town?"

Jules sighed and ran a hand through his thick hair. "They didn't say one way or the other. Do you want me to ask them at supper? I can send you word about their plans."

He sighed again when she visibly stiffened. He hadn't meant to make fun of her, he just didn't want to get into a discussion about Ethan, since that was who she was aiming at. He knew Ethan was avoiding Ammie, who was Dorrie's best friend in addition to being another honorary cousin to both of them. He also knew why Ethan was avoiding the dark-haired beauty, although he doubted if either Dorrie or Ammie did.

"What did you want to talk about?"

Dorrie bit her lower lip as she stared up at him. The top of her head barely came up to his chin, making her seem small and vulnerable enough that Jules instinctively took a step closer.

"What is it, Dorrie? I'll fix whatever it is." He frowned. "Is some man bothering you?"

She laughed. "No. And I wouldn't need your help to deal with that, Jules McKenzie. I have a da, not to mention a mam, and a whole passel of aunts who can shoot a gun better than most men."

That was true enough. Puzzled by why she'd come to talk to him, Jules gestured toward the two divans placed opposite each other in front of the fireplace. "Why don't we sit, and you can tell me what brought you here?"

It only took a few moments for them to get settled before silence once again fell between them.

"We'll sit here all night, if that's what it takes." Jules hoped it wouldn't, but that's what he'd do if he had to. Something was clearly bothering her, and he meant to get to the bottom of it.

"I don't know if I should have come here." She looked at him and rose to her feet. "Maybe my problem isn't worth a marshal's time."

Jules kept his seat. He had no intention of letting her leave until he knew what was going on in that head of hers. But he was a reasonable man. He'd give her a chance to decide on her own to stay before he picked her up and plopped her back onto the sofa.

Not that he would mind doing that.

"Anything you need help with is worth my time, Dorrie. Since you're here, why don't you tell me what's bothering you?"

He held his breath when she hesitated, then smiled as she slowly sank back onto the sofa cushion.

"Someone's following us."

The marshal sat up straighter. "Following you? I thought you said this wasn't about some man bothering you? Do you know who he is?"

Dorrie folded her hands in her lap and waited for him to stop barking out questions. "Are you done?"

Holding onto his patience, Jules rose and walked over to the fireplace. He stood in front of it, his arm leaning against the mantel. "Yes."

She nodded. "That's fine then. No. I'd never seen him before a week or so ago, and I only see him now when we're out. Mostly at the market. But he isn't always there. Just sometimes. And I think he's been watching Mam's shop. But not always."

Jules relaxed. "It could be he happens to live in that part of town."

"I don't think so," Dorrie said slowly. "It's a feeling I get. Whenever I've managed to get a sight of him, he's always looking at us."

"Us? Who's with you? Your da?" It was possible that even the level-headed Ian had made an enemy or two. Dorrie's father had a successful carpentry business, and her mother was one of the most sought-after dressmakers in the city. Successful people tended to have a rival or two who didn't always have the kindliest intentions.

"No. I've never seen him when I've been out with Da. Just when I'm with Mam or Anna."

"Your sister?" Jules' mouth thinned out. "How old is she now? Fourteen?"

Dorrie smiled. "She's almost sixteen and can still be a double handful of mischief."

"So you only see this man when the women are together?"

"Not all of us. When I've gone out on my own, I don't see him."

Jules crossed his arms over his chest. "You believe there's a man following the women in your family, and you still went out alone? Why?"

She shrugged, not seeming to be the least bit aware that she was making his temper spike. "To see if it was me, Anna, or Mam he's interested in. It isn't me." She raised her hands in a helpless gesture. "But why would he be following Mam and Anna?"

That's a good question. Jules let the thought take hold as he considered the possibilities.

"Have you told your da about this?"

"Not yet." Dorrie dropped her hands back to her lap and sighed. "You know how you all get."

He had no idea what she meant by that. "No. I don't. How do we all get?"

"The least little thing and you want to circle the wagons and toss the women and children into the center."

"That's usually the safest place." Jules' dry tone coaxed a smile from Dorrie. "But since we aren't on the trail, what are you trying to say?"

"No we aren't, which means there aren't any convenient wagons about. The next best thing is to keep us locked inside as if we need to be surrounded by cotton balls." She lifted her chin and her brown eyes flashed fire as she warmed up to the subject. "Ask my mam, or Lillian or Shannon. I'd bet even Doctor Abby would say the same. All your female cousins certainly would."

Since he'd been admiring how pretty she looked when she was getting herself all worked up, Jules felt an immediate jolt at the reminder that he and Dorrie Dolan were family, for all practical purposes. A flush of heat crept up his neck.

"Well?" she demanded. "What do you have to say about that?"

He let his arms drop to his sides and returned to his seat on the divan, with a table safely between him and where Dorrie was sitting. "You'll be waiting a long time for any of us to apologize for wanting to keep our families safe." He smiled at her. "And an even longer time for any of us to change."

"Oh, I know that well enough." Dorrie took a deep breath. And then another before she glanced over at him. "I'm sorry. That isn't what I came to say. I don't really know what you can do about this man. He isn't breaking any laws."

"No. He isn't."

She nodded. "All right. You're a marshal, and I understand that." She smiled. "Really, I do. Since Ethan is in town, maybe he'll be able to help. He's the best..."

"Tracker around," Jules finished for her. "Yes. I know. He's going to help me find a gang that robbed a train a couple of weeks back."

Dorrie's eyes went wide. "Oh. Then you're busy."

Jules didn't like that dejected look on her face. He preferred to see her smile. "Not so busy that I can't find time to help you."

"Maybe your brother has a bit of spare time?"

He tried not to be irritated when Dorrie brightened at the idea. His older brother, Cade, spent most of his time in town now, and left the chasing of outlaws across the countryside to Jules. "I'll talk it over with him."

"I'm not going to tell Mam that I spoke to you. She wasn't

too happy about me coming here when I mentioned it to her. She doesn't think this man popping up all the time is something we should be worrying about."

That surprised Jules. Maggie had always been as fiercely protective of her family as her husband, Ian, was. He tucked that away to also discuss with Cade.

When Dorrie rose, he did as well, crossing over the thick rug to put his large hands on her shoulders. "I don't want you worrying about this. I'll look into it. I promise."

She lifted a hand and placed it on top of one of his. "Thank you, Jules."

He quickly dropped his arms to his side and took a step back, but he couldn't tear his gaze away from hers. She finally broke the spell by turning to pick up the small purse she'd set on the table at the end of the couch. She looked back at him with a smile in her eyes.

"Ammie said that you have one of Rayne's horses now? She's green with envy."

Glad to latch on to a favorite topic in the family, Jules nodded. "Ammie should be. He's a beauty." He winked at her. "And now that I know one Miss Amelia Jamison is jealous of my new mount, I'll be sure to take him around so she can get a good look at my special gift from Rayne."

He grinned when she laughed.

"What's his name? And is it Spanish or Welsh?"

Each one of Rayne's horses were given a name in one language or the other. It was a tradition started by the twins who'd been the ranch foremen for decades before they'd retired to a small plot of land of their own, right there on Rayne's ranch.

"Welsh. It's Hafen. And his coat is such a dark brown you'd think it was black." Jules had loved the horse on sight, and Rayne for gifting it to him. Hafen was big, strong, and bred to run over rough country. The perfect horse for a US Marshal. So was the trick his honorary aunt had taught the animal.

"And?" Dorrie prompted. "What does it mean?"

"Haven." The name was also perfect. Haven was exactly how Jules had always felt about his home.

"Haven. It's a beautiful name," Dorrie breathed before her eyes took on a sparkle. "What did Rayne teach him to do? She always teaches her horses something special."

"To come home." Jules nodded when Dorrie's forehead wrinkled. "All I have to do is say 'barn', along with a hand gesture, and Hafen will come home." Jules showed her the double hand flip that their Rayne had taught him.

She smiled as she wrapped the strings of her small purse around her wrist. "That's perfect, Jules. And it's good to know that Hafen will always bring you home."

"And that you have a marshal in the family who will always be glad to help you." He walked beside her to the front door. "Don't forget my promise."

"I won't."

He watched her cross the porch and along the walk toward the small buggy with its horse waiting patiently out front. She gave him a final wave before taking up the reins and heading down the street. He wanted to go with her, but she was safe enough in the carriage. And he didn't want to be accused of wrapping her in cotton balls.

It wasn't until she'd disappeared from sight that he remembered he was supposed to have asked her to stay for supper.

4

The shop was one along a row set on a busy street in the market district. An ornately carved window box filled with blooming flowers hung under each of the three windows that spanned the front. The wooden clapboards on the shop's front were painted with a soothing cream color, and the solid oak door was a deep green. It made a lovely picture, and if Jules hadn't been so tired he might have appreciated it a bit more.

He stood outside, his hands in the pockets of his duster that came to the middle of his calves. It was splattered with mud from the long ride he'd started out on early that morning from Ethan's place. He'd spent the night with his friend, talking over plans to track down the Green Gang once and for all.

Jules had received word that the three outlaws had stopped by a small cabin not far out of town and helped themselves to whatever supplies had been on hand. The owner had come into town seeking the help of the sheriff, who'd directed him to the US Marshal's house. Since this gang had stolen from the US Government, the sheriff felt

that the homesteader's problem was already Jules'
headache, so the marshal had spent a good amount of time
scouring the countryside, looking for that gang.

So far he'd had no luck, except for coming across a set of
tracks that included a horse with two crooked shoes. But
he'd lost the trail on the hard ground of a well-traveled road.
There was no telling if his quarry had stayed on the road
and come into town, or had veered off toward whatever
place they were holed up in.

Either way, Jules instincts told him the gang was settled
in and didn't intend to move on, even with a US Marshal
looking for them. So he'd paid a visit to Ethan.

But he was overdue to have a talk with Dorrie about her
problem, and it weighed on his mind enough that he'd
taken the six-hour ride back into town so he could find out if
the men he'd hired to watch the shop, and the Dolan home,
had seen anything out of the ordinary. Now at least he had
something to tell her. It wasn't much, but it was enough to
have him more than half-convinced that Dorrie's imagination was not getting away with her after all.

As much as he wanted to talk to her, he still wasn't keen
on walking into the very fashionable dress shop. If he'd had
time, he would have stopped by home and gotten himself
cleaned up before walking into such a fancy place filled
with females.

He glanced around at Hafen who was tied to a post on
the other side of the wooden walkway. His horse needed a
good wash and a rubdown too, and Jules was sure that the
animal was glaring back at him. Just at that moment, Hafen
gave several sharp bobs of his head, as if to hurry his owner
along.

Jules sent his mount an exasperated look.

"I'm going."

It was Jules' bad luck that two women had decided to leave the shop at that very moment. They stopped and blinked at him before the older one raised her parasol and gave him a pleasant smile, while her younger companion's hand flew up to muffle a giggle.

Jules raised two fingers to the brim of his hat and gave a slight dip of his head. "Ladies."

He heard another giggle, followed by intense whispers, as they passed by him. They probably felt they had a thing or two to laugh about, seeing a US Marshal standing outside a dress shop and talking to his horse.

Thinking to hurry and get the ordeal over with, Jules straightened his shoulders and walked up to the solid green door. Turning the knob and pushing it open, he took a deep breath before he stepped inside.

The light filtering in through the three windows lent a cheery note to the soft and elegant atmosphere of the shop. Hats were set on narrow shelves stretching out from center poles that stood at intervals down the middle of the room. It looked to Jules as if there were shelves everywhere, and each of them straining to hold ribbons, feathers, and all manner of decorations for hats and dresses. Across the back of the shop, lined up like infantrymen, were colorful bolts of cloth.

Several women browsed among the rows of shelves, and every one of them looked over when he stepped across the threshold. Resigned to being viewed as if he were something completely foreign and out of place, Jules took off his hat and held it against his chest. It wasn't much of a shield, but it would have to do. He looked around, relieved when he spotted Kate. She'd been Maggie's assistant in the shop for as long as Maggie'd had a dress shop. With her red hair streaked with gray, plump curves, and wide smile, she looked both comfortable and welcoming.

But it was the squeal behind him that had Jules turning around just as Anna Dolan threw herself at him for a hug. "Hello, Jules! I haven't seen you in a witch's age."

Mindful of the frown from a nearby matron, Jules held her off with one long arm, but gave her a grin. "We were both at Lillian's for dinner just a few weeks ago, so it hasn't been that long." He cocked his head to one side and widened his grin. "Although I don't exactly know how long a 'witch's age' is."

"I read it in a book, so I'm not sure either." It didn't seem to concern his young honorary cousin much. She tossed her very red hair over her shoulder and grinned back at him. "I'll bet you're here to see Dorrie, aren't you?"

Before he could answer, Anna had leaned to the side and raised her voice so it could be heard across the shop. "Dorrie! US Marshal Jules McKenzie has come to call on you."

"I'm not calling on..."

"Dorrie! You need to get out here. He doesn't have much time."

When the mischievous girl straightened and gave him an impish smile, he pinned her with the same look Cade had always given him whenever he'd misbehaved. "Anna. You aren't too big for me to take over my knee."

She giggled. "No you won't. Da always says that but he never does."

Even though the almost sixteen-year-old gave him another cheeky smile, Jules knew he'd at least made his point since she'd lowered her voice and taken a large, cautious step away from him.

"*He* might not, but Mam certainly will if you keep disturbing the shop."

Dorrie's voice came from behind him, so Jules turned around, smiling at the glare she was sending her younger sister.

"Anna Dolan. You know very well that Jules hasn't come to call on me, he's here to talk to Mam about a business matter."

Dorrie had raised her voice in what Jules assumed was an attempt to quell any gossip. He looked around and was fairly sure that the ladies milling about the shop would stick with Anna's version of why he was there, rather than believing he was keeping a business appointment.

He gave a philosophical shrug. Dorrie's name connected with his wouldn't be the worst thing that could happen. Especially if it reached the ears of anyone who might be spying on her for a reason he hadn't figured out yet. Besides, gossip usually died down pretty quickly. Especially when nothing else came of it.

And nothing else would come of a story that he was calling on Dorrie.

Dorrie continued to glare at her younger sister, but she did lower her voice. "While we're having that discussion with Jules, you're going to stay out here and help Kate take care of our customers."

Dorrie motioned for Jules to follow her, and he almost laughed when Anna made a face at her sister's back.

"And you're too old to be sticking your tongue out at people," Dorrie said over her shoulder.

Jules grinned. Dina used to do that very same thing, calling him out about something she couldn't possibly have seen. He wondered what age they had to reach before a woman gained that secret skill. The grin stayed on his face while he followed Dorrie down a narrow aisle and through a heavy curtain hanging over an opening in the back of the shop.

It led into a cramped space, not much bigger than a good-sized closet from what Jules could tell. Maggie was at a small writing desk tucked into one corner. She looked around when Dorrie and Jules stepped into the room.

The older Maggie became, the more she looked like someone who should be living in a stone cottage in the Irish countryside. Her brown hair was shot through with streaks of red and silver, and she sat with her trim frame held ramrod straight. Brilliant green eyes sparkled a greeting as she nodded at Jules before looking over at her oldest daughter.

"I heard your sister. She's up to her usual mischief, I'm thinkin'." The music of Ireland still wove itself into Maggie O'Hearn Dolan's voice. "Am I needin' to go out and have a word with her then?"

"More than one word, Mam." Dorrie slanted a look at Jules. "She embarrassed the marshal."

"Did she now?" Maggie's gaze shifted to Jules. "Are you embarrassed then, Jules McKenzie?"

He took the short two steps forward needed so he could bend at the waist and place a kiss on her cheek. "No, Maggie. I've been accused of much worse than calling on a pretty girl."

"Pretty, is she?" Maggie laughed and set the quill in her hand down. "Well now. It's nice of you to say so."

"Accused?" Dorrie frowned at him. "Is that what you said? That Anna accused you of calling on me, like it would be some sort of crime?"

Dorrie's mother clapped her hands. "Somethin' for the

two of you to talk over later." She smiled at Jules. "What is it that has you droppin' in on me shop this mornin'?"

Not sure exactly what Dorrie had told her mother, Jules shot her a questioning look.

"It's about that man who's been following you and Anna, Mam. I told you I talked to Jules about it."

"You did," Maggie acknowledged. "And now he's here to tell us there's nothin' to any of it."

Dorrie put her hands on her hips and stared at him. "Is that what you've come to tell us, Jules?"

Acutely aware that he'd obviously stepped into the middle of a spitting match between mother and daughter, Jules shifted uncomfortably from one foot to the other. "Maybe a little of both."

"And what does that mean?" the two women said in perfect unison.

Dorrie started to tap her foot impatiently against the wooden floorboards while Maggie continued to stare silently back at him.

"It means I had a couple of men watching this past week. One at your house and one here. Neither one of them have seen anyone."

"There!" Maggie said triumphantly. "I told you. No one's been followin' anyone around." She shook her head at Dorrie. "Now you can sleep better at night. The marshal looked into it."

"But..." Jules interrupted before Dorrie could open her mouth. "Both of them were uneasy a couple of times. Joe, who was watching the shop, particularly said that he didn't see anyone specifically, but he'd swear there was someone watching at least twice." He shrugged at Maggie's snort. "He's a good man, with good instincts, that I would never dismiss out of hand. If Joe feels someone was watching, then there probably was."

For a full minute there was only silence in the small cramped room. Finally, Maggie pushed back her chair with a loud scraping noise as the wooden legs grated against the floor.

"He didn't see anyone, so no one was there. Dorrie's got you chasin' shadows."

"They aren't shadows, Mam," her oldest daughter insisted. "I've seen him, and now Jules' man has felt him"

"Seein' and feelin' aren't the same thing." Maggie lifted her chin at Jules. "Your man's instincts are playin' a trick on him."

"Two men then," Jules said. "Frank told me the same thing. He thought someone was there, he just couldn't get a sight of him."

"I'm not carin' if it's fifty men, Marshal McKenzie. If they didn't see anyone, then there isn't anyone to be seein'."

When Dorrie started to protest, Maggie held up a slender hand. "I'll keep our Anna close to the shop and home, and she won't be goin' out anywhere without someone else bein' with her. That should be enough for the both of you."

The seamstress stood up and had both Dorrie and Jules flattening themselves against the wall as she stalked past them. When she'd reached the curtain, she swiveled around to give them a stern look. "This should be the end of it. And I won't be havin' Ian bothered by any of this." After issuing that command, she turned on her heels and disappeared to the other side of the curtain.

"She is so stubborn."

Jules had to bite his tongue to keep from mentioning he

thought the daughter was every bit as stubborn, and settled for a much safer nod of his head.

Dorrie shook her head. She had to turn her face up to look at him in such close quarters. "Thank you for trying to reason with Mam."

"It's not much, but I didn't want you to think I'd forgotten my promise to you."

"I knew you wouldn't." Dorrie bit her lip and looked toward the curtain that was still swaying from her mother's exit. "But maybe we need something a little more than men watching the house and shop."

He knew what she was thinking and didn't want to disappoint her, but there were other more immediate dangers around. "You mean Ethan's tracking skills."

She nodded. "Yes." She placed a gentle hand on his arm and gave it a light pat. "I'm sure your men are very good, but Ethan is extraordinary. I know he doesn't like to come into town much, but I'm sure he will if you ask him. Or I can have Ammie ask him. He'll come if *she* asks."

Jules knew that well enough, but at the moment it wasn't possible. Ethan was already out looking for the Green Gang and wouldn't be reporting back to Jules for another week. Sighing, he shifted his hat to one hand and ran the other through his hair. "I'll talk to Ethan when he gets back."

"Back?"

"He's out doing a tracking job for me and won't be back for a week."

"A tracking job for you? So when he gets back, you'll be off chasing after whoever you sent him to find?"

The question took Jules by surprise. "Most likely. If Ethan can find who we're looking for."

"He always does."

Dorrie looked away, but not before he saw a slight quiver in her chin. He had no idea why she was suddenly upset.

"Are you worried about Ethan? He can take care of himself." When she looked back around at him, he smiled. "He'll be back in a week, and then he can work on finding out who's been watching you."

Dorrie continued to stare up at him, her brown eyes wide as her gaze lingered on each feature of his face. "I know you can take care of yourself too, Jules. Just be sure that you do."

Jules had to remind himself to breathe. Putting as much space as the little room would allow between himself and Dorrie, he clutched harder onto the hat brim he held in his hand.

"You do the same, Dorrie. Make sure you stay close to home, and don't go out alone until we can figure this out." He managed a smile for her. "That doesn't have anything to do with wanting to keep you in cotton balls. It's just plain common sense."

5

J ules glanced out the open door of the stable. Full night had descended, and it was pitch black beyond the ring of light thrown out by the lantern he'd hung on a peg inside Hafen's stall. Jules set the rubbing cloth he was holding on top of a barrel and picked up the stiffly bristled brush. He turned back to the big horse with the dark chocolate coat.

"Consider this my apology for leaving you standing in your own mud longer than usual." The marshal chuckled when Hafen shook his large head, sending his silky mane dancing across his now clean neck. "Well, whether you accept my apology or not, this last brush is all you're getting. And you'd best enjoy it. When we go out hunting the Green Gang, it will be a while before you have this cozy stall of yours to spend the night in."

"I'd be sorry to hear that."

Jules didn't turn at the sound of the quiet voice coming from behind him. He smiled and kept at his long even strokes over Hafen's back as the sound of heavy boots rang against the stable floor.

"Hello, Ian. I was wondering when you'd be showing up." Jules looked over his shoulder and smiled at the tall, muscular carpenter with the steady golden eyes.

Dorrie's adopted father had been raised on a farm with eight siblings, including his half-brother, Luke Donovan, Ethan's brother-in-law. Ian had come to San Francisco with the gold rush, but he'd chosen to open a carpentry business instead of pan for gold. He'd rescued Maggie during a harrowing night and then married her, a story that Jules had only heard bits and pieces of. He made a mental note to ask Dorrie about it.

"Do you talk to your horse on a regular basis?"

Jules could hear the amusement in Ian's voice. "Same as you do to the wood you're building with." He turned around and grinned at the carpenter. "I heard you often enough when Cade would send me over to help out on one of your jobs."

Now Ian laughed outright. "Help? That's what you and Ethan were doing? I seem to recall it a bit differently. We used to pass you boys around just so we could get some breathing space from all pranks. And when Robbie was visiting from The Orphan Ranch, we used to draw straws to see who had to keep an eye on you boys for the day." He leaned against a post, his smile growing wider. "It seemed to me that Charles drew the short straw a lot less often than Cade or me."

"That's what you get for drawing straws with a gambler." Jules walked over to the barrel and set his brush down. "Do you need something, Ian, or are you just visiting?"

"A little of both. I already stopped in and saw Cade, Abby, and the children. They're growing fast." He inclined his head toward Jules. "But then you all did."

"Not fast enough if you were drawing straws to choose who got stuck with our help for the day."

"Too fast. It's hard to believe Dorrie is full grown and my little Anna is well on the way to be as well."

When the big carpenter's gaze dropped to the ground, Jules closed the distance between them and put a hand on Ian's broad shoulder. "What's on your mind?"

Ian sighed and rubbed his hand across his chin. "My wife and daughters."

Jules had figured as much. Ian wasn't one to ignore anything he saw as a threat to his family. "Dina always leaves a pot of coffee on the stove. We can heat it up and have a talk, if that suits you."

"I guess with a doctor and two US Marshals in the house, you'd have a need for a pot of coffee at all hours of the night." Ian looked around the stable that was washed in shadows. "But I'd just as soon talk out here, if that suits you."

"It does." Jules stepped back and propped one arm on the open gate to Hafen's stall. "What's on your mind?"

"I think you know well enough. It's about this business of someone watching my family whenever I'm not around."

Not wanting to step into a marital argument, Jules was silent for a moment. "Did Maggie tell you about it, or was it Dorrie?"

"Anna did."

"Anna?" Jules' eyebrows shot up.

Ian lifted his gaze to the timbers over his head. "She's a good one for listening when she's not supposed to. And she was mad at her sister for telling her to mind the shop while you talked, so she thought she'd find out what was going on." Ian's gaze returned to Jules. "She doesn't much like the notion of being cooped up, or never being able to go anywhere by herself, so she came to me to demand that I fix it."

"I don't suppose she had any ideas how you're supposed to do that?"

"You know Anna. Of course she did." A ghost of a smile crossed Ian's lips. "She said I should come over here and tell you to find the man so you could shoot him, or arrest him, or run him out of town, whichever you prefer. Because you're a marshal and can do that."

Jules laughed. "Certainly sounds easy enough."

Ian was back to frowning as he crossed his arms over his chest. "Maggie hasn't said a word about it, though I knew something was bothering her. She's not any good at keeping things from me, and I'm always happy to hear what she has to say. But now she's keeping her silence."

"Doesn't sound like her." Jules knew that Maggie had said she didn't want her husband bothered with Dorrie's suspicions, but he'd ignored that the minute she'd said it. Dorrie's parents had a strong bond, and for as long as Jules had known them, they had never kept any secrets from each other. At least not as far as he knew.

"We don't keep secrets," Ian stated, voicing Jules' thought out loud. "Almost twenty-five years we've shared a life, a home, and a bed, and we've always told each other everything that's on our minds. But not this time." He narrowed his eyes as he looked at Jules. "My Maggie is keeping something from me, and it's scaring her. I can feel it." His gaze turned fierce. "And she's been crying. She thinks she can hide it from me, but I know."

A tingle of alarm went up Jules' back. Whatever this was, it was making the strong, outspoken Maggie cry? The very thought had those warning bells sounding even louder. He'd had a feeling that Maggie's lack of reaction to the idea that someone was watching her daughters was strange. And Ian's words were confirming his belief that Maggie knew more than she was telling. Jules suspected that Dorrie thought the same thing, and it was why she was so worried about her mother and younger sister.

"I know what you told Dorrie and Maggie this afternoon. What I don't know is if you think there's a real danger to my family?"

"*Our* family, Ian." Jules' quick declaration made the older man smile. "And I'm not sure. My men didn't see anyone, which Maggie was quick to point out meant there was nothing to see. But they felt like someone was there, watching the shop and your house." Jules shrugged. "And them."

Ian stayed silent for a long moment. "I'm still waiting to hear what *you* think, Jules."

"I think they're good men with solid instincts that I've trusted on more than one occasion. If they say they were being watched, then I'm leaning heavily toward believing them." He hesitated, weighing Ian's obvious frustration and worry with keeping Dorrie's confidence. Finally deciding in favor of Ian knowing everything so he could take steps to be sure the women stayed safe, Jules straightened away from the gate. "Dorrie has seen the man."

"What?"

Jules nodded. "She's seen the man. She first noticed him when they were at the market. She thinks he's only interested in Maggie and Anna."

"And how would my oldest daughter know that?"

This isn't going to make him happy. Jules was sure of that since he was still angry about it himself. "Dorrie's only noticed him when she's out with her mother and sister. When she's gone out on her own, she hasn't seen the man."

"When she's gone out...." Ian broke off as a tic formed along his jaw.

Jules could see the blaze growing in his honorary uncle's eyes.

"Are you saying that Dorrie knew someone was following them, and she deliberately went out on her own to find the man?"

The marshal nodded. It was a relief to talk to someone sensible enough to see how foolish Dorrie's actions had been. Now all they had to do was convince her of that. Jules had high hopes that Dorrie's father could talk some sense into his oldest daughter. She certainly hadn't seemed impressed when *he'd* tried to explain it to her.

"Is there anything else my Dorrie told you that I should know?"

"Not much." Jules smiled. "She wants to set Ethan on the man."

Ian's expression calmed down a bit. "That's a good idea. If anyone can track this man down, Ethan can."

"I agree. But he's out doing some tracking for me and won't be back for a week."

"Is he searching for the Green Gang?" At Jules' surprised look, Ian nodded. "Dorrie told me about them."

"She did?"

"She seemed worried about you." The tall carpenter raised an eyebrow at Jules. "She didn't mention that Ethan was already out looking for those men. I guess she isn't worried about him."

Jules frowned. "Seems more likly that Dorrie feels Ethan can take better care of himself than I can."

"I don't think that's it."

Uncomfortable at the sudden flush of heat on his neck, Jules broke his gaze away from Ian's stare and picked up his brush again. "When Ethan gets back, we'll find the man who's following the women."

"If Dorrie doesn't try to confront him first."

The marshal froze, the brush still held up in his hand. Jules slowly put it back down on the barrel, then turned to face Ian, his arms crossed over his chest and his legs braced apart in the usual stance he took to hear bad news. "Do you have a reason for saying that?"

"I know my daughter, Jules. She always gets a guilty look on her face whenever she and Ammie are up to something."

Taking a deep breath, Jules let it out very slowly. "And what are they up to?"

Ian rubbed his chin. "I don't know. But she asked me to find something to do around Maggie's shop tomorrow so I could watch over her mam, since she had plans to spend time with Ammie."

Jules relaxed. How much trouble could they get into sitting in Ammie's parlor?

"When I asked her what they'd be doing for the better part of the day, she got that look. Just before she told me they were going to go out to the shore and enjoy the fresh air." Ian rolled his eyes. "I know where they're going. Your aunts used to give each other shooting lessons out there. Maggie's taken my daughters there a time or two."

"Shooting lessons?" Jules' voice went up a notch. "Does Dorrie even own a gun?" His mouth dropped open when Ian nodded.

"She got a specially made one from Beth when she turned eighteen. It's a tradition among them for all the women to have one of those lighter-weight guns."

When Ian smiled, Jules shook his head. "I've always thought that Abby got that special gun of hers from Cade."

It was only a second or two before what Ian was telling

him hit Jules between the eyes. Ammie was going to take Dorrie out to the shoreline and give her shooting lessons? And Ian was likely right. It was so Dorrie could go out on her own to look for this man she'd seen on her own.

The very thought of her confronting a full grown, and most likely armed, man, had Jules' blood going cold. He wished he felt that she wouldn't do anything so foolish, but the certainty she was going to do exactly that, sat in the pit of his stomach like a lead ball.

"I need to have a talk with her." Which in Jules' mind went without saying. Dorrie was not going to be roaming about the city, toting a gun and looking for some stranger.

"I tried to tell her she'd better not be taking her gun out there, but I don't think it did much good. She just gave me that sweet smile of hers and said she heard me." Ian sighed heavily. "Though I noticed she didn't agree to leave her gun at home."

"She's going to listen to *me*." Jules' voice was firm and there was a determined look in his eyes. "We agreed to wait until Ethan got back, and she's going to stick with that."

"That's good, son. I'd be obliged if you'd talk sense into Dorrie."

Jules nodded. "You can count on that, Ian."

Ian rolled his shoulders back as if he were preparing for a fight. "And I'll go home and talk to my wife."

6

It was crisp and cool the next morning, with occasional wisps of the fog that had descended on the city the night before still lingering in the air. Jules let the quiet of the trees, rocks, and sand, along with the gentle sound of water lapping at the shore, take him into a calmer place inside himself. The way he did when he was riding the hills outside the city. Not far ahead was a grove of trees that went right to the shoreline, leaving only a thin strip of sand between them and the water. From the description Ian had given him, just beyond those trees the land curved into a small half-moon, creating a sheltered inlet that the women in the family had claimed as their own.

He'd never been there, although not from lack of trying. He and Ethan had decided to follow Ammie and Dorrie once, when they were younger and the four of them had been together. Dorrie had told him that her mam was going to take the two young girls to what she'd called their "special place", for lessons with Master Kwan. All of them had spent time with the Chinese fighting master through the years, including his aunts and uncles. And they still did. But Master Kwan had a rule that males and females did not train together. So of course he and Ethan had decided they were going to find out what was so special about this place where the girls went to practice.

Jules smiled at the memory. He and Ethan had followed Maggie's wagon some distance down the beach and had been as sneaky as polecats stalking prey. Or so they'd thought. Right up until Rayne had come up behind them on that huge bay-colored horse of hers. They hadn't even heard her until she'd said their names. They'd both frozen before swiveling around in their saddles, only to find their-dark-haired, expert-shot Aunt so close she could have reached out and nabbed them both by the collars. Jules wasn't certain, but he wouldn't be surprised if that was when Ethan had decided to start practicing his tracking skills every day.

The sound of gunfire had him pulling Hafen up short. He sat still and listened, not having to wait long before a second shot rang out, the sound muffled by the trees between him and the two people he was sure were doing the shooting. His calm dropped away, replaced by the same irri-tation he'd felt the night before when Ian had told him what his daughter was up to. Along with Ammie, of course. He was resigned to Ammie getting into trouble, but now he was wondering just how often she'd dragged Dorrie along with her. Probably more than he'd be able to tolerate hearing, if the women still used this secret place of theirs.

And for a great deal more than a harmless practice with Master Kwan, it seemed. Something Ian had known. But Dorrie hadn't ever bothered to tell him about the shooting practices, and who knew what other skills they were learn-ing. A sudden vision of Dorrie holding a knife and thinking she could defend herself against a full-grown man made him shudder in his saddle. With that image riding in his mind, he pulled his wide-brimmed hat lower on his forehead and set Hafen into motion. He clearly needed to have a serious talk with one Dorrie Dolan.

It was another ten minutes before he came around the edge of the trees and started across the sand of the small inlet. He recognized the two horses wandering along the water. His gaze rapidly quartered the space of open beach in front of him. It didn't take him long to spot the two women. Their backs were to him as Ammie took aim at a row of smaller rocks they'd placed along the tops of larger ones sticking out of the sand. He rode up closer before dismounting just as Ammie shot one of the smaller rocks off its perch.

It was a good shot. But he still didn't care to see it, or the gun Dorrie held, pointed away from her side.

He took another two steps and then suddenly stopped. Both women had quickly turned and were pointing their rifles right at his chest. Or at least Ammie's was. Dorrie clearly needed a little more instruction since her gun's barrel was dropped a bit lower.

"Whoa! It's me."

Both women lowered their rifles until the barrels were pointing at the ground. When he got a good look at them, he had to work at stopping his grin. They were dressed in overly large shirts and britches, and both of them had wide smiles on their faces. He crossed his arms over his chest and scowled.

"Something funny? Because I never have liked a gun pointed at me, much less two of them."

Ammie's cheeky smile had his lips twitching despite his annoyance with her antics. She was a hard one to resist, with her deep, turquoise eyes perfectly set off by the rich sable-brown color of her hair. Jules had heard her mother had been an unrivaled beauty in her day, but he'd always been dead sure that the daughter must have surpassed her parent. He'd seen men stop in their tracks the very second they'd laid eyes on her. Fortunately, none of that had ever seemed to impress Ammie much.

"Our guns aren't pointing at you at the moment, Marshal McKenzie." Ammie tilted her head to one side and raised a perfectly arched eyebrow at him. "We could hear you coming before you even cleared the trees. I hope you're quieter when you're tracking the bad men you chase about."

"I don't 'chase about' anyone, Miss Jamison. The general idea is to catch and arrest them." His gaze shifted to Dorrie, and he carefully schooled his features as he breathed through the sudden spike in his heartbeat.

He'd always been mildly aware that she had an effect on him, but it seemed to be getting worse lately. At least he'd sure been noticing it more. It didn't help much either when her smile grew, showing the dimple in her left cheek.

"Does that mean you've caught the Green Gang?"

She looked so pleased over the prospect that he was sorry he had to disappoint her.

"No." Jules shook his head before his gaze dropped to the rifle at her side. "I'm supposed to be out looking for their tracks before meeting up with Ethan, so we can share what we've found."

"Then why are you standing here?" Ammie leaned her rifle against the closest rock and put her hands on her hips. "I'm sure Ethan would appreciate the help, since he's supposed to be a rancher who's always delivering stock off somewhere, and you're the US Marshal."

"Ethan volunteered to help," Jules said, never taking his

eyes off Dorrie. Not so much as a movement of an eyelash gave away the fact he saw her try to slip her gun behind her back. *Guess she's got a good idea what I've come to say.*

He pointed at Ammie's gun. "Mind telling me what you two are doing?" He smiled at the instant blush on Dorrie's face. "You aren't big enough or sneaky enough to hide that rifle from me, Dorrie."

Dorrie gave an audible sigh and took two steps to the side to set her gun next to Ammie's. "I wasn't trying to hide it."

Jules rolled his eyes at that statement, but let it go. "What I want to know is why you're out here using it?"

"It never hurts to practice." Dorrie crossed her arms and mimicked Jules' stance. "Why are you out this way if you're supposed to be off chasing after the Green Gang?"

"Because your father came to see me last night. He told me you and Ammie would be out here getting practice in with a rifle." Jules narrowed his eyes. "I didn't even know you owned a rifle until Ian mentioned it."

"Beth gave it to me when I turned eighteen." Dorrie shrugged. "We came out to practice riding and shooting, and I didn't feel there was any reason to mention it."

"Riding and shooting," Jules repeated slowly. "Anything else you practice when you come out here?"

"Just the same lessons you also took with Master Kwan," Ammie broke in. "And it really isn't any of your business, Jules."

He glanced over at the brunette beauty. "When it comes to your safety, yes, it is."

Dorrie looked around. "Did you see a threat lurking close by?"

Jules ignored her question and went back to crossing his

arms over his chest. "You never told me what you intend to do with that rifle, and it had better not involve the man who's been following you."

"Uh oh," Ammie said, loud enough for both her child-hood friends to turn and glare at her. She held up her hands and took several steps backward. "I'm going to round up the horses."

Jules returned his attention to Dorrie and waited. The stubborn set to her jaw told him plainly enough that he'd have a long time to wait before he got an answer.

"I don't want you searching for that man, Dorrie. Whether he's been seen or not, we both know he's out there. And your father thinks your mam knows more about him than she's letting on."

Her shoulders slumped. "Yes, he does. I heard them arguing last night." She closed her eyes. "They never argue. And this morning my da was angry, and I could tell Mam had been crying."

"Do you agree with your father? Does Maggie know more about this man than she's saying?"

"I think so." Dorrie looked off toward the ocean. "But it's making Mam more sad than frightened." She looked back at Jules. "Which makes no sense to me."

"And doesn't make this man any less dangerous."

She shook her head. "To Mam and Anna, but not to me. He isn't interested in me."

Jules closed his eyes and sent up a quick prayer for patience. "You *think* he isn't, but you don't *know* that for sure. So don't assume you're safe going about on your own."

"Is that what you came out here to tell me? That you're so sure that I can't take care of myself?"

He blew out an exasperated breath and ran a hand

through his hair. "I am not going to get into one of your cotton ball arguments. We agreed to wait for Ethan. I want you to keep your word."

He almost ground his teeth together when she shook her head at him.

"You said you'd talk to Ethan about it. But I didn't agree to wait for him." She glared right back at him when his gaze narrowed. "I told you that Ethan should help you with that Green Gang, not go chasing after a man we aren't even sure exists."

"You're sure he does," Jules shot back. "Enough to come out here and practice shooting that rifle Beth was foolish enough to give you."

Dorrie's mouth dropped open. "Foolish enough?"

"That's right." Jules gave a sharp nod. "I'm sure she never believed that you'd do something stupid like go off to look for this man on your own with it."

"Now I'm foolish *and* stupid?"

Jules clamped his mouth shut. He'd meant nothing of the sort, but the thought of her putting herself into that kind of danger had his temper getting away from him. He tamped down his emotions and tried for a more reasonable voice.

"You aren't foolish or stupid."

"Why thank you, Marshal."

Her dry tone had him taking an even firmer grip on his frazzled patience. "That doesn't mean I want you out here practicing with a rifle, so you can sneak behind my back and go looking for this man while I'm out doing my job."

"No one's stopping you from doing your job, Marshal."

You are, Jules thought, but he let it go. "Stop calling me 'marshal' in that snotty tone, Miss Dolan, or I'll tell you the same thing I told Anna."

"If you're considering putting me over your knee, Jules McKenzie, I'd remind you I have a rifle here, and I know how to use it."

"You wouldn't get your hands on it before I got mine on you, Dorrie Dolan." His temper settled into a slow simmer when she gasped, her eyes going as big as saucers. At least she was taking his threat seriously.

"You aren't to go looking for that man until I get back here with Ethan." He emphasized his point by taking a long step closer to her, so they were barely a foot apart.

She tilted her head back so she could look into his face. "Is there anything else you don't want me doing?"

"Going anywhere by yourself or doing any more practicing with that rifle. Or spending too much time concocting mischief with Ammie."

"Is that all?"

The corners of his mouth tilted up into a fleeting smile. "That's a start."

Dorrie stared back at him, her brown eyes almost black, and Jules could almost see the steam coming out of her ears. He didn't care how mad she got at him, as long as she stayed safe.

"I don't care if you are a US Marshal, Jules McKenzie. You can't tell me what I can and can't do. You aren't my da or brother."

Neither said a word as their gazes locked as the seconds ticked by. Jules finally broke the silence by tugging on his hat brim.

"No. I'm not. But I want you to mind what I'm telling you." He turned on his heel and walked back toward Hafen, who hadn't moved from where Jules had left him. He easily lifted himself into the saddle and then looked back at

Dorrie, standing there, the curls tied at the nape of her neck moving slowly under the gentle breeze from the bay.

"You mind what I told you, Dorrie. Don't give your father more to worry about than he has already. I'll be back with Ethan at the end of the week."

"WELL?" Ammie said as she drew closer to Dorrie, both of their horses trailing behind her. "Did you get it all settled?"

Dorrie was still watching the point along the trees where Jules had disappeared from view. "As far as he's concerned we did."

Ammie followed her gaze. "And what do *you* think?"

"That our childhood playmate has grown up to be insufferable."

"Has he?" Ammie laughed. "They're both insufferable."

"Ethan's all right." Dorrie cast a sideways glance at her friend. Ammie rarely mentioned Ethan. "He's just not home much."

"You mean he's never home, and when he is, he certainly doesn't let anyone know. Except Jules, of course."

"Maybe Ethan should start taking Jules with him."

Dorrie's observation brought a burst of laughter from her friend.

"In the span of half an hour, he told me I'm foolish and stupid." She nodded when Ammie gasped. "And then demanded that I stop practicing shooting, riding, or anything else that didn't have his permission."

"Did he?" Ammie sniffed and glanced over at the rifles.

Knowing exactly what her friend was thinking, Dorrie couldn't have agreed more. As confused as she always felt around Jules, there was one thing she knew for certain. He could not go all high and mighty and tell her what to do. Walking over to the rock, she picked up her gun and aimed it at their impromptu targets.

"Do you want to continue our practice?" Ammie asked.

Dorrie gave her a wide smile and a nod. "Yes. Yes, I do."

7

"They come up to the house bold as brass, right in the middle of the day."

The hat in the big rancher's hands shook from the fingers gripping its brim. Ben Hanson was tall and carried a solid weight of muscle, attesting to a life of hard work. A neatly trimmed, dark beard covered most of his face and accented the bright burn in his blue eyes. He looked out of place in the soft hues of the parlor in the McKenzie home, and had only glanced at the divan before choosing to remain standing, his legs braced apart, and his shoulders slightly hunched over.

Since the man kept to his feet, so did Jules, nodding at Dina when she bustled in with a tray loaded with a large pot of coffee, mugs, and a plate piled high with biscuits. She set it on the table in front of the fireplace and nodded briskly at their unexpected visitor.

"Now you just help yourself, Mr. Hanson, and don't be shy about it."

"I'm sorry to barge in on you this way, ma'am." The rancher ducked his head in thanks when Dina handed him a mug of coffee, the steam rolling up and over its sides.

Dina smiled at him as she sent a questioning look to Jules who shook his head. "Don't you worry about that. A doctor and two US Marshals live in this house. We're used to having visitors at all hours of the day and night."

Jules waited until she'd exited the room and shut the parlor doors behind her before he said anything.

"Why don't you start from the beginning and tell me everything that happened."

"Not much I can tell you." Hanson's words were short and choppy, the fire in his gaze growing with each one. "My wife and kids were at the house, and me and the men were out checking on the cattle when my oldest son comes riding over the hill like a pack of wolves were chasing him. He's got blood on his face and he was shaking so bad it's a wonder he didn't fall out of that saddle. But he gets to me and tells me some men were in the house with his ma. She'd sent him and the littler ones out the back window. Told them to hide in the field behind the house." The rancher's chest puffed out and his voice was tinged with pride. "My boy tucked those little ones away and told them not to move, then he went back to the house to help his ma. But those men saw him coming and took a shot at him. They hit the rock next to the log he dove behind."

"Is that how he got the blood on his face? From rock chips hitting him?"

The rancher nodded. "That's what he said. Since he couldn't get closer to the house, he ran for the barn. Tater's horse was already saddled, so my boy jumped on him and came looking for me. Rode that horse right out of that barn with them men shooting at him. But he still managed to hear one of them yell out, calling for Patrick."

"Patrick? That's good to know." Jules frowned. "Who's Tater?"

"My foreman. We found him in the back of the barn out cold with a nasty gash on his head. They hit him from behind." Hanson set his still-full mug of coffee on the table and clenched a fist at his side. "Cowards. Sneaking up behind a man and putting a scare into my woman and children."

The marshal silently agreed with that. After a brief hesitation, he forced himself to ask the question he might not want an answer to. "Are the rest of your kids and your wife all right?"

"If they weren't I wouldn't be standing here talking with you. I'd be out hunting those bastards down. But Laurie didn't take to that idea much. She wanted me to come into town and talk to the sheriff. He sent me to you. The sheriff said you were already looking for those men."

Relieved that no one had been killed, Jules nodded. "I am. I have a man out tracking them, and intend to join him in the next day or so."

"That wouldn't be Ethan Mayes, would it?" The big man smiled when Jules nodded again. "I heard you two were tight. Met Ethan a time or two over a bit of horse trading. He's a good man." Hanson's shoulders relaxed. "And Ethan says the same about you."

Jules smiled. "We grew up together. I've known Ethan for seventeen years, ever since I was twelve years old."

"So you two work together?"

"From time to time," Jules said. "He's the best tracker in the territory. Did your wife happen to tell you what the men looked like?"

"She said there were three of them. They weren't real big

men, and kept their bandannas around their faces. She says they all had green eyes and talked funny."

"Funny? How?"

"Like they were from somewhere else. She's got a good ear for things. Plays a flute real well." He sighed and raised one hand to stroke slowly over his beard. "I'm going to have to leave extra men to guard the place while the rest of us are out working the ranch. I can't afford to do that for long. If you don't catch them, I'll have to bring my wife and kids into town for a spell."

Jules had every intention of catching the Green Gang, but it never hurt to use extra caution. "That might not be a bad idea, Mr. Hanson. We'll get them locked up. They killed a bank guard on a train, so you can't be too careful as long as they're running loose."

"A little heavier hand with whatever they hit Tater with, and he might be dead too." Hanson shook his head. "They'd kill a man just to get a sack full of supplies." At Jules' surprised look, he nodded. "That's all they took. Didn't even bother with going through my writing desk or they would have found the gold coins I keep in a box in the drawer. They took the coffee and flour mostly, waved their guns around after taking a couple of shots at my boy, and then left. And they don't shoot so good, either."

"Why do you say that?" Jules had been thinking the same thing. They didn't hit the boy or the horse when they came out of the barn, or even the log he'd hidden behind first. Either they didn't want to hurt him, or they were poor shots. And he was leaning toward that second explanation. Just a gut feeling he had.

"Doesn't seem like they can hit what they aim at," the rancher said. "Though I'm grateful for that."

"I am too. I don't care to bury good folks." Jules' forehead wrinkled in thought. "Your ranch is a couple of hours to the northeast, isn't it?" Jules waited for Hanson's nod. "Did your wife happen to see what direction they were headed?"

"She didn't see where they came from. The first she knew something was wrong was when they walked right into the house. But she watched them leave. They went over the hill behind the barn. So that'd be southwest of my place. Could be they took that direction because they knew we were working in the north pastures."

Or they were headed into town. If that were true, Jules wondered if they were holed up somewhere in the city, hiding among a population that swelled with new arrivals every day. It could be he and Ethan were looking in the wrong place.

TWO HOURS after Ben Hanson had headed back to his ranch, Jules opened the front door and smiled at his second unexpected visitor that afternoon. He stood aside and motioned for the tall man with the lean build to come on in.

Luke Donovan, Ethan's brother-in-law, flashed the smile that had melted hearts all over the city before he'd taken the fall himself and married Shannon Mayes. Once Jules had closed the door, Luke gave his honorary nephew a hard slap on the back.

"It's good to see you, Marshal." He stepped back and grinned at Jules. "Shannon sends her best, along with a complaint about you having her brother running all over the countryside looking for train robbers."

"I'll take that into consideration." Jules returned the grin. "Abby's out seeing patients and Cade is over at John's on business, but I'm glad to see you.

"I just came from John's so got to spend time talking with your older brother." Luke cocked his head to one side. "He sent me over here to check up on you."

"Is that a fact?" Jules frowned. Using one of Cade's favorite responses had made him sound just like his brother, and judging by the wide smile on Luke's face, his uncle obviously thought so too.

"I'm sure Dina has coffee on the stove if you've got some time."

"That sounds good. I could use a cup before I head home." Luke looked toward the hallway leading into the back of the house. "It's a long ride."

That wasn't any surprise to Jules. None of his uncles liked to leave their wives alone at home at night. It made them more nervous than it did the women. Of course every one of their wives had one of those specially made, lightweight guns that Beth seemed to enjoy handing out so freely. Setting the notion aside since it only got his temper up, Jules concentrated on the man standing in front of him. Luke had light-brown hair, and eyes that were the exact same color. But his usual easy-going smile showed some strain, and there were dark circles under his eyes.

None of the ranchers outside the city were getting much sleep lately.

Jules made his way to the kitchen with Luke following close behind. It didn't take long for him to stoke up the low embers in the stove and get the coffee heating. He turned and leaned against the wooden counter next to the stove and looked at Luke. He'd taken a seat at the table against the far wall. It was larger than the table Jules' had grown up with, but then the family was bigger too. And Luke had added to it with his three kids, all slightly younger than Cade and Abby's son and daughter.

It was a jolt to see the late afternoon sunlight that was coming in through the window reflect off the silver woven through his uncle's hair. Jules never gave much thought to the fact that as he'd gotten older, so had all the aunts and uncles. Most of the time it appeared that nothing had changed. Luke, Ian, his own brother, Cade, and all of them still stood tall and strong. But that tiny glint of silver had Jules seeing a vulnerability.

The thought made him uneasy in ways he couldn't explain to himself, so he set it aside and put his focus on why Luke had stopped by. He knew it wasn't because Cade had sent him to check up on his little brother.

"What's on your mind, Luke?"

"More of what's on Ethan's mind than my own. He wanted me to give you a message." Luke shifted in the chair. "It seems he found those tracks you've been looking for and he's going to see if he can find where those men are camped." Luke gave him a narrow-eyed look. "The same ones Ben Hanson probably just told you about." Luke shrugged when Jules' eyebrows beetled together. "I ran into him heading out of town. We talked for a bit."

"They're the same ones," Jules confirmed.

"Cade told me about this Green Gang." Luke let out a snort. "My brother-in-law hasn't been real talkative. All he said was that he was helping you out. And he wanted me to tell you he'd meet you at the crossroads in four days."

That was two days longer than they'd planned. Jules wondered if Ethan had caught a stronger scent of their quarry than he'd let on to his brother-in-law.

"He also said he couldn't make that stock delivery we've been planning," Luke quietly added. "He didn't say as much, but that told me he's got a reason to stay closer to home."

"That might not be a bad idea." Jules echoed the same thing he'd told Ben Hanson not two hours before.

Jules was also relieved. Even with Cade joining in the hunt, they could still use Ethan's help. At the hiss from the stove, he got two mugs off the shelf and proceeded to pour out the coffee.

Luke leaned back in his chair and stretched his long legs out in front of him as Jules set mugs on the table and took a seat. "I don't like the reason he's hanging around the ranch more than usual, but it will make Shannon happy. She hasn't seen as much of him as she's wanted to for the last five years." He glanced over at his honorary nephew. "Have you seen Ammie lately? I stopped by to check up on her, but Charlotte said she wasn't home. And didn't volunteer to tell me where she was, either."

Up to no good, and probably dragging Dorrie right along with her. Jules ran an agitated hand through his hair. "I ran into her and Dorrie yesterday. They were practicing with their rifles."

Luke's grin was back. "Uh oh. That can't be good. What's Dorrie talked Ammie into this time?"

Startled, Jules stared back at him. "I think you've got that backwards."

A smiling Luke shook his head. "Not as I recall. Dorrie used to start the mischief just as often as Ammie did. Maybe more so since Charlotte's niece spent so much more time with you boys when you were growing up, so she had you and Ethan to keep her in line. Dorrie spent more time out at that shooting beach than Ammie did. At least when you were younger. Beth told me she's been doing some catching up on that the last few years."

Jules was having a hard time adjusting his view of

Dorrie to match what Luke was saying. He didn't remember her getting into any trouble when they were growing up.

"Our Dorrie's a pretty one, and fits right in with all the women in the family," Luke laughed. "Easy on the eyes, but she's no angel, and has a mind of her own."

"I know that," Jules grumbled.

"It's a good thing to remember, son." Luke's grin slowly faded as he picked up his coffee and took a healthy swallow. "And speaking of Dorrie, Ian dropped by John's while I was there. He was asking to have a few guards arranged for his home and Maggie's shop. He told us what he thinks is going on. He also said he's talked to you about it."

The marshal nodded. "He was here. The only one who doesn't believe someone is watching the Dolan women is Maggie."

"And that's a puzzle." Luke rubbed the side of his jaw. "Maggie's always been like a mother bear protecting her cubs when it comes to her family."

"That's how Dorrie feels about it too."

"How else does Dorrie feel?"

"She has this notion that the man is only following Maggie and Anna, and a foolish idea that she might be able to catch him on her own." Jules' voice gathered steam as he warmed up to the subject that had been plaguing him since he'd seen Dorrie on that beach yesterday, holding a gun. "I told her to wait for Ethan, but she's sure I need him more than she does. And I know she's out there practicing so she can go chasing off on her own while I'm busy tracking the Green Gang. And I..." Jules trailed off when he spotted Luke's huge smile.

"What are you grinning at?"

"It's just nice that you're paying attention to what Dorrie

thinks about the situation." Luke lifted his coffee mug, effectively hiding his smile.

"More like trying to rope it in," Jules snapped. Annoyed that his temper had gotten the best of him again, Jules relaxed his jaw and shook his head. "She's a handful."

"Aren't they all? I know she was adopted, but Dorrie's certainly taken after her mama." Luke nodded at Jules' grunt. "Maggie's been known to take on a grown man or two when she should have left it to Ian to deal with. Drove Ian crazy at the time. Just like Dorrie is doing with you."

Jules ignored that last part as he aimed his gaze at Luke. "Maggie? When did she do something like that?"

Luke took another deep sip of his coffee before setting the mug on the table and getting to his feet. "Next time you're out our way, you should ask Shannon to show you that book of hers. She keeps a family history of sorts. You might find out a lot of interesting things about your elders."

"Elders?" Jules snorted in disbelief. Any impression he'd had of Luke being vulnerable evaporated at the sight of the tall man with the broad shoulders standing in front of him. Jules also got to his feet and extended his hand.

"I'm glad you stopped by, Luke."

"Glad to see you too. Just wanted to give you Ethan's message, and to tell you to take care of Dorrie's problem." He winked at Jules. "Not that you needed to be told that."

8

T wo days later, Jules was once again standing outside Maggie's shop. But this time he walked right up to the solid green door and turned the handle, stepping inside as he removed his hat.

He looked around and spotted Robbie, lounging against a wall on the far end of the room. Both surprised, and more than a touch annoyed, Jules gave his friend a curt nod, only to have Robbie wiggle his eyebrows and jerk his head to the side. Jules' gaze tracked in the direction Robbie had indicated. A smile crossed his lips as he saw Dorrie, standing behind a counter, listening intently to a customer.

After a few minutes, the older heavy-set matron nodded and moved off toward a rack holding several hats, leaving behind a man who continued to talk to Dorrie. Jules' eyes narrowed as the unknown man, dressed in a black suit and a white shirt with a stiff collar, leaned far over the counter as he nodded and smiled at something Dorrie was telling him. If he bent any further, the dandified gentleman would be lying on the counter.

He glanced back at Robbie who rolled his eyes and

pointed a finger at Jules and then at Dorrie. Jules shot him an exasperated look but walked over to stand right behind the man who was obviously bending over backwards to impress Dorrie. *Or bending forward*, Jules thought.

Since he was almost a head shorter than Jules, the marshal towered over the man as he stood with his arms crossed over his chest and his blue-eyed gaze narrowed on Dorrie. She shot him a quick glance, then ignored him for a full minute, clearly expecting him to get her message and retreat into a corner and wait for her to finish talking to the man. But Jules didn't budge. She finally took her attention off what Jules assumed was a would-be suitor and glared up at him.

"Can I help you, Marshal?"

"Marshal?" The single word came out in a squeak as the man took a step back and wheeled around, which put his nose square into the middle of Jules' chest.

"Oh my." The man lifted his chin and tilted his head all the way back until he could look up into Jules' face, his eyes as large as saucers.

"I'd appreciate it if you'd take a step back." Jules accompanied that request with a hard stare which had the man quickly taking a hop backward.

"Certainly, um... Marshal. That is, I'd be glad to."

Jules pretended not to hear Dorrie's loud sigh, or see the glare she continued to direct at him, but kept his gaze on the man who was trapped between him and the counter. Jules didn't move an inch.

"Graham?" Dorrie smiled when the man's head swiveled around. "I don't know if you've met Marshal McKenzie?" She raised her gaze to Jules. "And Marshal, this is Graham Tucker, of the St. Louis Tuckers. He's here visiting his sister. He came in on the train just yesterday."

"Visiting." Jules gave Graham Tucker a smile that didn't quite reach his eyes. "Is that right?"

"Yes, sir, Marshal, sir," Graham stuttered, looking frantically past Jules to where his sister was still looking over the hats. "Frannie, that's my sister, she and her husband live here." He gave Jules a weak smile. "But I won't be in town long."

Jules shrugged. "Spend all the time you'd like in the *rest* of the town, Mr. Tucker."

Graham rapidly bobbed his head. "Certainly, certainly." He carefully began to slide sideways. "I'm sure there's a lot for me to see here in San Francisco. It's a lovely place.

"We like it." Jules didn't bother to hide his smile at the sheer relief on Mr. Tucker's face when he'd sidestepped far enough away from Jules that he'd managed to regain his freedom.

"Yes, yes, I'm sure you do." He gave a brief nod to Robbie, who was grinning at him, before rushing over to tap his sister on the shoulder. After a brief whispered conversation, he hurried out the door. The now stiff-backed Frannie turned and gave the marshal a cool glance and very brief nod, before her gaze passed right over Dorrie as if she wasn't even there. Sweeping her skirts around with a wide arc, she marched out of the shop.

Jules hadn't liked the way the woman had snubbed Dorrie. He took an automatic step toward the door.

"Don't, Jules."

Dorrie's soft command had him stopping and turning to face her. "She had no call to be rude."

"She's a frequent customer who pays her bills on time." Dorrie's shoulders lifted in a quick shrug. "That's more important to Mam's shop than her high-and-mighty ways." She lifted one hand and wagged a finger at him. "And you weren't very polite to her brother either. That might have had something to do with it." She picked up a bolt of cloth, wrapping both arms around it. "I'll put this away and then you can tell me why you've come by today."

He watched her move off, not taking his eyes off her even when Robbie strolled over and leaned against the counter beside him.

"Entertaining, Marshal. But can't say Mr. Tucker was much of a challenge." He followed Jules' gaze. "A man should have to work for something he wants so badly."

Jules reluctantly glanced over at his friend. "I don't think Mr. Tucker's spent much of his life working. I doubt if those boots he had on have ever seen a speck of mud."

Robbie laughed as he shook his head. "You and Ethan. You're a pair if ever there was one. But since he's not here and you are, I guess I'll just have to show you how things are done."

Already exasperated with what he'd come to tell Dorrie, and with finding a strange man fawning all over her, Jules wasn't in the mood for Robbie's teasing. "What are you talking about, Smith? I don't have time for games."

Robbie straightened up as Dorrie made her way back to them. "That's too bad, McKenzie, because sometimes those games can be fun." He turned his back on Jules and gave Dorrie a big smile.

"If you have any more, I'll be happy to help you put them away."

When Dorrie shook her head, Robbie took a step toward her and reached over to capture one of her hands. "Let me help you get back around that counter, Dorrie." He lifted their joined hands to his chest. "And has anyone..." Robbie paused and shot a sideways glance at Jules. "... told you how pretty you look today?"

Dorrie's dimple made an appearance as her eyes sparkled back at Robbie. "No, they haven't, as a matter of fact. And to borrow words from Mam, what do you want for all that blarney coming out of your mouth, Robbie Smith?"

"I've already told you that, darlin'. I want you to come out to the ranch and cook for us. I promise everyone will pitch in to help, so you'd mostly just be giving us orders on what to do."

Jules stepped up and firmly clasped his fingers around Dorrie's wrist, pulling her hand away from Robbie's. "That's enough of your fooling around, Robbie. I need to talk with Dorrie."

"Uh huh. So do I." Robbie's expression turned serious. "It isn't a bad idea, Jules. Dorrie coming out to the ranch. There's no threat to her out there, and knowing she's safe would take a worry off her father and off you. Anna could come out too, for that matter."

Jules fell silent as he thought it over, not even aware that he'd kept hold of Dorrie's hand. It would be a relief to be sure that she was somewhere safe. The problem was, he didn't know just where that could be. The Green Gang was likely holed up somewhere between Luke's ranch and Robbie's. At least that's what his gut was telling him.

Not willing to discuss that in front of Dorrie, Jules settled on a more obvious reason why Robbie's idea wouldn't work. "I don't have time to take her out to your place."

But Robbie snorted at that. "I can take her with the supply wagon. We have double the men with us, to be sure we don't run into any trouble."

Jules glared at him. "I said 'no', Robbie."

His friend's shoulders went rigid. "And you're acting too much like a marshal who thinks he's everyone's boss."

"And both of you are forgetting to ask me how *I* feel about going out to Robbie's place." Dorrie snatched her hand away from Jules and put the counter between herself and the two men she'd been friends with for a good part of her life. "You're both acting ridiculous." She looked over at the rancher. "And you don't even know if I *can* cook, Robbie."

The indignation left Robbie's eyes as his mouth twitched at the corners. "No I don't, darlin'. Now that you mention it, I don't believe I've ever tasted your cooking." He leaned his elbows on the counter. "Care to invite me over for supper?"

"No, she doesn't." Jules gave his friend's foot a hard nudge with the tip of his boot. "That's enough of this nonsense. I need to talk to Dorrie, then have a word with you about the Green Gang."

Robbie's whole demeanor changed. Within an instant he and Jules were back to their familiar understanding of each other. "I'll wait for you. Take your time." He winked at Dorrie. "And you give him a piece of your mind about trying to run your life for you." He laughed and stepped away, barely avoiding a harder push from Jules' boot.'

Once Robbie was on his way to the far side of the shop, Jules turned his attention back to Dorrie. He thought the easy-going Robbie was right about one thing. Dorrie looked very pretty today in her light blue dress with a matching sash around the middle. A wide white ribbon tied her long fall of rich copper curls at the nape of her neck. He'd always liked that she rarely wore her hair up. He'd often admired the look of it cascading down her back.

"What did you want to talk to me about, Jules?"

Dorrie's question interrupted his thoughts, bringing him back to his most pressing problem.

"I thought we agreed that you wouldn't go out by yourself?"

Dorrie rolled her eyes. "No. You said I shouldn't go out by myself. I didn't agree to anything."

Jules didn't like that answer one bit. "It isn't safe, Dorrie."

"It isn't safe for Mam or Anna," she insisted. "I'm fine." She narrowed her eyes at him. "And how did you know I went out by myself? Are you spying on me?"

"Your father has guards watching the house and shop."

"Oh. So my father's guards told you I went out?"

Jules shifted from one foot to the other. It would have been easy enough to agree with that, but he didn't want to lie to her. "No. My own men told me."

"So, you are spying on me." Dorrie put her hands on her hips. "With Da's guards keeping an eye out, why do you need your own men doing the same thing? They'd make better use of their time by helping you with that Green Gang, not lingering about watching us."

Jules ran a hand through his hair. What she'd said was true enough. The fact was, he didn't know why he'd kept the men watching her. Or why he'd told them to keep her in their sights and leave his aunt and Anna to Ian's guards. But he wasn't about to admit to that.

"You've got your wish. They'll be heading out with Cade soon. I've already had to give them other tasks until then." Which was also true, although it didn't sit well with Jules. But there wasn't much help for it. They were experienced men, and he couldn't cover everything on his own with Cade being gone so much lately.

Dorrie's arms fell back to her sides, and she fixed her gaze on Jules. "Will you be going with Cade?"

He shook his head. "I'm heading out in two days to meet up with Ethan."

She bit her lower lip. "So Ethan will be coming into town to meet you?"

Jules gave her a puzzled look. "No. We're meeting at the crossroads. Why?"

"Except for those few minutes at your house, I haven't seen him in a long time. Even when he's home on the ranch, he doesn't come into town. It's as if he's avoiding something."

Or someone. Jules only shrugged. He wasn't going to make any comments on how Ethan chose to live his life. Right now he was more concerned about the woman standing across the counter from him.

"I need your promise that you won't go out alone while I'm gone, Dorrie." When she pursed her lips, he dipped his head to one side and added "please."

She finally sighed. "I promise. And you need to give one in return that you'll keep yourself safe."

He smiled. "You have my word on it." He lifted his hat and placed it on his head, putting two fingers to the brim as he nodded at her. "I'm heading back to my place today, but I'll see you in a few weeks."

"I'll be watching for you."

Pleased with the warmth in her response, Jules' step was light as he headed for the door, motioning for Robbie to follow him out.

Once the two men were on the sidewalk, Robbie raised an eyebrow at him. "You look like your talk ended better than it started out."

"Let it be, Robbie. I had a visit from Ben Hanson yesterday, and there's something you need to know." Jules glanced back at the windows spanning the front of the shop. "Let's take a walk."

9

"I'm tired of sitting in the shop for days and days."

Anna's whiny tone grated across her older sister's nerves.

Dorrie stoically ignored the sixteen-year-old as she continued to rearrange hats on the shelves near the front of the shop. She usually enjoyed the quiet hours before they were open for customers, walking down the long aisle split in two by the racks of hats and what Mam called "bits and bobs" used to adorn any piece of ladies' attire. But Anna's constant stream of complaints the day before had had Dorrie going to bed with a headache, and waking up this morning with it still lurking at the base of her skull. A night of sleep apparently hadn't improved Anna's mood because her younger sister had started up again the minute they'd arrived at the shop.

"I don't know why I can't go out, at least to the morning market. Mam would let me."

"Mam isn't here." Dorrie glanced over at her sister. "And she didn't say you could go out alone."

The pout on Anna's lips grew bigger. "She didn't say I couldn't go out. That's as good as saying I can."

"No, it isn't, and you well know it Anna Dolan."

"She'd say it was fine if you came with me. You don't need to mind the shop until half past ten. There's plenty of time for us to go to the market."

The change in Anna's tone from a whine to a wheedle was making Dorrie's lingering headache radiate up to her temples. She closed her eyes and rubbed them with two fingers.

"Anna, I don't want to spend another day arguing with you. If you're so sure Mam would let you go to the market, then you can wait for her so she can take you."

"It will be too late. You heard Da. He told Mam he wanted to talk with her and then practically threw us out of our own house." Anna flounced over to a straight-backed chair next to the counter and plopped down, folding her arms around her waist.

"I believe it's Da's house." Dorrie's dry tone echoed through the shop. "And we didn't come here any earlier than we usually do."

Dorrie deliberately turned her back to her sister so Anna wouldn't see how troubled she was. Mam and Da never argued, at least not with any real heat in it. Except for now. And having grown up with her mam's Irish temper, it wouldn't have bothered Dorrie much if there had been a little shouting and carrying on. But this was different.

It was the cold, polite exchange between her parents that had her on edge. She'd never seen them act this way. Never. And she wasn't sure how to react to it, or deal with it. Dorrie glanced over at Anna who sat slightly slumped over, her lip still stuck out as she stared at the floor. She was sure the barrier between her parents was affecting Anna even more. It really wasn't like her little sister to be so grumpy and annoying.

Or her, either.

But it wasn't just Mam who weighed on her mind. It was Jules. Tomorrow he'd be off to join Ethan in hunting for the Green Gang. A gang who'd killed a man, and likely wouldn't hesitate to gun down a US Marshal. Her dreams had been plagued with a vision of an ambush with Jules fighting for his life. And maybe losing. A sudden chill had her shaking from a hard shiver, even though she was standing in a patch of sunlight streaming in through the window.

The bell over the shop's door tinkled as Kate stepped into the long room. She greeted Dorrie with her cheery smile which faded a bit before she glanced over at Anna. Kate had been her mam's first friend when Maggie had made the trip from Ireland with her da and brothers, and Dorrie had always considered the genial woman a second mother. So when Kate put her hands on her wide hips and turned a frown on her, Dorrie felt a twinge of guilt at giving her such a poor welcome.

"Now then. What's the matter with the two of you?"

"Anna's tired of being cooped up." Dorrie drew in the clean whiff of air that had followed Kate into the shop.

Her mam's oldest friend unpinned her hat and set it aside, along with the large bag with the woven hemp handles that she always carried, before placing her hands back on her wide hips. "And what's given *you* the long face?"

Dorrie immediately schooled her features into a pleasant smile. "Mostly listening to Anna's complaints. A chore I'll now be able to share with you."

"It's one I'm thinkin' you should keep for yourself." Kate

picked up her hat and bag and disappeared through a curtain leading into the dressing and sewing rooms in the back of the shop. When she reappeared a minute later, she was tying a long apron around her waist. "I also think there's a wee bit more to your worryin' than Anna." She stepped closer to Dorrie and lowered her voice. "How's your mam and da doin', then?"

"The same as yesterday," Dorrie whispered back. "They're barely speaking to each other."

Kate shook her head without dislodging even one hair of the tightly coiled braid at the nape of her neck. "She's a stubborn one, Maggie is. Always has been. And I imagine she's givin' poor Ian fits by not tellin' him whatever's been botherin' her."

Dorrie quickly pounced on that. "So you think something's wrong with Mam too?"

"I do too," Anna declared. She jumped out of her chair and rushed over to where the two older women were standing. When they simply stared at her, Anna stared right back. "She's my mam as much as yours, Dorrie Dolan, so I get to hear what Kate thinks, same as you."

Knowing Anna was right, and whatever was affecting their parents affected both daughters as well, Dorrie put an arm around Anna's shoulders and drew her in so the two of them were facing Kate together. Her headache receded when Anna put an arm around her waist and gave her older sister a quick hug.

"Has Mam told you what she's been upset about these last few weeks?" Dorrie's brown eyes looked steadily at Kate. Whatever it was, not knowing was putting too much worry in the family. And she had Jules riding into danger to add to it.

Dorrie exchanged a disappointed look with her sister when Kate shook her head.

"She hasn't said a word to me, more's the pity. And it's not for lack of naggin'. But she's keepin' her mouth closed and her thoughts to herself." Kate's ample bosom heaved in a big sigh. "And that's not like her either."

The three of them stood in a gloomy silence until Kate clapped her hands together.

"That's enough of this." She put a smile on her lips and nodded at the pair standing in front of her. "Some things are best left to a husband and wife to work out. It's not for us to be blatherin' on about." She glanced out the window. "It's a bright day, and another good hour before we have to open the shop, even if your mam isn't here. She'd expect that. But until then, you two should go out and enjoy a bit of fresh air and sunshine. It will help your mood," she said, smiling at Anna before switching her gaze to Dorrie. "And that headache I can see in your eyes. Go to the market and fetch us a bunch of flowers for the shop, and maybe a fresh vegetable or two for our noon meal. It will get your mind off your mam, and a certain marshal."

"Marshal?" Anna's ears perked up. She turned wide eyes to her sister. "Is Kate talking about Jules? Are you pining for Jules?"

Dorrie narrowed her eyes at the sudden grin on Anna's face. "I'm not pining for anyone, and if you want me to take you to the market, you'd better be quick about getting your shawl.

She watched Anna scamper away before giving Kate an exasperated glare. "You shouldn't put notions into Anna's head."

The short cheery Irish woman's eyes crinkled as she laughed. "Why not? They're in yours. And don't you be shakin' that head of yours at me, Dorrie. I helped your mam raise you. I know that look you get whenever Jules is around. And he's lookin' back at you exactly the same way."

He is? Dorrie wasn't even aware of the smile on her lips, even as she rolled her eyes in response. "He's like a brother. Of course I worry about him. Marshalling is a dangerous job."

"I'm ready," Anna declared, much to Dorrie's relief. She was happy to have an excuse to close Jules as a topic of discussion with Kate.

"Then you'd best be goin'." Kate stepped forward. "I'll tie your cap on for you while Dorrie gets her shawl."

TWENTY MINUTES LATER, Dorrie was truly enjoying herself as she and Anna wandered among the wagons laden with a wide variety of goods for sale. She greeted the merchants who'd become friends over the years, stopping to chat for a minute or two with several of them. She strolled along, hoping to find Brenna's wagon in her usual spot.

Aside from Ammie, Brenna Quinlan was the only other close friend and confidante that Dorrie had. The two had hit it off over a decade ago, when Brenna had come to live on a neighbor's farm, several miles east of the city. She'd taken to helping them sell their produce in the market, which is where Dorrie had first met her. She grinned when the familiar voice rang out through the crowd of people milling around the wagons.

"Dorrie!"

Latching onto Anna's arm, Dorrie dragged her sister along. She wove her way around groups of bodies as she made her way to Brenna's wagon. Her friend was standing near the lowered tailgate, waving frantically over her head.

Topping Dorrie by a good three inches, Brenna was dressed in her usual attire of britches, with a rope belt holding them in place on her slim waist, and a coarse linen shirt, accompanied by an oversized shirt. It wasn't the most acceptable attire for a lady, but Brenna only shrugged at the censuring looks from the women around her.

Since she had to leave before dawn and drive a team and wagon through the fog and dark, and then back again in the afternoon, Dorrie's friend had always maintained she didn't have time to mess around with skirts and petticoats. In Dorrie's opinion, Brenna's choice of attire was certainly more practical, but it was too bad. The battered straw hat and boy's attire hid the natural beauty of her friend's rich black hair and striking blue eyes. She'd always suspected if Brenna ever had a chance to don a pretty dress, she'd seriously rival Ammie and Lillian as one of the most stunning women in the city. But it wasn't Brenna's priority, and never had been.

Surviving had always come first.

The Quinlans had taken Brenna in when her parents had died in a fire when she was seven, and had always treated her like a grandchild since their own son and his family lived too far away for them to visit often. So at least Brenna had been blessed with a roof over her head and good people to help finish raising her. And she'd certainly more than earned her keep with all the work she did on the farm.

When Dorrie finally made it to where her friend was standing, waiting for her, the two women greeted each other with a long fierce hug.

When they parted, Brenna stepped to the side and

gave a clearly startled Anna the same hug. "Before your sister and I get into our usual gab, how are you doing, Anna?"

"I'm fine. I wish I could wear britches. Mam is the only one of the aunts who never does. So we can't either."

"Speak for yourself." Brenna pointed a finger at Dorrie and grinned. "I believe I've seen that one in a pair of them a time or two."

Anna giggled. "When Mam isn't looking."

"Which is the smart way to do it," Dorrie declared. "How've you been, Brenna?"

"Working mostly. Memaw hasn't been feeling well, and Gramps needs more help with the chores."

Dorrie carefully studied Brenna's face. "How bad is Memaw? I can ask Abby to make the trip out to the farm. I'm sure she'd be happy to look in on her."

Brenna gave her a smile filled with warmth. "Thank you. I might have to ask you for that favor." She pointed a thumb toward her wagon. "What can I get for you? I'll give you the friend price. You won't even have to haggle for it."

"What's the friend price?" Anna asked, craning her neck to study the vegetables in the wagon.

The tall dark-haired Brenna laid a hand on the younger woman's shoulder. "A smart person values their friends and never asks for anything in return."

Anna wrinkled her nose. "What does that mean?"

"That I don't take money from friends." Brenna tweaked the lacy edge of Anna's cap.

"Kate said we should bring back some flowers and a vegetable for dinner."

"Anna!" Dorrie admonished before glancing at Brenna. "Flowers would be nice. We need cheering up today. But only if you'll let me pay for them. Friends know each other's worth too. And you work too hard for me not to pay you out of respect for your labors."

"You get that from your mam?" Brenna grinned. "I've got really nice sunflowers from Memaw's garden. Brought them along in case one of those fancy houses wants them."

Dorrie looked over Anna's head at the bright yellow flowers tied up and standing tall in a bucket near the back of the wagon. But she was more interested in the pail next to them that was filled with white daisies.

Brenna followed her gaze then hopped up onto the wagon bed. She quickly retrieved the flower-filled pail and set it in front of Dorrie before easing herself back to the ground.

"They are pretty." Brenna smiled at Anna. "Would you mind getting me a cup of water from the bucket on the floor of the front of the wagon? It was a dusty ride in today."

As Anna moved off, Brenna took a step closer to her best friend. "Why do you need cheering up? You can't tell me that marshal isn't helping you any."

"Jules?" Dorrie blinked.

"I don't want him hurting your feelings because he refused to help you."

"Jules?"

Her friend laughed. "You sound like one of those parrots I've heard about, repeating the same thing over and over again. Yes. I'm talking about Jules. The one you go all soft-eyed over every time you mention his name."

"I do not," Dorrie instantly protested. "He's part of my family."

"Not a blood part he isn't." Brenna removed her straw hat and shook her head. "So is he the reason you need cheering up?"

"Not entirely," Dorrie admitted. "I mean he is family, and

he's about to go off to hunt for some very dangerous men, but mostly it's Mam. And now Da as well."

"Tell me everything."

Grateful to have someone she so completely trusted to talk over her worries with, Dorrie proceeded to relate everything that had happened. From the first time she'd noticed the man following them, to the conversation with Jules the day before. When she was finished, she gave a relieved sigh.

"You've been seeing a man following your mam and your sister around?" Brenna bit the inside of her cheek. "But not you?"

"I don't think so. I've only seen him when Mam or Anna are around. What do you think of how Mam's acting? It isn't like her to ignore this, especially if it involves Anna."

"Or you," Brenna stated as she leaned to the side and looked toward the front of the wagon. "But it's Anna I'm thinking of right now. She's taking a long time to get that water."

"What?" Dorrie whirled around, her skirt flaring out as she jumped to the side of the wagon so she could see all the way to the horses standing patiently in front of it. Anna was nowhere in sight.

"Where is she?" Panic had Dorrie's stomach doing flips as she picked up her skirts and sprinted toward the horses. Even though it was ridiculous, she couldn't help but peer into the opening below the wagon's bench seat before turning to scan the surrounding area. Still no sign of Anna.

"Come on. We can see better from the seat."

Brenna grabbed a handhold on the wagon's side and hefted herself up. Without any hesitation, Dorrie lifted her skirts up to her knees with one hand and grabbed the handhold for support with the other. She scrambled up to the narrow bench seat and stood on it, frantically looking over the heads of the crowd.

"There." Brenna pointed to her left. "She's over there next to that wagon filled with cabbage."

Dorrie finally spotted Anna, but her relief was short-lived. Her little sister was having a lively conversation with the same man who'd been following them. Even at this distance, Dorrie was sure of it.

10

Not registering what Brenna was saying to her, Dorrie dropped to the seat, held onto its side, and jumped from the wagon. Giving up a small prayer of thanks that her skirts hadn't tangled around her feet, Dorrie quickly started to push and shove her way through the crowd, not stopping to offer any apologies at the offended looks directed at her as she made a straight line to where she'd seen Anna. She broke through the solid wall of bodies just in time to see the stranger reach out a hand encased in a rough leather glove and place it on Anna's slender shoulder.

Dorrie leaped over the last few feet and grabbed her sister by the back of her dress, yanking her away from the man as she knocked his hand off Anna's shoulder.

"Get away from her."

The man pulled his hat low over his face and ducked his head so all Dorrie got a clear look at was his mouth and chin. He wasn't much taller than she was, and his body was whip thin.

"You have no right to interfere."

She may not have been able to see his face, but Dorrie could certainly hear the menace in his voice. She stepped around her sister, putting herself between Anna and the man.

"She's my sister, and I'm telling you to stay away from her. And from my mam."

"Your mam, is it?"

Dorrie frowned. Now he sounded amused. Having had enough of whatever game this man was playing, her temper led the way and she reached out, grabbing onto his arm before he could step away.

"Who are you?"

"You're no blood kin of mine, so I've no reason to listen to you girl." He abruptly twisted his arm, easily dislodging Dorrie's hold on him. "And you'd best stay out of me business."

With that low guttural warning, he turned and walked swiftly away. It only took seconds for him to become lost in the crowd.

As much as she wanted to follow him, Dorrie's feet stayed right where they were. She wasn't about to leave Anna alone.

"Who was that?" Brenna's voice came over Dorrie's shoulder as she peered after the stranger.

"I don't know." Frustrated, Dorrie spun around and put her hands on her hips. She glared at Anna.

"Why did you wander off? You were supposed to stay close to the wagon."

Anna mimicked Dorrie's pose and stuck her chin out for good measure. "I did. He came up and talked to me. Then we just started walking. I didn't even notice how far we'd gone."

"You shouldn't have talked to him, Anna. You should

have walked away or called out for me." Dorrie's fear lent a sharpness to her words that had Anna's face going beet red.

"He didn't mean any harm. All this fuss is over nothing."

"Nothing?" Dorrie sputtered into silence and stared at her sister. Didn't she realize how much danger she'd been in? The man had been luring her off, for goodness' sakes!

Brenna put one arm around Anna's shoulders and the other around Dorrie's. "Let's take some breaths here." She looked at Anna. "You gave us both a good scare. Your sister nearly collapsed trying to get to you. And stepped on a lot of toes to do it." She winked at Anna. "And I mean that's exactly what she did."

Dorrie shook her head, trying to clear it. Her hands were still trembling from the shock of trying to get to her sister before something terrible happened, and then hearing the low-voiced threats from the stranger.

"What did that man talk to you about?" Brenna's calm voice and practical question helped Dorrie latch onto some control of her own.

She pinned Anna with a stare. "Yes. What did he say to you?"

Still looking mutinous, Dorrie's sister waved a hand in the air. "Nothing. He asked if I was Anna, Maggie O'Hearn's daughter, and when I said I was, he laughed. He said he'd have known me anywhere." She glared at Dorrie. "He had the most friendly smile, and kindest eyes. And he was easy to talk to."

"Fine," Dorrie snapped out. "What else did you talk about?"

"We didn't have time to say much since you practically pounced on us." She lifted her chin even higher. "And I don't have to tell you anyway. It was a private talk."

Dorrie crossed her arms and started tapping her foot rapidly against the dirt. "Private?"

"Yes." Anna gave her a smug look.

Dorrie dropped her arms to her side and reached out, snagging one of Anna's hands in her own. "We'll see about that."

"You're too old to be tattling on me to Mam." Anna pulled against Dorrie's tug, but it didn't get her anywhere. Dorrie kept walking, dragging Anna along behind her.

"Not to Mam." Dorrie stopped and looked over at Brenna. "I'll stop by on the next market day. Will you be here?"

"Most likely." Brenna gave Anna a sympathetic look. "I know it might not seem like it, but Dorrie's trying to do what's best for you." She nodded. "You might consider that."

"She doesn't have to be so mean."

Anna squeaked when Dorrie gave another hard tug on her hand. "I'll see you in a week, Brenna." Without another word, Dorrie kept marching right out of the market, turning left instead of right to head back to the shop.

"Where are we going?"

Dorrie looked at Anna long enough to raise one eyebrow. "To the warehouse."

"The warehouse?" The color drained from Anna's face and she began to put serious effort into resisting the pull on her hand. "I'm not going to see Da. We should go talk to Mam. She's who the man was interested in."

"Which is what you're going to tell Da."

Dorrie refused to respond to any more of her little sister's pleas as she marched down the boarded walkways, heading straight for the large building where her father kept his tools and lumber, as well as made furniture he sold to the owners of the large houses that dotted the hills around the city. She was anxious to hear what Anna had to say, but their da would be too, so Dorrie was willing to wait until she could drag Anna in front of him. There was no doubt in her mind that Da would have Anna telling him every word of the conversation she'd had with the mysterious man who was so interested in their mam.

It took a good half an hour for them to cover the distance from the market to their da's warehouse. Dorrie was exhausted from the constant battle with Anna to keep her moving along. The large double doors, painted in a dark brown with a sign hung on them stating it was the business of Ian Dolan, Carpenter, were a welcome sight. Using her free hand to push one side of the heavy door open enough for them to slip through, Dorrie pulled Anna into the cool interior of the large space as she glanced around for her da.

Ian was standing next to a long wooden bench, talking to a man whose back was to Dorrie. But she didn't need to see a face to know who was talking to her da. Only one man stood with that kind of ease and confidence. Dorrie groaned as both men looked around, undoubtedly alerted to their presence by the loud rasp of the door swinging on its hinges. She gave a last yank to bring Anna up beside her as she smiled at her da, and then at his visitor.

"Hello, Jules."

THE FLASH of pleasure Jules felt when he spotted Dorrie standing just inside the doorway faded into the background as she drew closer, dragging a squirming Anna with her. He could tell by the set of Dorrie's mouth and the way she quickly averted her eyes from him that he wasn't going to like whatever had brought her to Ian's workshop. Even as a pit grew inside his gut, he told himself it was probably only a harmless prank by her younger sister that had gotten under Dorrie's skin. At least he hoped that's all it was.

"Da, I have something I need to confess." Dorrie's voice was soft and her hold on her wiggling sister was firm.

Her father smiled. "I'm not a priest, Dorrie. You can tell me what your sister's done to have you hauling her here without making it sound like a confession."

Dorrie took a deep breath. "I know you told us to stay close to the shop."

From the corner of his eye Jules saw Ian's expression change, and that pit in his gut grew another notch wider.

Anna finally managed to wrench her arm free. She took a quick hop away from her sister and glared at her. "I'm the one he was talking to, so I should do the telling."

Jules' gaze darted to Dorrie before he went very still. *He?*

When Dorrie opened her mouth, Ian held out one hand as he kept his stare on his youngest child. "Tell me all of it, Anna."

His quiet command had the young woman wetting her lips, but she dutifully nodded.

"We needed a few things, so we had to go to the market." She paused. "And Dorrie agreed to walk with me."

"I'm sorry, Da." Dorrie's soft apology had her sister back to glaring at her.

"There's nothing to be sorry about. We were only there a few minutes, and most of that time we were talking to Brenna." Anna ended on a sniff before returning her attention to her father. "And that's what we did. Go to the market, talk to a few people, and now we're here."

Ian's stare stayed pinned on his daughter, who began to squirm under its intensity. Jules kept his gaze on Dorrie, watching as her eyes narrowed and a stain of red crept across her cheeks.

"So you just came from the market?" Ian asked, waiting for Anna's nod before continuing. "Because you needed a few things? What things?"

"Um. Flowers and a vegetable for supper." Anna smiled. "Kate asked us to fetch them."

Her father sent a pointed look at her empty hands. "And where are they?"

Anna looked down and then back up, holding her hands out as if she was surprised to see them empty. "We didn't have time to get anything before Dorrie wanted to come here."

The big carpenter shook his head. "You're playing word games with your da, Anna. And I'll not have it. Why did your sister come here to 'confess', as if she'd committed a sin by walking with you to the market?"

When Anna hung her head, Dorrie let out a loud sigh. "It was my fault, Da."

"What was your fault, Dorrie?" Jules asked when Ian remained silent.

"We saw the man who's been following Anna and Mam."

"Saw him?" Jules repeated. "At the market?"

Dorrie nodded and then her whole body went rigid. "And spoke to him. Although he and Anna did most of the talking."

Ian's quick indrawn breath echoed through the shop. "He got close enough to speak to you?"

"I was getting water, Da. A cup of water for Brenna." Anna took a step closer to Dorrie and partially hid behind her sister. "They were busy whispering to each other so when this nice man said 'hello', I didn't want to be rude.

Especially since he was older. Maybe even older than you, Da." She ended in a rush of words.

"That is old," Ian said, a distinctly dry note in his voice. He folded his arms over his chest and took a wider stance. "What else did he say, Anna? I'm thinking a hello isn't enough to get Dorrie riled up."

"It would have been coming from him," Dorrie muttered. She nudged Anna's foot with her own. "Tell Da all of it, Anna."

Anna's chin began to quiver. "He only asked if I was Maggie O'Hearn's daughter, because I had the look of her. I said that I was, and he asked about the shop, and about Mam. How she was doing. And he wanted to know if it was Mam's shop, or if you owned it.

Dorrie frowned. "He did? You didn't tell me that."

Anna ignored her sister. "He was very polite, and never laid a hand on me." She jerked her head toward Dorrie. "At least not like he did with her. But then she came running up and started yelling at him. Everyone in the market was looking at us."

Dorrie snorted. "You'd walked away from the wagon, Anna. I couldn't see you in the crowds. And when I finally did, there you were talking away with the man who's been watching you. He had no business talking with you, and he was leading you away."

Ian's face drained of all its color. He reached out a long arm and pulled his daughter out from behind Dorrie. "You left your sister and went off with this man?"

The young woman looked close to bursting into tears. "We were just talking, Da. I didn't realize I was out of Dorrie's sight."

Jules looked at Ian who glanced between the marshal and his oldest daughter.

"I'm going to take Anna out back and have a talk with her." He frowned at his youngest child who now had tears running down her cheeks. "And I'd better be hearing the whole truth, Anna Dolan. You aren't too big for me to take over my knee."

"Oh, Da. You've never taken either of us over your knee," Anna sniffed.

"Maybe I should have." Ian pulled Anna along, right out the back door of the shop.

"I'm thinking the same thing." Jules took a step closer until he was only a boot length or two away from Dorrie. "Did I hear your sister right? That man put his hands on you?"

Dorrie tilted her head back and smiled up at him. "It was more the other way. I grabbed onto his arm."

"*You* grabbed *him*?" Jules snapped the words out. "And it's not something to smile about, Dorrie."

His temper went to the roof when she kept her smile and shrugged.

"I had questions for him."

"So you confronted a grown man? Did he have a gun?"

"Not that I saw."

"Meaning you didn't bother to look." Jules shut his eyes out of pure frustration, and so he wouldn't take hold of her shoulders and shake some sense into her. She'd walked up to an armed man and, if Anna was telling the truth, grabbed his arm and started yelling at him? It's a wonder his heart hadn't stopped beating right then and there.

"I didn't mean to get you so upset." Dorrie gave his arm a light pat. "But I had to get Anna away from him, and there wasn't any other way but to go chasing after them."

"I'm not upset, Dorrie, I'm angry." Jules ran a hand through his hair. "He could have hurt you. Either of you."

Dorrie frowned. "Not me. I keep telling you, he isn't interested in me. It's Anna and Mam he has his eyes on." She wrapped her arms around her waist. "Everything he asked Anna was about her and Mam. He didn't want to know anything about me or Da."

Jules was silent for a long moment as he wrestled with his temper. Finally managing to get a lid on it, he took a deep breath and stared into Dorrie's upturned face.

"What else did the man say?"

"That since we aren't blood he didn't have to tell me anything, although I doubt he'd tell his kin much either if he didn't want to. And that I was to stay out of his business."

"Good advice even from a bad mouth." Jules looked off into the distance, his forehead wrinkled in thought.

It did seem that the mysterious stranger was more inter-ested in Anna and Maggie than he was Dorrie. The relief of that made him feel guilty, which made his tone sharper than he'd intended.

"What did he look like?"

Dorrie closed her eyes. "Smaller than you. Not so much height, and not as solid. He was skinny and his clothes were baggy." She sighed. "He pulled his hat so low I couldn't see much of his face except for his mouth and chin. And the cloth around his neck was up so high, I didn't see much of that either." She pursed her lips. "It also needed a good wash. You could barely tell it was green, it was so covered in dust." She opened her eyes and shrugged. "But then so was the rest of him."

Jules considered that for a moment, forming a picture in his mind. "So he wasn't dressed like he was from the city?"

"No. More like a ranch hand, although there's enough of those that come into town."

The marshal tucked it away into his mind to be sure and

ask at any of the ranches he stopped at about a hand who wore a green bandanna. But aside from that, there wasn't much else he could do. He was sure the man was long gone, but he still intended to go to the market and ask around. Maybe someone had noticed Anna with him. And he still had a more immediate problem.

"Dorrie. Promise me you won't go anywhere but your home and the dress shop while I'm gone." He glanced at the closed door on the far side of the shop. "Your da will make sure that Anna does the same." He looked back at her. "I can't leave town unless I have that promise from you."

She gasped. "You have to go, Jules. You made a promise of your own. To Ethan. If you don't meet him now, he might not stick around long enough to help you catch that gang, and then you'd be doing it on your own." She reached out and wrapped a hand around his upper arm. "Tell me you'll keep your own promise."

The muscle under her hand went rock hard as Jules stared into her eyes, his heart pounding thickly in his chest. He withstood the exquisite agony for several long seconds before he took a step back, breaking the contact between them.

"We'll both keep our word, if you'll give me yours."

She clasped her hands in front of her as she nodded. "You have my word, Jules."

11

J ules walked into the spacious foyer of his home, using his heel to close the door behind him. He winced as it banged back into place, casting a guilty look up the stairs. His sister-in-law, Abby, kept odd and sometimes very late hours looking after her patients, and if she was still sleeping, he didn't want to wake her. The distinct sound of voices floated through the air, but they weren't coming from the floor above him. He set his hat on the wide table along the entryway's wall, smiling when he saw his brother's wide-brimmed hat was already taking up the space on one end.

He followed the voices to the back of the house. A sudden burst of deep masculine laughter, accompanied by the high-pitched giggles of his niece and nephew, greeted Jules as he walked into the kitchen.

"What's so funny?"

His demand brought squeals of delight from his thirteen-year-old niece and her younger brother. Emily was out of her chair in a flash, but still wasn't as fast as young Sam. The boy was plastered to Jules' side before his uncle had time to brace himself. Catching Emily as she threw herself into his arms, Jules took a quick step back before he lost his balance and they all ended up in a heap on the floor. He gave a one-armed hug to his niece with the golden curls, and a quick head-rub to his dark-haired nephew.

"Back to your meal now, children. You need to eat, and your uncle needs to breathe." Dina beamed at them from her place by the stove.

The children's bottom lips came out, but they unwound themselves from their smiling uncle and returned to their chairs at the table. They usually weren't so easily persuaded to let go of him, but when Jules glanced at their plates, he knew why. Each had a small iced cake on their plate. He looked over at his brother and grinned.

"I guess your wife isn't home?"

Cade and Jules shared the same height, with wide shoulders and lean waists. They both had deep-blue eyes, but Cade's hair was lighter than his younger brother's, and he had a long thin scar that ran from his cheekbone down to his chin. A memento of a knife fight he'd been lucky to walk away from.

"Abby had to go out early this morning. The Morrison baby is coming. She left me to mind these two."

Jules turned his head and winked at Dina who rolled her eyes. They both knew who it was that Abby depended on to tend the kids. Cade doted on them, so they could get pretty much anything they wanted from their father. Which most likely explained why they were having cake in the middle of the morning.

"Interesting breakfast you've given them. Or is that their noon meal a couple of hours early?"

Cade reached over and ruffled a large hand over the top of his son's head, sending strands of hair flying in its wake.

"What do you say to that, Sam? Your uncle doesn't think you should have cake before a meal."

His ten-year-old nephew, who was very proud that he could now claim two numbers for his age just like his sister, turned wide hazel eyes toward Jules, who couldn't help but smile at him. He looked so much like his grandfather, that every now and then Jules found himself staring at the boy in pure astonishment.

"Sometimes it's good to eat the sweet first in life."

Jules laughed. "Is that a fact?"

Dina pointed a long wooden spoon at Cade. "Your brother has turned a piece of cake into a life lesson. Which is how I imagine he'll be trying to convince his wife that it was a good idea to allow the children to have cake at ten in the morning."

"If that doesn't work, I've got other ways of persuading her." Cade's slow smile brought a shaming look from Dina.

"You haven't asked your brother if he wants cake for *his* breakfast." She looked over at the children who were avidly listening to the adults talk. "Which, since we're giving lessons this morning, would have been the proper and polite thing for your father to do."

"But they're brothers. Papa doesn't have to be polite to Uncle Jules." Sam issued that pronouncement with a huge smile.

"Samuel McKenzie!" Dina put her hands on her hips and shook her head at the boy. "Whoever told you such a thing?"

"Robbie," Sam, his father and his uncle said in unison.

"Or maybe Ethan?" Jules added.

"Well I don't care which of your sorry uncles told you that. It simply isn't true, and you aren't to believe a word of it. Do you hear me, young man?"

"Yes, Dina." Sam sounded disappointed as he stuck his fork into his cake and pried off another piece that he popped into his mouth.

Cade smiled. "I'm afraid Robbie is going to be in Dina's bad graces the next time she sees him."

Jules shrugged. Out of the three of them, Robbie had always been the one who'd landed in the most hot water with their many aunts, and also the one who'd been best at charming his way out of any punishment.

"What can I fix for you, Jules? You left this morning before you had any breakfast." Dina frowned when Jules shook his head.

"I'm not hungry, Dina, but I appreciate the offer. I need to get some work done." Jules really wasn't hungry. His simmering temper over Dorrie's escapades that morning, and the fact his asking around at the market hadn't yielded even a scrap of information, had soured his mood and his appetite.

With one last wink at Emily, and a nod to Cade and Dina, he left them to their fun and laughter and headed for his study. He shut the door and immediately walked over to the desk, taking out a whiskey bottle and one of the glasses that he and Cade kept in there. He'd barely poured out a healthy portion and settled into the chair behind the desk when the door opened and Cade walked in. His gaze traveled from Jules' face, down to the whiskey glass, and then back up again.

"Hard morning?"

"Hard enough," Jules grunted as Cade made himself comfortable in one of the leather chairs set in front of the desk. He lifted the glass in his hand. "Can I pour you one?"

"I'll wait until I hear how your morning was and then judge if it warrants a drink."

"It surely does." Jules sighed and set the full glass onto the desk top before running a hand through his hair. When he glanced over at Cade, his brother was leaning back in his chair, silently watching him.

"I don't recall you ever having a drink before dark, much less before noon." The older marshal's eyes narrowed. "Are you worried about Ethan stopping over at Robbie's ranch for a few days?"

"No. He tracked the Green Gang into that area, so it's good he's helping Robbie set up a proper guard for his place. And that he gets some rest before we both set out. He'll head this way when he's ready, and it gives us more time to get the men together."

"Then what's got you having a whiskey before noon?"

"Dorrie." Jules lifted his glass and took a swallow before setting it back on the desk with a heavy thump.

Cade's eyebrows shot up. "Ian's oldest girl?"

"Dorrie Marie Dolan." Jules sighed. "She'd drive any man to drink."

"We are talking about the same Dorrie, aren't we? Seems to me she has a pretty sweet disposition. Not to mention that you grew up with her. Why all of a sudden is she making you turn to drink?"

Jules lifted his glass again and scowled at the amber liquid. "Because the woman doesn't have any sense, and I can't always be around to make sure she stays out of trouble."

"What kind of trouble has she gotten into?" Cade frowned. "It doesn't have anything to do with the reason Ian hired guards for his house and Maggie's shop, does it?"

"It does." Jules set his glass down again and leaned forward. "I had to pull a promise out of her to stay away from the man those guards were supposed to be keeping an eye out for."

Cade watched his brother pick up the whiskey glass and hold it in front of him. "Jules, drink it or set it aside, but either way, tell me what's going on with Dorrie. I thought you weren't sure that she wasn't imagining a man following Anna and Maggie about."

Jules put the whiskey glass down and pushed it to the side before he leaned back in his chair. "It turns out he's real. He had a nice talk with Anna this morning, and then a not so nice one with Dorrie."

Cade's gaze went flat and his mouth thinned out into a straight line. "Tell me all of it."

Not needing any further urging, Jules related what had happened at the market that morning. He wasn't aware that his temper bled through his voice when he described the man's threat to Dorrie to stay out of his business or she'd regret it, until his brother let out a low whistle.

"What bothers you more? That he threatened Dorrie or put his hands on her?" When Jules glowered at him, Cade smiled. "I was just wondering. It was hard to tell."

"He needs a good lesson for doing either one." Jules' flat tone left no doubt who he thought should give those lessons to the stranger. "And Dorrie needs a good talking to about walking up to a man she doesn't know and giving him a piece of her mind."

"So why didn't you take care of that, little brother?"

The younger marshal sighed and ran a hand through his hair. "I was too angry. I thought it might come out so hard that she'd be upset." Jules didn't like the smile that suddenly appeared on Cade's face. "What are you smiling about?"

"Like that glass of whiskey, there seems to be some unusual behavior going on. I've never known you to be reluctant to upset Dorrie. Never bothered you when you were kids."

Jules ignored that and went back to what he considered unacceptable behavior by Dorrie. "She isn't a kid anymore, and she should have better sense than to go up to someone she knows has been following her." He waved a hand in the air. "She didn't even notice if the man had a gun strapped to his hip."

"She's not used to noticing that kind of thing. Since you said you pointed it out to her, now she'll look for it."

Jules snorted. "She'd better not be. She promised me she wouldn't go anywhere except for home or Maggie's shop."

Cade rubbed a hand across his scarred cheek. "Hard to get any of the women in the family to agree to be that penned in. How did you get that out of Dorrie?"

"I promised her that I'd go out and meet Ethan and not stay in town to keep an eye on her."

His brother dropped his hand back to his lap. "Did you also tell her that wouldn't be for a few more days? So until then, you *will* be staying in town?"

"I might have to leave before then," Jules hedged. He still intended to leave and hunt the Green Gang with Ethan. He just hadn't told Dorrie that the plans had changed. "She needs to be reined in. She was out taking shooting lessons from Ammie. And that's not all."

"You might as well tell me," Cade said, settling back into his chair and stretching his long legs out.

"She has this crazy notion about dealing with this man herself. First she comes to me for help, then she acts like she doesn't need it and I should go off with Ethan because *I* need *his* help. Next thing I know, she's off taking shooting lessons on that stretch of beach all the women in the family go to. And when I give her sound advice about staying away from that man and letting me look into it, she starts arguing with me, and won't let up."

"Did you give her advice, or was it more like an order?"

Jules glared at his brother. "It was advice. And I told her to mind what I was saying."

Cade cocked his head to one side. "I'm not sure that was the proper way to handle it, Jules." He looked up at the ceiling. "Why don't you let Ian deal with Dorrie? She's his daughter."

"He's got his hands full with his wife and Anna."

"So you're helping him out?" Cade didn't even flinch at the heat in Jules' glare. "Since you're a US Marshal and all."

"Yes, I am," Jules snapped out. "And Dorrie's old enough she shouldn't need her father to ride herd on her. And she ought to listen to what a marshal tells her. We aren't kids any longer."

"Is that a fact?"

His patience completely in shreds, Jules scowled at his brother. "What's that supposed to mean?"

There was silence for a full minute before Cade cleared his throat. "I knew a woman once who was a little like Dorrie." When Jules looked over at him, Cade nodded. "She didn't show much sense either about where she went chasing off to. I talked to her about her foolish thinking, but she didn't listen."

"What's that got to do with Dorrie and me not being kids anymore?" Jules demanded.

"I'm getting to it." Cade lifted his foot off his knee and dropped it to the floor. "This woman wouldn't listen to me, and one day a man did the same thing that stranger did to Dorrie. He put his hands on her and made a threat."

His interest caught, Jules frowned when Cade went quiet. "What happened?"

"I found it necessary to teach that man a lesson."

Jules smiled with satisfaction. "Just like I said."

Cade rose to his feet and laughed.

"Just like you said," Cade agreed. He grinned at his younger brother. "And then I married her."

12

J ules stepped into the fashionable teashop on one of the busy streets near the central square in the heart of the town. Katherine's Teashop had been a favorite of the women in the family for decades, and so was Katherine, who still ran her establishment with a huge smile and a welcome for everyone.

He'd been here a time or two with Abby and Emily, but he still felt out of place among the dainty tables and chairs, not to mention the decorative and fussy place settings Katherine favored for her shop. But it was a half-step better than going into Maggie's dress shop. Still, he lingered in the entryway, peering around the edge of the wall that separated it from the main dining area.

He didn't even have to look over the room. His gaze went right to the slender female, sitting by herself at a table near the back wall. Even though she was facing away from him, he'd still know her by the way she held herself, and the rich caramel color of her hair. Today she wore it in a thick, coiled rope at the back of her head, with several ribbons weaving in and out. It looked delicate and appealing all at the same time.

When Jules' thoughts turned to picturing himself undoing it, one coil at a time, he blinked and pulled back behind the wall. Cade's words still echoed in his ears, and unless he was going to give them serious consideration, which he wasn't, he had no business entertaining those kinds of notions about Dorrie. They were childhood friends and playmates. Remembering her as a young girl had him shifting from one foot to the other, making him feel lower than dirt.

"Friends. More than that, we're family. You'd better keep that in mind," Jules muttered to himself.

He glanced over his shoulder at the door. He wished he'd let Cade come on this errand. After all, Dorrie had sent for his brother and not him. But when her note had come, he'd been irritated that she hadn't wanted to see him. Kind of like a mild itch that he couldn't scratch. So he'd told Cade he'd take care of it before his brother could mount any objections. And now it was too late to be having his doubts. He couldn't leave her there alone while he tracked Cade down and told his brother to meet Dorrie at the teashop after all. But he didn't want to sit across from her right at the moment either. He needed time to get his head back into the right place.

"Who are you talking to? And what are you doing standing alone back here?"

The female voice cut into his thoughts and brought a wave of heat up his neck. Jules carefully put a smile on his face before turning his head to look right into the surprised expression of Katherine herself.

"Hello, Miss Katherine."

"Hello yourself, Marshal McKenzie." She peered around him. "What's back there that has you so fascinated?"

"Nothing. I was just looking around."

She planted both hands on her wide hips and stared at him, amusement dancing in her eyes. Dressed in a plain skirt and blouse, with a long white apron covering her from her neck to her hemline, she looked like she belonged in a fancy teashop. Jules wished he'd wiped the dust off his boots before he'd left home.

"Why don't you hang your hat up on one of those pegs right beside you and go let Dorrie know that you're here."

Trapped so his decision was made for him, Jules stuck his hat on an open peg. "Why do you think I'm here to meet Dorrie?"

Katherine laughed before she leaned over, lowering her voice to a conspiratorial whisper. "Because I know every person in your family, and the only one here today is Dorrie." She straightened up and smiled at him. "Doesn't take any great amount of intelligence to have figured that one out."

"Family. Right."

Jules drew in a deep breath and ran a hand through his hair before he stepped around Katherine and slowly walked toward Dorrie. Since he now had his back to her, he completely missed the raised eyebrow and the speculative look Katherine gave him before she continued on into the kitchen.

Dorrie didn't look up until he was standing right next to her table. He smiled at the surprise in her eyes. At least she didn't seem annoyed to see him standing there instead of Cade.

"Hello, Dorrie. I got your note." He glided right over the fact that it had been sent to Cade rather than him.

"I was expecting Cade. I thought you'd already left to meet Ethan."

That soothed his pride. She would have sent for him, but she'd thought he was already gone. He pulled out a chair and sat a bit more carefully than he normally did. He wanted to be sure the delicate looking piece would hold his weight. When it didn't let out even one creak of protest, he settled himself on its small surface. "I'm going later. Why did you want to come here?"

He relaxed when she smiled.

"Cade doesn't like coming to Mam's shop any more than you do, so we always come here instead."

"You do?" Jules wondered just how often she met with his brother.

"Whenever Abby manages to drag him along." She hesitated. "I also didn't want to talk at the shop, where Mam might overhear us."

That got his attention. As far as he knew, and all of his uncles would have agreed, the women in the family didn't keep secrets from each other. At least, he amended silently, until recently.

"What is it you don't want your mam to hear?"

She gazed at him, her eyes soft and a slight smile on her lips. At that moment Jules couldn't have looked away from her if his life had depended on it.

"I think you're going to be angry with me."

"No. No, I won't be, Dorrie. Tell me what's bothering you. I'll fix it."

The rest of the room faded completely away when warmth and amusement mingled in her eyes.

"You can't fix everything, Jules McKenzie, and I don't mind if you get angry. You never stay that way long."

He grinned. "Is that a fact?"

"Yes, it is."

She sounded pretty sure of herself, which had his whole insides lighting up. He badly wanted to take her hand in his, but he settled for a shake of his head. "All right. So what is it I'm not going to be mad at for very long?"

Dorrie's smile dimmed. "I was upset yesterday, and angry at Anna wandering away like that. And scared for her, too."

Jules wished she'd been a little more scared for herself, but he let it go. He kept his gaze on Dorrie as Katherine came over with a tea tray and set the pot, cups, saucers and a plate of biscuits with a pot of jam in the center of the table. Once the shop owner had retreated to see to other customers, Dorrie poured out a cup of tea and set it in front of him before preparing one for herself.

"When I was home last night, I kept hearing his voice over and over in my head, telling me he didn't have to listen to me, and to stay out of his business."

"That's not so unusual," Jules assured her. "It happens after a good scare. You just need a little time. It will stop."

Dorrie shook her head. "It wasn't the scare. It's like I was trying to remember something." She raised her eyes from her teacup and looked directly at him. "Last night when everything was quiet and settled in, I remembered."

"He said something else to you?"

"No. It wasn't what he said, but how he said it." A shadow of a smile crossed her lips. "I think it didn't mean anything to me at the time because I've heard it most of my life. And so has Anna, so it probably didn't strike her as strange either."

Jules held his gaze steady on hers, even as his heart rate picked up a beat. "What did you hear, Dorrie?"

"Irish," she said softly. "I heard Irish in his voice, Jules. I'm sure of it."

Jules showed no reaction on his face, but he leaned forward and took her hand that was resting beside her teacup into his. "You're sure?"

"Yes." She didn't pull away from him, leaving her hand where it was. "But I don't know what it means. Only that he's Irish."

She stared back at him for a moment and must have seen what he was thinking in his eyes, because she sighed and finally withdrew her hand from his. Jules immediately felt the jolt of the break of their connection.

"Just because he's Irish, doesn't mean Mam knows the man." Now her eyes held an edge of defiance. "Lots of Irish came looking for gold at Sutter's Mill, and now the silver in the Comstock Lode. Mam says most came to escape the great famine, the way she, her da, and brothers did. So that man could be just another person from Ireland who came to seek his fortune." She shrugged. "Mam certainly doesn't know every Irishman who's set foot in town."

He sighed and leaned back in his chair. "Anna said the man was as old as your da."

"I know." Dorrie shrugged again. "And we'd be in agreement about that. Although I can't be absolutely sure. I didn't get a look at this face."

"There weren't so many people in San Francisco when Maggie and Ian first came here," Jules said quietly.

"There's nothing to say this man arrived when Mam did."

"No. There isn't." He kept his voice low. "But we have to consider it, Dorrie."

"I know."

He was sorry she sounded so unhappy over that, but it

didn't make it any less of a problem. Given the closeness in their ages, it was a very real possibility his Maggie had run across this man somewhere in her past. The question was, though, why hadn't he stayed in her past?

"There's a bit more." Dorrie sounded even more upset than she had the moment before. "Da questioned Anna last night about what the man looked like. She didn't remember much more than I told you, except she thought he had a nice voice and one other thing. He had green eyes."

"Green eyes?" Every muscle in Jules' body went completely still. Suddenly a clear path appeared in his mind and he didn't like where it was taking him. Was it possible his Maggie knew a member of the Green Gang? He drew in a slow deep breath, careful to keep it even and not draw attention to his racing heartbeat.

"Have you told you da about the Irish in the man's voice?" he asked slowly. When Dorrie shook her head, he nodded his. "You need to do that. Let your da talk to your mam. She's his wife. She can't keep secrets from him forever."

Dorrie sighed. "If she really does know this man, she's been doing well at not telling Da about it." When Jules raised an eyebrow at her, she pursed her lips. "I'll tell him. But don't you be telling everyone else in the family about this until we know something for sure. Not even Ethan."

Jules found a smile. "I promise." He looked around the shop before returning his gaze to her. "And speaking of promises, how did you get here today?"

She raised a hand and wagged one finger back and forth. "Oh no you don't, Jules McKenzie. You aren't going to demand I stay inside forever because I broke a promise. One of Da's guards walked here with me, and he's waiting outside to walk me back home."

He still didn't like her being out in the open, but knew he'd have to settle for her being accompanied by one of Ian's men.

"Now it's your turn."

"My turn to what?" Jules held up a hand, his palm facing her.

"Why aren't you on your way to meet Ethan?"

"He sent word that he'd ended up at Robbie's, and he'd meet me here in a few days when he was finished helping Robbie set up a watch rotation for his place."

Dorrie smiled and nodded. "Oh. When did he let you know that?"

"A couple of nights ago. Luke stopped by to deliver his message," Jules answered absently, his mind already circling back to the possibility it was a member of the Green Gang lurking about town. It was a good thing, then, that Ethan was headed back this way.

"So before you asked me for that promise and gave me yours in exchange?"

"Hmm." What she'd said suddenly hit Jules. "What?"

"You heard me, Jules McKenzie. You knew you wouldn't be riding out to meet Ethan anytime soon, and let me think you were to get that promise from me to stay inside all the time."

"I'm going to be riding out to meet Ethan at some point in our search. Just not today."

"Oh, I see." Dorrie rapidly blinked her eyes at him to go with her pasted-on smile. "So then I guess *my* promise will start just as soon as you do that."

"Dorrie." Jules let the exasperation show in his voice. He didn't want to have to order her to stay home all the time, but he would if he had to. And leave a man to be sure she did. He doubted if Ian would have any objections, especially not once he learned the man following his wife and daughter was Irish. The carpenter would come to the same conclusion he had. His wife somehow knew this man.

"Jules," Dorrie repeated right back at him. "I thought we'd already had this 'cotton ball' discussion. But just in case you've forgotten, I can take care of myself, thank you very much. Although I do appreciate your concern."

When she started to get up, he reached out a long arm and brought his hand down on top of hers. "We aren't leaving here mad at each other, Dorrie. I don't like it when we're mad at each other."

Her mouth dropped open. "You don't? But we got mad at each other all the time when we were growing up."

His jawline tightened, and he kept his hand right where it was. "Well, we aren't kids anymore, and now I don't like it."

She slowly lowered herself back to her seat. "All right. Then I'm a little vexed but not mad. How's that?"

He studied her face through narrowed eyes. "That's fine, if it's true."

She suddenly laughed, causing his own mouth to turn up at the corners.

"It's true. I suspect I'll even think of you as my good friend again once I get home."

Jules easily rose to his feet and held out one hand. "Then just to be sure that you do, I'll be the one escorting you home."

She rolled her eyes at him, but accepted his hand and stood up. He firmly tucked her hand into the crook of his elbow.

"Thank you, Marshal."

Jules smiled back at her. "My pleasure, Miss Dolan."

13

"I cannot believe I let you talk me into this. I must be out of my head." Ammie buried her face in her hands and groaned.

"Stop being so dramatic," Dorrie hissed. "You're just being a good friend. And all you need to do is go into the shop until Mam leaves, and then come out of the shop so I'll know if she went out the back door."

Ammie peered out the carriage window. "So will that guard Ian's hired. He's sure to notice your mam leaving her shop and follow her, the same way you're intending to do."

"She'll find a way around him. Which is why I need you to be inside to let me know when she leaves."

"I don't know why you're so sure your mam is going to sneak out of her own shop." Ammie flopped back against the carriage seat and eyed her friend. "Or that it's such a grand idea that you follow her dressed that way."

Dorrie fingered the cotton on the sleeve of her oversized shirt peeking out from beneath the big jacket. She'd shrugged into it just moments before Ammie had pulled the carriage to a stop a little way past the shop's door. The britches Dorrie had on were also too big for her, but, along with the jacket that hung to her knees, and the thick gray scarf around her neck, they did a good job of transforming her into a slender boy. She'd pulled her hair back into a tail with a piece of twine and stuffed it down the back of her jacket, and had a thick knitted wool cap pulled low over her eyebrows, while the scarf hid the lower half of her face. Aside from being a bit taller than the average young boy, she could easily pass for any one of the number of urchins who wandered the streets.

"Mam won't notice me dressed this way."

Her friend continued to frown at her. "What makes you think she'll be coming outside to notice you at all?"

"Because she was acting funny last night, telling Anna and me she didn't want us at the shop today because we were becoming too much of a distraction, and going misty-eyed every time she thought Da wasn't looking." Dorrie had a feeling that her mam was up to something. The outspoken Maggie had never been good at hiding her feelings or masking her thoughts, so odd behavior and a weepy face only convinced her oldest daughter that something was afoot.

Which was probably why her beloved parent had also avoided her husband most of the evening, finally pleading a headache and retiring early to bed. Dorrie couldn't even remember the last time her mam had claimed any kind of malady, much less taken herself off to her bed without her husband.

"What do you think Jules will have to say about your little charade?" Ammie smoothed out her skirt. "If he gets wind of this, he might make good on that constant threat of his when we were younger and take you over his knee."

"He still makes that threat to Anna. I'd tell him, but I

haven't seen or heard from him in two days, and besides, he can't say a thing since he's still in town."

"What has that to do with anything, for goodness' sake?"

"I'll explain later." Dorrie pointed to the wooden walkway. "Will you get going?"

"Fine. I'll go into the shop. I don't suppose you have an excuse for me to give about why I'm showing up on the doorstep before it's even open?"

Dorrie smiled. "Because you thought you were supposed to be there to pick out the material for the new dress you're needing."

"What new dress?"

"There must be a dinner or entertainment you're expected to show up at in those high-society houses you've been gracing with your presence lately." Dorrie airily waved her hand back and forth.

"Only because most of my clients come from those houses." She pushed Dorrie's hand away when her friend tried to get her to move out of the carriage. "I'm going. But the next time I come to you for a favor, Dorrie Dolan, you'd better say 'yes'."

"When have I ever told you no?" Dorrie made a shooing motion. "Go on. The shop will be open before you get one foot inside."

Ammie stepped out of the carriage and made a face at Dorrie from over her shoulder, before strolling leisurely down the walkway. Since the shop wasn't open yet, she passed by the front door and turned into the alley.

Once Ammie had disappeared from sight, Dorrie climbed out of the confines of the two-person coach and walked over to lean against its wheel, doing her best to look as if she were merely watching the conveyance while its owner was off on an errand.

Shoving her hands into the large pockets of her jacket, Dorrie hunched her shoulders and cautiously looked around the street, trying to locate the guard her da had hired. She soon focused on a short, stocky man, sitting on a bench outside the tailor shop next to her mam's, and reading a newspaper print he held up in front of him. Or pretending to. Dorrie noticed that his eyes were constantly moving over the street and the people passing by.

She settled into her own wait, trying not to count off the seconds as the front of her mam's shop remained quiet. When a woman appeared at the entrance to the alley, Dorrie straightened away from the carriage. She had the bright blue shawl her mam had worn that morning covering her hair, and a good part of her face, before it was wrapped around her shoulders. As she hurried along the walkway, Dorrie watched the man with the newsprint hastily fold it in two and tuck it under his arm as he fell into step behind her.

Dorrie frowned as her mam walked off. There was something about the way she looked that wasn't right. Dorrie stepped away from the carriage and stood in the center of the walkway. Since it was still early, there weren't many people around, so she had no problem keeping her mam in sight from her position just a few steps away from the carriage. It didn't take her long to realize that the shawl and clothes were right, but her mam seemed to have lost several inches of her height and gained a bit of weight.

When Ammie didn't make an appearance, Dorrie went back to her place next to the carriage's wheel. She would bet her last gold piece on one of Charles' games of chance that her mother had switched clothes with Kate and sent her out to lure the guard away. Not two minutes later, Ammie strolled back out of the shop, waving to someone inside before she shut the door behind her and walked briskly to the carriage.

"You'd better make yourself scarce. I'm sure Maggie will be coming out that alley any minute." Ammie smiled. "She sent Kate out with her shawl, which I can see didn't fool you. What about the guard?"

"He's following Kate." Dorrie gave Ammie's arm a grateful squeeze. "Thank you."

"I'll be back to pick you up in one hour. That's when the shop opens and I'm sure your mam will be back by then. And if you aren't here, I'm going straight to your da."

"Fine." Dorrie quickly stepped away, keeping her face averted as her mam stepped out of the alley. She kept her head down until her parent was a good shop's length away before starting after her.

It only took Dorrie a few minutes to realize they were heading for the market. The thought had her pulse jumping. The market was where they usually saw the man who Jules was certain her mam knew somehow. Dorrie told herself to wait and see, but in her heart she believed it too. And from the argument she'd heard her parents having after she'd told Da about the Irish in the man's voice, Ian was also sure his wife knew the man. Dorrie sighed. Whatever reason her mam had for keeping her secrets, it must be important to her. But that didn't set the danger aside.

She was careful to keep her distance as her mam wandered through the market, barely stopping to look at the produce. When she'd reached the far end, Maggie turned about and slowly headed back in the same direction she'd just come from, once again not stopping to talk to any of the farmers or merchants selling their wares.

Dorrie kept to the sides, moving at the same pace as her

mam. She stayed close to the rotting walls of an old warehouse that bordered the market, with her eyes firmly fixed on her mam. Suddenly an arm shot out from a gap in the building's side. Before she could let out a single sound of protest, a large hand covered her mouth and nose, while a sinewy arm locked itself tightly around her middle dragging her backwards. Dorrie clawed at the hand on her face, fighting for air.

"Why are you following Maggie Dolan, you little dock rat?"

The harsh voice hissed in her ear as he continued to force her back into the semi-darkness of the deserted warehouse, despite the flailing of Dorrie's arms and legs. When they were well within the empty depths, he tossed her to the ground before hauling her back up by the front of her shirt.

Green eyes narrowed on Dorrie's face as she took in great gulps of air. "Well. What have we here? It seems the whelp who's no blood of hers is followin' our Maggie around."

Forced to stand on her tiptoes to keep her feet on the ground, Dorrie leaned as far away from him as the tight grip on her shirt would allow.

"Who are you?" she demanded.

"It makes no difference, girl. I'm thinkin' you were spyin' on your mam to try to get a look at me." He gave her a good shake, making her head snap back and forth. "I told you to stay out of me business." He shook her again. "I would have thought that husband of Maggie's would have taught you to mind your elders."

Dizzy, and scrambling to keep her balance, Dorrie still managed to glare back at him. "My da will be seeing to you. And so will Marshal McKenzie."

His smirk showed a set of rotting teeth. "A marshal, is it? Well. I certainly don't want to be tanglin' with any marshal. I'd best be sure to get a good start on the man." In a lightning fast move, he had his hand across her mouth again and was dragging her further into the darkness. Within a minute he'd stopped by a barrel.

"When I spotted you, I copped a few things from a couple of those farmers. I knew they'd come in handy." He unwound the cloth from his neck and stuffed most of the dirty rag into her mouth. With his hand gone and her mouth blocked, Dorrie desperately breathed in through her nose, her eyes wide as he uncoiled a length of rope.

"You really need to practice how to properly follow someone without bein' seen." His voice was low and even, as if they were having a friendly conversation and he hadn't yanked her hands in front of her and was winding the thick rope around them.

Once he had her hands tied, he forced her to sit next to the barrel. A moment of sheer panic almost had her passing out when he drew a long, wicked-looking knife from his belt. But he only cut the rope and proceeded to tie up her feet and then wound the rope around the barrel. By the time he was finished, she could barely move. He gave the barrel a solid push, but it didn't budge.

"That should hold you until someone realizes you've gone missin' and comes lookin' for you."

He squatted down and put his face just a few inches from hers. "You'd best be prayin' it doesn't take them too long." He unwound the long scarf she had around her neck. "Since I've given you me neck cloth, I'll just be takin' yours, then."

He laughed as he stood up and casually threw his prize around his neck. "I'm hopin' this is the last we'll see of each other, girl." He nudged her outstretched leg with the tip of his boot. "And you'd best be hopin' the same." He pulled his lips back into a sneer. "You're in fate's hands now, girl."

Without another word he walked off, leaving Dorrie alone in the dark.

14

"Cade? Jules? Are you here?"

Jules took his eyes off the map he'd been studying to glance over at the doorway into his study. His brow wrinkled in concern. The voice yelling from the front of the house sounded like Ian. Dina rushed past his doorway with his sister-in-law, Abby, on her heels. Curious, Jules set the map on the desk and got to his feet, covering the distance across his study in long strides. When he reached the hallway leading toward the parlor, he could hear the distinctive low tones of his older brother. A second later, Cade's voice rolled through the house.

"Jules. Come into the parlor. Now."

The younger marshal's step went from a walk to a run as he burst into the front parlor and skidded to a halt. Ian was standing by the divan, his hat still on his head, and surrounded by Cade, Dina, and Abby.

"What's happened?" Jules took another two steps into the room then halted and braced his legs apart. Whatever reason had brought Ian here, it wasn't going to be good.

The tall carpenter slowly turned his head toward his

nephew. Jules could plainly see the mix of rage and fear in Ian's eyes.

"Dorrie's missing."

"Missing?" Jules' gaze shot to his brother who gave a sharp nod, then looked back at Ian. "What do you mean she's missing?"

"She was supposed to stay at home with Anna this morning." Ian snatched the hat off his head and crushed the brim beneath his long fingers. "But Ammie came to my shop and said she took her to the dress shop instead."

Jules took a long step forward, so he stood directly in front Ian. "Ammie? Dorrie and Ammie went to Maggie's shop?"

"Well that doesn't sound so bad." The tone of Dina's voice was unnaturally bright.

Cade reached over and gave her shoulder a gentle pat. "We need to hear all of it." He nodded at Ian. "Go on."

"They didn't go into the shop together. Ammie went in to watch Maggie. Then when Maggie left the shop before it opened, Ammie went back to the carriage to tell Dorrie."

"Whyever would she do such a thing?" Dina asked.

Jules' fist clenched at his side and heat flooded his veins. He knew exactly what Dorrie had been up to. "She followed her mam, didn't she?"

Ian nodded, then gave a grunt of surprise when Jules grabbed onto the front of his shirt and twisted the rough cotton with a jerk of his hand. "Where did your wife go?"

Cade immediately pushed Dina behind him. He brought his arm between the two men, grabbing onto Jules' wrist and giving it a hard squeeze. "Let go of Ian, Jules, and calm down. You won't do Dorrie any good by getting into a fist fight with her father."

Jules looked at his hand. He hadn't even realized he'd

grabbed onto Ian. He dropped his arm and stepped back, shaking out his hand and wrist to ease the sting left by his older brother's iron grip. But his stare stayed glued to Ian's face as he took deep breaths, locked in an internal struggle for control. "You didn't say that Maggie was missing, just Dorrie."

Ian's jaw twitched, but he stayed where he was, making no move toward the younger man standing across from him. "Maggie's home. I left her crying at our table while I took the guards to go look for Dorrie." He held up a large hand to fend off his honorary nephew when Jules leaned forward. "Maggie went to the market. We searched there, and all the way back to her shop. Then I came here to ask for your help."

"You have it," Cade assured him. He settled a heavy hand on his brother's shoulder. "Let's get the facts, and then we'll decide what to do next."

"We go back and search the market, ask questions." Jules' eyes narrowed. "If anyone saw her, they'll talk to me about it."

"Hopefully you aren't thinking of pointing your gun at anyone." Abby's calm, practical voice cut across Jules' boiling rage. "That won't help."

"Simmer down, Jules."

Cade's sharp command had Jules' back going rigid, but he managed a nod. His brother was right. He needed to hear everything Ian had to say, and the seconds were ticking by.

"I'm sorry, Ian." He accompanied the stiff apology with a quick dip of his head. "Did Maggie know Dorrie was following her?"

Ian shook his head. "She did not. Maggie said she never saw Dorrie. She didn't know our daughter was even about until Ammie came into the shop looking for her." Ian sighed. "Ammie was supposed to meet Dorrie back at the shop, and when my daughter didn't appear, Ammie went to the house thinking maybe Dorrie had gone straight home. But Anna said she hadn't seen her all morning, so Ammie came looking for me."

"That's good." Cade sent a sideways glance toward Jules. "Then you went to talk to Maggie?"

"I expected to find Dorrie there, thinking she'd been distracted by something and was late getting back. When I told Maggie that our daughter had followed her and was supposed to have met Ammie outside the shop, and now hadn't shown up at home either, my wife told me she'd only gone to the market." Ian's broad shoulders slumped. "That she'd hoped to see the man who spoke to Anna, but she didn't catch sight of him, so she came home."

Jules tensed. "Did Maggie tell you who the man is? She knows, doesn't she?"

"She didn't at first. She said because she couldn't be sure. Green eyes and Ireland in his voice would describe almost every man she'd known back home, or any Irishman she's met here. But when I told her about Dorrie going missing, she gave it up pretty quick." He glanced at Abby. "She isn't sure, but she thought from Anna's description, he had the look of Connor."

Abby blinked behind the lenses of her gold wire-rimmed glasses. "Connor? Her brother?"

Jules frowned. He vaguely remembered a mention or two that Maggie had had a brother. Maybe even more than one, although he couldn't recall.

Abby put a supportive arm around a gaping Dina's shoulders. "But Maggie's always said that he was dead."

Ian rubbed his chin. "She thought he was. So did I, since she hasn't heard a word from him in almost twenty years."

He glanced over at Jules. "But that's why she wasn't worried about him hurting her or the girls. She's sure her brother would never do that." He switched his gaze to Abby. "She says she can't be sure it was Connor, but I could see it in her eyes that she thinks her brother has come back."

"But she isn't sure it's her brother." Cade ran a hand along the scar on his face as he frowned at Ian.

"And if he has, he might not treat Dorrie the same way he would Maggie or Anna," Jules spit out. "He made a point of telling Dorrie that she wasn't his blood."

There was a beat of silence in the room before Cade cleared his throat. "Let's deal with what we do know. Dorrie followed Maggie, and Maggie went to the market and then back to the shop." He gave his scar another quick rub. "How long was Maggie at the market?"

"She said she only made one pass up and down between all the wagons before she returned to the shop, so she could open on time." Ian's shoulders slumped a bit further. "She'd sent Kate out with her shawl and wasn't sure when Kate would be back. Maggie wanted the guard to follow Kate thinking it was her, and then she could go to the market alone."

"But she didn't fool Dorrie." If Dorrie had been standing in front of him right at that moment, Jules might very well have put her over his knee.

Or kissed her senseless.

He shook off the thought and concentrated on the immediate problem first. Finding her.

"Not with Ammie's help," Ian said.

"Those two could always get into mischief," Dina declared.

"It's the last time that's going to happen," Jules snapped out. He turned on his heel and headed for the foyer. The heavy thud of boots followed him. Jules grabbed his jacket and his gun belt off the peg next to the door. He stepped aside so Cade could do the same.

"Are your guards outside?" Jules directed his question to Ian, who nodded back at him.

"Two of them are. I left the third one with Maggie and Anna at the house."

"That's good." Jules slapped his hat onto his head and opened the front door, crossing the porch and heading for the stable. In less than five minutes he was swinging up into the saddle as Hafen danced beneath him.

Ian was already holding the reins of the team hitched to his wagon. Jules set Hafen into a fast trot. Cade rode on his own mount right beside him. The two US Marshals didn't exchange a word as the headed for the town market.

It only took them fifteen minutes to reach the edge of the wagons where farmers sold their produce. Jules dismounted and stood beside Cade, looking over the layout of the wagons in front of them as Ian's wagon rattled to a stop behind them. Once Ian and his two guards had joined the two marshals, Jules pointed off to his left. "You three go that way and look in, under, and around every wagon and into every face. Ask everyone if they've seen Dorrie." He glanced at Ian. "What was she wearing?"

Ian pursed his lips and looked off into the distance. "A brown jacket that was too big for her, a white shirt, britches, and a knit hat."

"Sounds like an outfit my wife has," Cade grumbled before he raised his voice so the guards could hear him. "Then you're asking about a skinny and slightly tall boy."

Jules and Cade started down the right side, stopping at every wagon, making sure their badges were visible, and questioning everyone they came across. Jules was ahead of

Cade as the end of the line of wagons came into view when someone called out to him.

"Marshal?"

He turned to the side and searched for the voice, quickly spotting a tall, slender young woman with black hair in a thick braid trailing down her back, waving at him. He almost nodded and continued on when Dorrie's voice, talking about her dark-haired friend with the Irish name who wasn't Irish at all, whispered from the back of his memory. He changed course and rapidly closed the distance between them. As he drew closer, the woman looked him up and down before nodding as if she were satisfied about something.

"You're Jules, aren't you?"

"I am. And your Dorrie's friend." Jules searched his memory for a name. "Brenna?"

The young woman smiled. "You look exactly the way Dorrie described you." Before he could come up with a response to that, she put her hands on her hips and glared at him. "Has something happened to her?"

"Why do you say that?"

Brenna turned and deliberately looked at Cade who was two wagons away, talking to a man. "I saw her mam here earlier, but she didn't stop to talk like she usually does. I also saw a man who looked the way Dorrie always described her da, poking around all the wagons, just the way you are. And now you're here. And so is another marshal, who Dorrie told me was your brother. I figure if something happened to her mam or sister, Dorrie'd be here looking with you." Brenna glanced around. "But I don't see her."

"Did you see her earlier today? When her mam was walking through the market, or maybe some time after that?"

When Brenna shook her head, the small flame of hope that had flickered to life inside Jules died.

"If she'd been here, she would have stopped by." Brenna crossed her arms in front of her. "Why do you think she was here?" When Jules looked into the back of her wagon, Brenna snorted. "I'm not hiding her. And I know about the man who's been following her sister and mam. I was with Dorrie when she had to rescue Anna from him."

Jules' gaze snapped back to Dorrie's friend. "You saw him?"

"Just the back of him. He'd already turned away by the time I caught up with Dorrie and Anna." She paused. "Are you looking for him, or for Dorrie?"

"Both." Jules sighed, removed his hat, and ran a hand through his hair. "You might not have recognized Dorrie. She was wearing britches and a large jacket."

Brenna gave a short laugh. "Wouldn't have made any difference. I've seen her in her boy's garb before. I'd have recognized her, and she knows I would have. So if she was trying to avoid being seen, she wouldn't have come too close to my wagon no matter how she was dressed."

Startled, Jules stared at her for a moment. He'd been wondering how Connor O'Hearn, or whoever the man was, would have managed to grab Dorrie in the middle of the market without anyone noticing. He carefully studied the surrounding area.

If Dorrie had followed Maggie this far, she most likely would have made a wide path around her friend, Brenna. There wasn't much but open space to his left, but off to his right was a sagging building that looked as if it had seen better days. He went still at the ripple of awareness that climbed up the nerves in his arms and neck. His eyes narrowed as he considered it. Earlier that morning, the side wall would have been covered in shadows.

Thanking Brenna, he walked off to pick his way past several wagons until he reached the rotting wood that didn't look strong enough to be holding up the roof. It only took him a few moments to come across the gaping hole left by several missing boards. He easily stepped through it and then stopped and listened. That ripple became a constant hum.

Jules didn't hear anything from the interior of the building. Only the noise from the market taking place on the other side of the wall. But his gut was tight and his breathing shallowed out. He closed his eyes and slowly began to draw air in and out, the way he'd been taught in his childhood lessons with Master Kwan. He could feel her. She was here. He knew it.

He raised his hands to cup around his mouth. "Dorrie?"

Greeted with silence, he took several more steps deeper into the darkness that loomed in front of him. "Dorrie?"

This time he heard a thump, and strange sounds that weren't made by any rat or stray animal.

"I'm coming, honey. Keep making noise." He grunted with relief when there was another thump, this time much closer.

Jules only stopped long enough for his eyes to adjust to the dark. He kept moving forward, his gun drawn, until he saw the dilapidated barrel next to a thick post, and the rope wound around it.

In the next second he was down on his knees, his gun on the ground beside him, as he was pulling at the thick cloth covering Dorrie's mouth. As soon as it was free, she gulped in huge gasps of air.

Jules' large hands cradled her face and he leaned over so

he could get a good look at her in the dark. "Are you all right?" His gaze swept along the length of her body and outstretched legs. "Are you hurt anywhere?"

"No." Dorrie's voice came out in a croak. "Thirsty."

Jules closed his eyes at the sweet sound of her voice before he leaned down and placed a gentle kiss on her lips. Even the brief contact sent a jolt all the way to his toes.

"I'll get you out of here." Reaching into his gun belt, he withdrew a long-bladed knife from a leather loop holding it in place. He swiftly cut the ropes, frowning when she winced as he sliced through the bonds around her wrists. When he saw the blood and bruises on them, his eyes went dark, but he kept working on the knots until she was completely free. He stood and drew her up with him, but when her legs started to collapse from beneath her, he quickly scooped her up into his arms. Dorrie sighed and wrapped an arm around his neck and laid her head against his shoulder.

"I'm too dirty for you to carry."

"I don't want to hear another word from you, Dorrie, until Abby's had a look at you."

"I'm fine," she breathed softly, the air moving gently across Jules' neck. "I just need some water."

"And a bed and rest," Jules said firmly. "Not another word unless you want me to take you over my knee."

Dorrie gave a weak laugh, then settled in against him.

15

J ules carried Dorrie into the sunlight, ignoring the startled looks of the merchants and shoppers as he threaded his way around the wagons toward the front of the market. He'd almost reached Ian's wagon when the big carpenter came rushing up, his arms outstretched, already reaching to take Dorrie away from him. Jules tightened his hold and sent Dorrie's parent a warning look that had him stopping dead in his tracks.

Ian looked at his daughter and then back at the man who was holding her close against his chest. "Is she all right?"

Dorrie lifted her head and managed a weak smile. "I'm fine, Da. I just need water, and then we can go home."

Her rescuer wasn't having any of that. When Dorrie started to squirm, Jules tightened his grip. "Her wrists are bloodied, and she almost suffocated under the cloth he'd stuffed in her mouth. Abby needs to have a look at her."

"I'm fine," Dorrie croaked out.

"You are not," Jules countered. "And I don't want to hear another word, remember?"

Ian reached over and ran a wide palm over her disheveled hair. "Daughter, you'll see the doctor. Then I'll take you home to your mam and sister."

Jules wasn't having any of that either, but he kept his silence as he lifted Dorrie into the back of the wagon and climbed in after her. He didn't hesitate to lean against the rough wooden side and settle her against him. Once her head was again nestled beneath his chin, he looked over at Cade who was standing behind Ian.

"Bring Hafen, will you?"

Sure that his brother wouldn't leave the big stallion behind, Jules took more of Dorrie's weight onto his lap so he could cushion her against the bumpy ride home. Ian gave the young marshal one more long look before he walked to the front of the wagon and stepped up to the high bench seat at the front. Picking up the reins, he set the horses into motion, keeping them to an easy walk as he wound through the streets and past the main square, heading toward Nob Hill and the McKenzie house.

When Dorrie leaned away from him, Jules tilted his chin down so he could look into her face.

"Are you all right? We'll be home soon."

"I'm fine," Dorrie whispered back. "Really." She peeked around him to the man driving the wagon. "I don't think Da is happy with you ordering him around like that."

"You aren't fine, and I'll take care of your da."

The dimple appeared in Dorrie's cheek. "Will that include an apology? Even Da only has so much patience."

Not needing that reminder, because now that he had her safe in his arms and his blood had cooled considerably, Jules was well aware he'd need to apologize to Ian. Not only because he was family, but mostly because he was Dorrie's father.

Inwardly wincing at his behavior, Jules knew he was lucky that Ian hadn't simply hauled off and given him a good wallop or two. Of course, there was the distinct possibility that he still might do just that. Deciding there wasn't anything he could do about it at that moment, Jules concentrated on cushioning Dorrie as the wagon rattled its way along the busy streets. He clenched his teeth even harder every time she winced. He let out a sigh of relief when Ian finally pulled the horses up in front of the large two-story house with greenery plants next to the walkway.

Scooting to the end of the wagon bed, Jules lifted Dorrie out and carried her up the porch steps. Abby and Dina were waiting for him, with Dina holding the front door wide open and Abby leading the way up the stairs to the second floor. Familiar with Abby's routine in emergencies, Dina disappeared down the hallway and into the kitchen, leaving Ian and Cade standing alone in the foyer, staring at each other.

Ian gazed up the stairway for a full minute before he turned and scowled at Cade. "How long do you think it will be before your brother allows me to talk to my own daughter?"

Cade slapped his hat onto the peg near the door and unbuckled his gun belt. "He does seem to have a head of steam up." The marshal hung up his gun and pointed toward the double doors on his right. "I could use a whiskey."

After one last glance up the stairway, Ian turned and followed Cade into the parlor.

JULES WALKED past his own room and into the one next door.

He walked over to the wide bed jutting out from the far wall and carefully set Dorrie down into its center. She wiggled backward until she was sitting up with her back against several large pillows. Jules sat on the end of the bed and started to remove her boots.

"Jules, I can take off my own boots."

He glanced over at her. "Abby hasn't looked at you yet."

Dorrie turned an exasperated look on Abby who was standing a few feet away. "Can you please examine me? Jules said I can't talk until after you do."

Abby smiled. "I see. Well then, I'd best get on with it." She walked over and sat on the edge of the bed and gently lifted one of Dorrie's hands. Abby held the wrists up and carefully felt around the bloody scrapes in the skin. She looked at Dorrie over the rim of her glasses. "Were you tied up? This looks like something you did trying to get free."

Dorrie bent at the waist and looked at her wrist along with the doctor. "Yes, I was. I thought if I could stretch the rope a bit, I could make enough room to slip my hands out." She lifted her shoulders in a small shrug. "It might have worked eventually, but Jules came along and took care of the little problem for me."

Abby nodded as she examined the other wrist before gently laying it on the coverlet. She carefully felt along Dorrie's ribs.

"Any pain? Are you having any trouble breathing?"

"No." Dorrie smiled at Abby. "I'd just appreciate a drink of water."

Jules immediately got to his feet, but before he could take one step, Dina bustled in carrying a large tray with two pitchers of water, a bowl, cloths, and a tin mug. She marched over to Jules and put the tray into his hands.

"Now, you stand there and make yourself useful." She

picked up the smaller pitcher from the tray and poured water into the tin mug, handing it to Dorrie before placing the pitcher on the stand next to the bed.

Jules watched Dorrie take tentative sips of the water, tilting her head back slightly with each one. Once the cup was empty, she put it next to the pitcher and held her hands out to Abby.

Dorrie didn't utter a sound while the doctor cleaned the abrasions on her wrists, and then wrapped a clean, thin cloth around each one. Jules never took his gaze off Dorrie's face, so he noticed the exact moment she averted her eyes and her chin began to quiver. As soon as the doctor had finished her handiwork and stood up, he thrust the tray at Dina and took Abby's place by the bed.

Dina silently shook her head at Abby and motioned her out of the room. Laying a gentle hand on Jules' shoulder she leaned close to his ear. "I'll be leaving the door open, and I'll be standing right on the other side, Jules. So you mind your manners."

He barely nodded, and didn't even notice when Dina tiptoed away as he clasped Dorrie's hands gently with his own. "Now you can talk, Dorrie. Tell me what happened. I know you followed your mam to the market. What happened there?"

She took in a deep breath but kept her gaze on the coverlet. "Mam was coming back. She hadn't talked to anyone, but just walked through the market. I had to keep off to the side to avoid a friend."

"Brenna," Jules supplied. He smiled when her gaze flashed up to his and then back down again. "I met her when we came looking for you. She said she'd have recognized you no matter what you were wearing."

"Which was why I kept out of her sight." Dorrie sighed.

"I didn't know the man was in that old warehouse until he pulled me inside." She finally looked up at him, rapidly blinking against the mist forming in her eyes. "He had his hand over my mouth and around my middle so hard I could barely breathe." She looked down again. "I was so scared."

He reached over and gently pushed a caramel-colored curl away from her face. "He won't scare you again. I promise."

Her generous mouth curved into a tiny smile despite the tears swimming in her eyes. "I know it's your duty as a marshal to keep us all safe, but you can't promise that, Jules. And I would never hold you to it."

"My job," he repeated softly.

She nodded. "I haven't thanked you for finding me." She looked toward the partially open door and lowered her voice. "I imagine Da will come to take me home soon, but I need to tell you something." She cast another quick look at the door.

"You're staying the night here." When her eyes widened and her gaze flew to his, Jules nodded. "So Abby can keep an eye on you."

"But, I'm fine," Dorrie protested. "And Da..."

"I'll take care of explaining it to your da." At least Jules hoped an explanation was all it would take. But no matter what protest her family put up, Dorrie was staying here tonight. He'd worry about tomorrow when the sun came up again.

"Now, what was it you wanted to tell me?"

Dorrie bit her lower lip and stared at him. Jules kept silent, letting her think it through. Whatever it was, she either trusted him, or she didn't. Having her trust meant everything to him. He quietly held his breath as he waited for her to decide.

"The man," she slowly began. "He knows Mam. I'm sure of it. He wanted to know why I was following 'our Maggie'." When Jules frowned, Dorrie squeezed the hand he still held in his. "He knows her. I could see it in his eyes. And he knows she's married, and that I'm not her blood."

Jules sat very still, his eyes narrowed in thought. Our Maggie? He finally focused back on Dorrie. She had trusted him. Now he needed to show her the same trust. "Maggie thinks he might be her brother."

"What?" Dorrie's mouth dropped open but no more words came out.

"Maggie called him Connor. Has your mam ever talked about her family from Ireland?"

Dorrie frowned. "Not for many years, and Da has never even mentioned them. Mam once said he's still angry that they deserted her so they could go mine for gold. And they never came back."

"They?"

"Her own da and brother."

Jules breathed in carefully. "Did she have more than one brother?"

Dorrie's forehead wrinkled. "The only name I ever remember hearing was Connor, so I think she only had one." Dorrie's eyes misted over again, and she raised a hand to rub her temple. "I'm sorry. I just don't know."

Jules leaned over and placed a gentle kiss on her forehead. "You're tired. You need to get some rest. Lie down now." He stood and retrieved the white quilt folded over the end of the bed. Opening it up, he waited while Dorrie slid into a flat position, and then spread the quilt over her.

"You rest." He sat on the edge of the bed and smiled at her. "I don't want to hear another word out of you until you've had some rest."

She gave a weak laugh as she shut her eyes. "You're very bossy, Jules McKenzie."

He watched her until her breathing evened out and he was satisfied she'd fallen asleep. He ran a finger lightly over her soft cheek. Her hair was a tangled mess, and despite Abby's efforts to wipe most of the dirt off Dorrie's face, there was still a smudge under her chin.

"And you're beautiful, Dorrie Dolan."

16

Jules took his time making his way to the parlor. He'd left Dina and Abby upstairs with Dorrie. The doctor had told him that Ian and Cade were in the parlor. Ian wasn't going to like what Jules had to say. Which was why his pace slowed as he crossed the foyer toward the open parlor doors. Just as he expected, the minute he stepped inside, two sets of eyes immediately turned in his direction.

Ian stepped forward first. "Is Abby finished taking a look at Dorrie?"

"She is." Jules held up a hand to keep Ian from moving forward. "But Dorrie was tuckered out from everything that happened. She's sleeping. It's best not to disturb her, and let her get her rest."

The big carpenter's mouth dropped into a scowl. "Are you telling me I can't see my daughter?"

Jules was more than a bit leery at the annoyance in Ian's eyes, but he held his ground. "I'm telling you she's asleep."

"I need to take her home. Maggie will worry until she's sick and has to take to a bed herself."

Dorrie's self-appointed protector shook his head. "She needs to stay here, so Abby can see to her."

"Now you're telling me what's best for my daughter?"

Since Ian looked more astonished than angry, Jules breathed a little easier. He didn't want to fight with Ian, but he wasn't going to let Dorrie out of this house, either. Here he could be sure she was safe.

"Dorrie told me that the man who attacked her called her mam 'our Maggie', knows that she has a husband, and that Dorrie isn't yours by blood." Jules watched the tall carpenter's mouth thin out. "I'd be interested in what Maggie has to say about that." He glanced over at his brother. "I'm going to go take care of Hafen. He needs a good rub down."

As Jules left, he could feel the stares of the other two men boring into his back. He knew he'd been insulting to the point he deserved the beating Ian was likely itching to give him. But he needed time alone to wrestle with everything that had happened today, and it wasn't even dark yet. He crossed the foyer just as Abby was descending the stairs. Jules paused long enough to send her a questioning look.

"She's fine. Sleeping very soundly. Dina's sitting with her."

Jules nodded his thanks and kept on walking toward the back of the house.

LESS THAN AN HOUR LATER, he heard the heavy boot steps crossing the stable floor, but Jules couldn't bring himself to get up off the small bench and face whoever it was. He stayed sitting, his head bent and his hands clasped in front of him.

"Abby told me to give you some time. I figured you've had enough."

Jules lifted his gaze to his brother's face. "I could use more."

"You've had enough time to talk things over with your horse." Cade crossed his arms over his chest. "I had to apologize to Ian on your behalf, and I expect you to do the same when you've come to your senses."

Knowing his brother was right, Jules nodded. "I'll go see him tomorrow."

Cade rubbed the scar on his cheek. "You can talk to him when he comes by the house in the morning to pick up Dorrie. He'll be here with Maggie, Anna, and Ammie."

That did get Jules' attention. "Why's Ammie coming?"

His brother lifted up a hand and started counting off fingers. "Ian's coming because he's her father, Maggie because she's her mother, Anna's her sister, and Ammie's her closest friend. None of them need another reason." He dropped his hand and looked up at the wooden beams crisscrossing overhead. "And they're coming here because no one is sure you'd be willing to let Dorrie go home. Abby also told Ian to bring them all here."

"Why'd she do that?"

Cade lifted his shoulders. "I don't know, and I've learned not to ask her about such things. I find out eventually."

Jules picked up the brush he'd set next to him on the bench and stood. "Dorrie should stay here. Maggie's brother threatened her, and he might well make good on those threats." Jules' fist clenched at his side. "Because she isn't his blood. And he knows where Maggie lives."

"Did Dorrie tell you that?"

"She told me about the threat, and that he said again that she isn't his blood. And if he knows when Maggie goes to the market, then he's been watching her, so it's a good bet he knows where she lives."

"Seems reasonable," Cade agreed. "Maybe Dorrie wouldn't object to staying with Ammie and her Aunt Charlotte for a while."

"She's not staying there." Jules couldn't believe his brother had even suggested it. Three women lived in that house, and two of them were almost defenseless. Dorrie might end up having to protect them.

"What about Charles and Lillian's house? Do you have an objection to them?"

Jules narrowed his eyes at the amusement laced into his brother's voice. Of course Dorrie would be safe enough with Lillian and Charles, so Jules didn't bother to argue that point. He simply shook his head. "Not there either."

"Let's send her home with Ethan. She can stay a spell with Luke and Shannon."

"No."

Cade laughed. "Don't even trust your friend with her? What about your other friend? I hear Robbie needs a cook."

Not even bothering to respond to that, Jules walked over to Hafen's stall and opened the gate. The big stallion looked around and bobbed his head. Jules put the brush to the horse's broad back and moved his arm in long, even strokes. Cade walked over and rested his arms on top of the low wall separating Hafen's space from the rest of the stable.

"What do you think of the notion that he's Maggie's brother?" Jules asked over his shoulder as he continued to brush his horse.

"It's looking that way. I imagine Ian's having quite a talk with his wife about now."

"Maggie should have said something when she first thought it might be her brother watching her and Anna."

Jules gave Hafen a hard enough stroke that the animal craned its neck around to look at him.

"I imagine it can't be easy thinking you've seen someone you believed was dead and buried years ago," Cade said quietly. "Just as hard to realize it's taken him all this time to come find out what happened to her."

Jules stopped in mid-stroke and rested an arm across Hafen's back. "So this brother and father really did leave Maggie in San Francisco to go pan for gold?"

Cade nodded. "That's what Abby told me a few years ago. I gather Maggie had to fend for herself, and Ian had his hands full getting her out of a bad situation, though I'm not sure of the details." He smiled. "You know Shannon writes those stories for the penny press back East? Well, she also keeps the family history. The women have told her their stories, and she's written them all down in this fancy journal she got after she married Luke."

"I've heard that." Jules had never given much thought to Shannon's journal. Until now. He wondered if it would reveal any more secrets about Maggie and her brother. Maybe he'd have Ethan ask his sister if Jules could borrow the journal for a spell. He looked over at Cade. "Have you ever read it?"

"No. I've never had the time, and whenever I've been out at Luke and Shannon's place, it never came to mind." He grinned. "But I probably should since I'm sure Abby has contributed a story or two. It wouldn't hurt to get her perspective on what happened when we first met."

Jules snorted. "No mystery there. She didn't like you."

His brother immediately frowned. "Did Abby tell you that?"

"No. But I was there, remember? I might have been young, but I could still see and hear things."

Cade snorted. "Your memory needs work." He fell quiet and watched as Jules went back to brushing Hafen. "What's eating at you, Jules?"

"He made her cry." Jules' temperature rose at the thought of the tears sliding down Dorrie's face. It had torn him up inside, and it still was. "He scared her so badly she was shaking with it." He glared at Cade. "And probably will be having nightmares."

"Probably."

"She sat in the dark for hours, all trussed up like a Sunday supper chicken, hardly able to breathe. And he left her there, not caring if she lived or died." Jules brushed Hafen's coat harder and faster. "He had no way of knowing if we'd find her or not. She could have stayed that way until she'd died of hunger and thirst, or maybe suffocated on that filthy rag he'd stuffed into her mouth."

"I realize that."

"He deserves to get a beating within an inch of his life."

"Are you volunteering for the job?"

Jules clenched his teeth together. "I could. And be sure it would be one Connor O'Hearn wouldn't forget. He'd stay away from Dorrie then."

"He'll stay away once he finds out she's under your protection," Cade pointed out. "He's already proven to be a coward by spying on his sister and niece, rather than come out into the open and possibly be confronted with Maggie's husband. He won't take on a US Marshal."

Since he felt exactly the same way about it, Jules shrugged. "I can't be with her all the time, and especially not if she's living in her father's house."

"I don't suppose you've come around to a solution for that?" When Hafen stomped a hoof hard on the stable's floor, Cade smiled. "And you'd better stop brushing your horse before he gives you a good kick."

Lifting his brush, Jules took a long step away from Hafen.

"Well?" Cade demanded.

Jules raised an eyebrow at his brother's impatient tone. "Well, what?"

"What do you think the solution is for keeping Dorrie safe? Especially when you can't be around all the time?"

"I already told you I was around when you married Abby. I remember the reasons too. You're thinking I'm facing the same problem with Dorrie, so I ought to consider the same solution." Jules ran a hand through his hair. The truth was, he had been mulling over the same thing. It's what had driven him out to the stable. But he still didn't have an answer.

"If you give her your name, Jules, she'll have that protection."

"I know it." His gaze dropped to his boots. "What I don't know is if she'll see it that way." He shrugged. "She might not want to get married."

"You could ask her. That's usually the simplest way."

That same jittery feeling skittered along Jules' back and had him shifting from one foot to the other before he glanced over at his brother. "She might have other ideas on why she should get married. Most women do."

"And she might be amenable to the idea." Cade grinned. "What I'm noticing is that *you* don't seem to have any objections to the idea."

Jules snorted. "I just haven't gotten around to voicing them yet. Not sure I need any since she probably won't take to the notion." He couldn't stop from rolling his eyes. "She thinks of us as family, like cousins."

"Well, you aren't cousins. You'll just have to point that out to her."

That jittery feeling intensified and had Jules rolling his shoulders back and forth to ease it up. "I haven't decided if I'm going to be pointing anything out to her yet."

Cade's chuckle had Jules back to glaring at him. "What's so funny?"

"I'm amazed at just how smart my wife is. Now I understand why she told Ian to bring Maggie, Anna, and Ammie with him tomorrow." He wiggled his eyebrows at Jules. "All you have to do is talk to Dorrie, and get a preacher to the house."

That jittery feeling turned into a sudden tremor as Jules gaped at his brother. "What?"

"Oh, you've made up your mind, little brother. Probably did the minute you heard Dorrie was missing." Cade shook his head. "Just look at how you've acted all day, and how you risked a beating from Ian because you want to keep her close. Not to mention that you intend to beat this Connor O'Hearn to a bloody pulp for scaring Dorrie and making her cry. You've grown into a calm man, Jules, and one who has good control of himself and his temper. Until today. Take a good look at yourself and the truth will hit you right between the eyes. That kind of truth usually does."

Cade pushed away from the wall, winking at a stunned Jules. "I'll ask Dina about supper. Come in when you're ready." He smiled at Jules. "And stay away from your horse. He's been punished enough."

17

T he next morning Jules stood outside the partially opened bedroom door, listening as Dina chattered away. If he hadn't known that Dorrie was also in there, he'd have thought his cousin was talking to herself.

He'd spent the better part of the night lying awake, thinking about what Cade had said in the stable. He'd thought about it while he was getting dressed for the day, and then some more while he'd poured himself a cup of coffee and listened to the sleepy responses his niece and nephew had given their mother over breakfast. He'd still been thinking it over as he climbed the stairs to the second floor.

Halfway up he'd decided there were two things he was sure of. That he'd rather face an army of bank robbers than the woman he'd known since he was twelve-years-old, and he wanted to marry her. If he didn't, he doubted he'd ever get another good night's sleep. And it was the reason why he'd already sent for the preacher.

Now all he had to do was convince her to come around

to his way of thinking. Taking a deep breath, he stepped through the doorway.

Dorrie looked over at the sound of his boot steps and smiled. "Good morning."

He nodded before looking past her to Dina, who was wagging a finger at him.

"You'd better not be here to demand I make you hotcakes for breakfast, Jules McKenzie." She chuckled as she winked at Dorrie. "That's been his favorite since he drew his first breath. If he didn't have hotcakes at least twice a week, I'd be in for a whole day of serious pouting."

"Is that a fact?" Dorrie grinned when he rolled his eyes at her use of one of his favorite phrases.

"It certainly is." Dina glanced back toward the man she'd helped raise. "If not hotcakes, what's brought you upstairs when you're usually out and about at this hour?"

Jules inclined his head toward the hallway. "We have guests, Dina."

The older woman wiped her hands on her apron and looked over at the ornate clock sitting on the bureau across from the bed. "Of course, of course. They're earlier than I'd thought they'd be."

"Who are you expecting?" Dorrie asked.

Dina smiled. "With two marshals and a doctor living in this house, there's always somebody dropping by." She nodded at Jules. "We'll just go on downstairs, then, and Dorrie can join us when she's ready."

Since that didn't suit his plans, Jules shook his head. "You go on down, Dina. I need to talk to Dorrie."

His cousin was back to wagging a finger at him. "I am not leaving you alone with her, Jules McKenzie. You know better than that."

"It's all right, Dina." Dorrie shrugged. "We're family and have certainly been alone before."

The older woman put her hands on her hips and pursed her lips together. "You aren't children any longer, and this is a bedroom. It wouldn't be right."

Jules' patience was running thin. Now that he was set on talking to Dorrie, he wanted to get it done. Even this small delay had his nerves jumping higher, which wasn't doing anything to improve his mood. "No, we aren't children. We're both old enough to maintain the proprieties for a few minutes, and what I have to say to Dorrie needs to be said between the two of us."

"Oh. I see." Dina slowly moved off toward the door. "But I'll be standing right outside and keeping an eye on that clock at the end of the hallway. You should be able to say whatever you need to in five minutes. Any more than that, and I'll be coming in to fetch you, Marshal McKenzie. And keep in mind that you *are* a US Marshal. Remember that oath and code of honor you're sworn to uphold."

"That'd be hard to forget," Jules muttered as he closed the door behind Dina. When he turned around, Dorrie was looking back at him, her hands clasped in front of her.

"What do you need to tell me that you didn't want Dina to hear? Is it about what happened yesterday?"

Jules ran a hand through his hair. "In a manner of speaking." He crossed the room until he was standing just a foot or so away from her. "Your parents, Anna, and Ammie are downstairs."

Dorrie's eyes lit up with amusement. "All of them came to escort me home? Even Ammie?"

"That depends."

She blinked. "Depends on what?"

He opened his mouth and then closed it again, as heat

crept up the back of his neck. This was harder than he'd thought it would be.

"It's likely the man who tied you up is your Uncle Connor." He wasn't surprised when she nodded since he'd told her that the night before. But he wanted to go slowly with what he had to say next. It would be hard for her to hear. "He doesn't see you as family in the same way he looks on your mam and sister."

Dorrie surprised him when she simply nodded.

"He made that clear, Jules, by reminding me that I wasn't his blood."

"And he appears to have taken a dislike to you, Dorrie."

"I gathered that when he tied me up and left me in the dark."

The picture permanently etched in his mind of Dorrie tied to that barrel, barely able to breathe, still made Jules' blood boil. And he fully intended to have a word or two with Connor O"Hearn over it one day soon, but right now, he had other things to consider.

"I don't believe he's going to leave you or your family alone, Dorrie. It's clear he wants something from your mam, and he wants to cause trouble for you."

Her eyes went wide. "Do you think he might hurt my family?"

Jules shrugged. "Maybe not on purpose, but if he sees another opportunity at getting you out of his way, he might." He clasped his hands behind his back. "You should stay here."

His shoulders tensed when she quickly shook her head. "I don't want to bring trouble to your house, Jules. Abby and the children live here, and Dina is here most of the day, too."

He relaxed again. At least she hadn't dismissed the idea of living here with him.

"It would only be temporary," he assured her. "And I doubt if Maggie's brother would come near this house. He's only watched the women when Ian wasn't around to catch him, and at the market when you're alone. He strikes me as a coward, Dorrie. He won't come around to a house where two US Marshals live."

Dorrie's brow wrinkled. He hoped she was giving it a fair thought.

"Connor O'Hearn, or whoever he is, did mention that he had no intention of tangling with a US Marshal."

That surprised Jules. "He did? So he knew I was looking for him?"

"I don't know if he did before I told him." She smiled as she gave that little confession. "Actually, it was more of a threat that you'd come looking for him."

Absurdly pleased that she'd thought of him as her protection, he gave her a solemn nod. "You told him the truth. I'm glad he took it to heart."

She looked around the room with a sigh. "How long would I need to stay here?"

"Until I can find us a house of our own. I'll start asking around."

"A house of our own? Jules, we can't share a house together."

The look on her face had him smiling. She looked stunned. Which was a whole lot better than outraged.

"We can if we're married."

"Married?"

Jules took a short step forward and wrapped his hands around her upper arms. All the color had drained from her face and he was afraid she might faint on him. He didn't want her to hit her head on anything if she suddenly collapsed to the floor. It only took a few seconds before the color rushed back into her face and her eyes narrowed.

"That isn't funny, Jules."

"I wasn't meaning to be, Dorrie." He kept his gaze on hers so she could see how serious he was.

She blinked several times before lifting one hand and touching it to his forehead. "You don't feel feverish."

"I'm not sick."

When she dropped her hand and continued to stare up at him, Jules thought he needed to spell things out more plainly for her. "It solves a problem for both of us, and our families." When she frowned up at him, he loosened his grip and unconsciously started to rub a big hand soothingly up and down her arm.

"You don't want to bring trouble to your mam and da's house, do you?" He waited until she gave a small negative shake of her head. "Because this Uncle Connor of yours is sure to do that if you stay there."

Dorrie wrinkled her nose. "He made it clear he isn't my blood, and thank heavens for that. But what you're suggesting, Jules, will just move the trouble from my da's house to yours. And I've already told you, you aren't the only one who lives here. Abby and your niece and nephew call this home as well, remember?" She shook her head. "I won't bring trouble to them."

Jules gave an inward sigh and took a firmer hold on his patience. "Which is why I'll be looking for a house of our own. And some reliable guards until I can get my hands on Connor."

"You're going to arrest him?"

Or something like that, Jules thought, but he knew better than to voice that out loud. Dorrie was sure to object, and might refuse to marry him. "If I have to." He ran a hand through his hair. "Dorrie. Having my name will give you protection. Connor isn't going to take on a US Marshal. It will also help to have a marshal attached to your family. There's a good chance he'll move on, rather than cross a lawman."

She chewed on her lower lip. "He said as much to me." She drew the words out slowly. "And it might keep him away from Anna and Da. But he seems determined to talk to Mam."

"We'll find a way to deal with that."

She glanced away before lowering her gaze to the floor. "You're offering something you won't be able to take back, Jules. And I'm grateful beyond words." She drew in a big breath and lifted her eyes to his. "But I'm not your problem. I could leave town for a while. Maybe go visit Rayne or Shannon, or stay with Robbie for a spell. I could help Shue with the cooking and cleaning."

Jules didn't care much for that solution, and even less for the growing enthusiasm in her voice. Nope. She definitely was not going to be spending any time under Robbie's protection rather than his.

"If you think I'm going to let you step out of my sight, then you're mistaken, Dorrie."

Her eyes widened.

"And if Anna isn't too big to take over my knee, then I'd remind you that you aren't any bigger than she is."

"You wouldn't!"

He grinned. "No, probably not. But I'd sure give it some serious consideration." When she narrowed her eyes, he reached up and ran a finger down the side of her cheek.

"I should ask you," he said softly. "Is there someone else you'd rather marry?"

Dorrie's curls floated over the hand he still had on her arm, causing his whole body to tense up.

"No, Jules. There isn't."

"Do you object to me as a husband?"

She laughed. "No woman would. You'd be a fine husband, and I doubt you need me to tell you that."

Feeling the whole matter was settled, a heavy weight fell away from Jules' shoulders. "And I don't object to you being my wife."

"Oh? How kind."

Jules was too caught up in the plans racing through his head to notice the overly sweet response from his future bride. "It's a good start."

"Do you think so?"

He smiled at her before lowering his head and giving her a solid kiss square on the mouth. When she continued to stare at him without uttering one word, he was delighted to have found such a pleasant way to keep her quiet and win an argument.

"I'll send the women up. They can help you get ready."

"Ready?" Dorrie sounded dazed.

"I'm sorry, and I'll make it up to you, but we need to be quick." He glanced at the clock on top of the clothes chest. "The preacher should be here any minute."

"The preacher? Now just a minute, Jules McKenzie..."

Deciding what worked once would work again, Jules pulled her closer and gave her another kiss, this one a good deal more thorough than the last one. When he finally lifted his mouth from hers, they were both breathing unevenly. Remembering Dina's words, Jules was suddenly acutely aware of the bed not two feet away. He gently set Dorrie away from him.

"I'll send the women up. Don't take too long."

18

J ules stepped out into the hallway and softly closed the door behind him. He was vaguely surprised that Dina was nowhere in sight, but quickly shrugged it off as he strode down the hallway toward his own bedchamber. It took him less than thirty seconds to cross over the threshold, and he headed straight for the tall wardrobe in the corner. Opening the highly polished oak doors, he dropped to one knee and reached into the back, pulling out a small wooden chest with an ornate rose carved on the top. As was his lifetime habit whenever he held it, he ran a finger across the rose.

"Hello, Mama." He smiled. His mother had been his father's second wife, and died giving birth to her son, so Jules had no conscious memory of her, but he always thought she'd appreciate a smile from her only child. Jules lifted the lid and picked up a small object wrapped in a velvet cloth. He put it into his vest pocket before closing the chest up and once again ran a finger across the rose. "Thank you, Mama. Dorrie's a good woman. I know she'll cherish it."

He carefully returned the chest to the bottom of the wardrobe and rose to his feet. Closing the doors, he headed back out to the hallway and down the stairs. When he'd reached the foyer, he stopped and took several deep breaths, not at all certain exactly what was waiting for him behind the parlor doors. This was new territory for him. He'd had many conversations with the man he'd always thought of as an uncle, but never before had he faced the carpenter as Dorrie's father. But no matter what the man had to say, or anyone else in her family, he was going to marry Dorrie. Today. So he'd better get the formalities out of the way before the preacher he'd sent for earlier that morning arrived on the doorstep.

Running a nervous hand through his hair, Jules took one last deep breath before walking up to the parlor doors and pulling them open.

Every eye in the room turned in his direction. Cade and Abby were beaming at him while Dina sniffled quietly into a white kerchief she was holding up to her mouth. When Jules shifted his gaze to the group gathered around each other next to the divan, he wished they looked as happy as his brother and sister-in-law did. But Ian was staring at him, his large arms crossed over his chest. Maggie's eyes narrowed on his face and Anna chewed on her lip as her gaze darted between him and her parents. Ammie stood slightly apart, her lips trembling with what Jules assumed was suppressed laughter at his predicament. When she gave him a cheeky smile and an exaggerated wink, it reminded him so much of the girl he'd grown up with, that his nerves settled back into place.

Smiles or frowns, this was his family. He'd been dealing with them most of his life and now was no different.

He stood up a little straighter and looked his honorary

uncle, who would soon be his father-in-law, right in the eye. "Ian. Can I have a word with you?"

The carpenter gave a short nod. His hand settled briefly on his wife's shoulder before he stepped around Maggie and Anna to follow the younger man out of the room.

Jules headed for his study, waiting by the door for Ian to precede him, then stepping inside and closing it behind him. Since Dorrie's father didn't take a seat but simply turned to face him, Jules chose to stand as well.

The two men stood silently staring at each other. When Ian finally quirked an eyebrow at him, Jules cleared his throat.

"There're two men I need to talk to," Jules began. "One is my uncle, and the other is Dorrie's father."

Ian snorted. "I'm both those men, Jules. Go ahead and say what you need to, and then I'll have my say as well."

The marshal sighed and ran a hand through his hair. "Fair enough. I need to apologize to my uncle. I shouldn't have been so disrespectful yesterday, and I hope you'll accept my apology."

"That depends." Ian cocked his head to one side. "On why you were so disrespectful in the first place. I gave it some thought last night, and can't say I've ever known you to be. Except for yesterday."

"Thinking Dorrie might be hurt, or worse, made me crazy."

The simple statement had Ian smiling. "I remember feeling that way about a woman once." He ducked his head. "I still do." With a sigh, Ian nodded at the man standing in front of him. "Your uncle accepts your apology, son. Now what is it you want to say to Dorrie's father?"

"I'd like your permission to marry your daughter, sir." Jules unconsciously braced his legs apart, as if he were readying for battle. "As soon as possible." At Ian's sudden frown, Jules was quick to add, "because of the threat from this man who we believe is Maggie's brother, Connor. He doesn't consider Dorrie his blood, so has no problem with hurting her. It would be best if she had the protection of my name."

"You don't think I can protect my family?"

"You have your hands full keeping your wife and Anna safe." Jules paused for a moment, hoping Ian wouldn't take offense at what he was going to say next. "And you aren't a US Marshal. Connor doesn't want to tangle with a marshal. He told Dorrie as much."

Ian's eyebrows shot up. "Did he? How did he come to know that you're a marshal?"

Despite the seriousness of the conversation, Jules couldn't help his sudden grin. "Dorrie told him that I'd be looking for her."

"She did?" Ian raised a large hand and rubbed it across his chin. "You're the man she thought of as her protector, instead of her da?"

"Yes, sir."

Dorrie's father sighed and turned his head to look out the window. But not before Jules caught the sheen of moisture in his eyes.

"A father always knows this day will come, when he's no longer the only man in his daughter's life."

Not knowing how to respond to that, Jules kept his silence, shifting uncomfortably from foot to foot until Ian finally turned his gaze back to him. The marshal was glad to see there were no longer tears forming in the big man's eyes.

"I'm assuming you've talked this plan of yours over with Dorrie?"

Jules nodded. "I have, and we're in agreement."

"So am I." Ian held up a hand at Jules' quick smile. "But I can't say what her mam will think of this. When were you planning on having this wedding?"

"This morning. As soon as the preacher gets here."

Ian had a sudden coughing fit, his eyes bulging out as they stared at Jules. "This morning? Maggie will have both our hides."

Well aware that Ian was right about that, Jules was determined to stand his ground. He and Dorrie were going to be married today, and Maggie would have to settle for a celebration later on.

"I know. But Dorrie's agreed, and there's a reason for the haste. With your daughter's safety at stake, I hope Maggie won't object too much."

Ian let out a loud snort. "You go ahead and hope that if you want, but we're both going to be in for one hell of an argument." He rubbed his chin again before holding out his hand. "But you have my permission to marry Dorrie." As Jules took Ian's hand with a firm clasp, Dorrie's father smiled. "I'd welcome you into the family, but you're already part of it, so I'll just give you my best wishes for a long and happy life together."

"Thank you, Ian."

"You might want to practice making that 'Da', since you'll be my son-in-law instead of honorary nephew."

Jules grinned. "Yes, sir."

The two men shook hands in perfect accord before heaving identical sighs as they turned to leave the safety of the study to face the women in the parlor. Or at least one of them in particular.

They walked in together, but Ian signaled for Jules to wait behind him as the carpenter moved to stand in front of his wife. Taking her hands in his, Ian leaned down and whispered into Maggie's ear while Jules waited for his aunt's reaction. When she leaned to one side to look around her husband, Jules wasn't surprised to see the frown on her face.

"I've no objections to you marryin' me daughter, Jules McKenzie. But I'm thinkin' I didn't hear me husband correctly when he said it would be happenin' today."

Jules felt the heat creeping along his cheeks under his aunt's cool stare. "I'm sorry, Maggie, but it has to be today." When she continued to stare at him, he looked over at Cade for help. His brother gave a quick shrug and turned toward his wife. Abby shook her head at both of them.

"Well, a quiet ceremony today and a huge party next week sounds perfect," Ammie chimed in. She stepped to the side and put an arm around Anna's waist. "You can help your mam make the perfect dress." She winked at the young girl. "It will be wonderful practice for making one of your own someday."

"In the far future," Ian said firmly.

Jules would have gladly kissed Ammie for her enthusiasm, and for enlisting Anna's help in persuading her mam. But a sideways glance at his aunt's face told him that Maggie was far from convinced.

"And you say Dorrie has agreed to this?" Maggie demanded.

"She has," Jules said calmly.

Maggie darted away from her husband and stood with her hands on her hips, glaring at him. "And you've agreed with our daughter bein' married today?"

"Yes. It's for the best." Ian gave his wife a steady look. "Whether the man is your brother Connor or not, he tried to hurt Dorrie. She'll be safer under the roof of a marshal."

A brief look of uncertainty passed over Maggie's face before her lips thinned out again. "Well. I'll be needin' to talk with me daughter about this."

Without another word, she turned on her heel and marched out of the room.

Jules looked from Ian over at Cade.

"You're sure Dorrie's in agreement?" his brother asked as he stared after Maggie.

Jules nodded. "We talked it all out. She's agreed to marry me today."

"THE MAN HAS CLEARLY LOST his mind." Dorrie paced the floor in front of the bed where Ammie sat watching her.

"I'm sure I just heard you convince your mam that you're in favor of this marriage, as well as the wedding taking place today." Ammie tilted her head to one side. "Are you saying you didn't mean a word of it?"

"Well, I couldn't have Mam going back downstairs and calling Jules a liar, now could I?"

"Sure you could," Ammie said cheerfully, then laughed when Dorrie made a face at her. Rising from the bed, she went over and gave her friend a warm hug. "We're a pair, aren't we?"

Dorrie dropped her forehead to rest it briefly on Ammie's shoulder before straightening up and taking a small step back. "How did we get here, Amelia Jamison?"

"I have no idea, Dorrie Dolan, but I do know one thing. Why shouldn't at least one of us have her dream?"

"I don't know." Dorrie bit her bottom lip. She'd buried her feeling for Jules McKenzie so deeply and for so long, she wasn't sure what to do with them now as they bubbled so close to the surface. And even though she'd never spoken of them to Ammie, she'd always known her best friend had never been fooled. She sighed and wrapped her arms around her waist. "I don't know what to do."

"Marry Jules, what else?"

"But he didn't really ask me."

Now Ammie grinned. "He didn't? Well, that's not staying true to the family tradition, and I'm sure all the aunts will have something to say about that. But in the meantime, what *did* he say to you?"

Dorrie rolled her eyes. "That he didn't object to me being his wife."

"That he didn't object...?" Ammie trailed off into a gale of laughter. "So romantic," she managed to choke out. "It's a wonder you didn't faint after hearing such a charming proposal."

The corners of Dorrie's mouth turned upward. "It did lack a bit of something."

"Lack a bit of something? The man is aware that you own a gun, isn't he?"

Now Dorrie started laughing. "Yes, he is. And that all my friends do, too."

"He's a very brave man," Ammie said solemnly before bursting out into a fresh round of laughter.

"He's a US Marshal," Dorrie declared before she joined in the laughter.

It took them a good five minutes to calm down. Both of them plopped back onto the bed, next to the fresh skirt and blouse that Dina had laid there for Dorrie to change into.

Ammie turned her head and grinned at her best friend. "Tell me everything. I promise to take it all very seriously."

"Uh huh." Dorrie doubted that, but she quickly related her conversation with Jules, then gave the stunning brunette a questioning look. "Well, what do you think?"

"I think you gave him a way to back out, and he didn't take it, that's what I think."

Dorrie sighed. There was no denying that. Jules seemed set on marrying her, and she certainly wouldn't mind marrying him, but it bothered her that it wasn't for the right reasons. "He never said he loved me."

"According to Lillian, they usually don't at first. She says it takes most men time to make that particular declaration. And Lillian knows about these things." Ammie declared.

Since t Lillian had once owned the most successful brothel in San Francisco, Dorrie couldn't argue with that.

"What if he doesn't feel that way and never says it?" she fretted. The possibility left a gaping hole in the pit of her stomach.

Ammie grinned. "After the way he was acting when you went missing? Not a chance."

She said it with so much confidence that Dorrie's spirits immediately lifted.

Ammie rose from the bed, grabbed Dorrie's hand, and pulled her to her feet. "Don't be a ninny, Dorrie. Get dressed, go downstairs, and marry that man. He's everything you want. And trust me, you're everything he wants, too." Ammie gave her a wink. "And think of the fun you'll have convincing him to say the words."

Heat flooded through Dorrie, and she was sure her face had turned bright red. "I'll get dressed and marry him if you promise not to say such things when he's around. Or to Mam or Da either. They'd both faint dead away."

"Your da might, but I don't think your mam would." Ammie gave her another wink. "I've never been allowed to read Shannon's journal on the family history. Whenever I've asked, she said it isn't time yet. But I've heard a snippet or two of most of the stories."

Dorrie gave her friend's arm a light swat. "Oh be quiet and help me get dressed for my wedding."

19

"I now pronounce you man and wife." The heavyset preacher with the kind smile nodded at Jules. "You may kiss your bride."

Acutely aware of all the eyes trained on them, Jules leaned down and placed a chaste kiss on Dorrie's cheek. When he heard her small sigh, he moved his lips slowly over to her ear.

"Later, Mrs. McKenzie," he whispered. He lifted his head and grinned at the blush rapidly spreading across her face.

Dina clapped her hands together. "Congratulations. You're a perfect match!"

Ammie, who was standing right next to the half-laughing, half-crying Dina, raised an eyebrow and gave Jules a broad wink when he glanced over in their direction. He put an arm around Dorrie's slim waist and turned them both to face their audience, keeping her close to him as the rest of the family rushed up with hugs for his bride and a few good-natured slaps on the back for him.

Within minutes, Dina was passing around tall glasses of lemonade as everyone melted into a happy confusion of best wishes and toasts for a long life together. Jules smiled through it all, pulling Dorrie even closer when he felt her tremble. It seemed so natural and right to have her tucked in against his side that he wondered why it had taken him so long to get her there.

He did tense up when Maggie approached them. The Irish woman pulled Dorrie away from him and gave her daughter a fierce hug before gently pushing her back toward her husband. Jules' new mother-in-law then turned to him and rose on her toes to place a brief kiss on his cheek.

"You'll take good care of me girl, or I'll be knowin' the why of it." She softened her words with a smile. "I know you'll be a good husband to her. I'm warnin' you, though. She needs a firm hand at times." Maggie reached over and cupped a hand around her daughter's cheek. "She can be a wee bit stubborn, this one can."

"Mam!" Dorrie protested with a laugh. "You don't need to tell him all my faults when we've only been married for an hour."

Maggie's smile bloomed until it lit up the room, reminding Jules of just why Ian was still under his wife's spell.

"I'm rememberin' that you grew up with this new husband of yours. I'm thinkin' there isn't much about your faults that he doesn't already know. But he's just findin' out that your mischief makin' wasn't always started by Ammie." She turned her smile on Jules. "You always were a bit blind to that."

Jules looked down at his bride and grinned. "Is that a fact?"

"No, it is not," Dorrie sniffed. "Ammie got us into a lot more trouble than I ever did."

"No she didn't," Ammie called out from several feet away

where she was talking with the preacher. "I'd hate to have to call you a liar on your wedding day, Dorrie McKenzie."

Dorrie looked up at her husband, her eyes sparkling as she whispered loudly enough so her friend would also hear her. "I'm your wife. Don't listen to her."

Jules used one finger to lift her chin higher. "Yes, you are," he said softly, bringing the blush back to Dorrie's cheeks. He was so captured by the soft look in her deep-brown eyes that he was lowering his head for that kiss he'd been craving ever since she'd said, "I do", when Abby clapped her hands loudly to get everyone's attention.

Jules pulled back and took in a deep breath. Some privacy and a bed would suit his mood about now, but instead he gave Dorrie a rueful smile before they both looked over at Abby.

"We have a mountain of food in the kitchen that Dina needs help with, and a family party to plan." She smiled at Dorrie. "We're going to have the bride to ourselves for a few minutes while the men enjoy something stronger than lemonade."

Within seconds there was a flurry of skirts as Dorrie was pulled away from Jules and whisked out the parlor doors, surrounded by the women in the family with the preacher trailing behind them.

Jules watched her go, already feeling the absence of her warmth by his side. He was still staring at the empty doorway when Cade came up behind him and slapped a large hand on top of his shoulder.

"Why don't we go into the study and you can explain your plan to Ian. He might want to give it a try himself."

Ian's eyebrow quirked up. "What plan is that?"

Jules glanced over at his uncle-turned-father-in-law. "For catching Connor O'Hearn."

A few minutes later, the three men were standing around the large cherry-wood desk in the study, each with a glass of whiskey in front of him. Jules looked at the other two men and frowned. Somehow discussing a plan that involved Dorrie without her there just didn't seem right. He excused himself and quickly went down the hall to the kitchen. He stopped inside the doorway.

"I need to borrow my bride for a few minutes," he announced when everyone froze in midmovement and looked over at him. "We're talking over a plan that involves her." He smiled when Dorrie immediately set down the bowl she was holding and walked over and took hold of his outstretched hand.

Maggie looked at her daughter's face and sighed. "Don't keep her too long, Jules."

He only smiled as he pulled Dorrie out of the kitchen and back toward the study. Once they were in the hallway and out of sight of curious eyes, he whirled her about until her back was against the wall. Bracing his arms on either side of her, he smiled into her startled eyes. "Now for that proper kiss, Mrs. McKenzie." Jules didn't wait for an answer, but lowered his head until his mouth covered hers. He moved his lips and tongue across her softness. When she opened up for him, she kissed him back until they were both fighting for breath. He broke it off before he lost his control completely, but couldn't stop his mouth from trailing across her cheek and down her long slender neck.

"We're waiting, Jules."

Cade's voice was loud enough that Dorrie gasped and put a hand to Jules' chest, giving it a firm shove. It wasn't enough to move him, but he obligingly took a step back to put some space between them.

"Behave yourself, Marshal," Dorrie whispered, casting a

clearly worried glance over at the wide-open door to the study.

"You do the same, Mrs. McKenzie." Jules grinned when Dorrie glared up at him. Giving her a wink, he took her hand in his and walked into the small room where his brother and father-in-law stood, carefully looking everywhere but at the open doorway.

Ian turned to his daughter and studied her face for a moment before directing a frown at Jules.

The younger marshal quickly cleared his throat and inclined his head toward Dorrie. "Since this involves my wife, I thought she should hear it too."

"Wasn't aware that you were talking to her," Cade observed, laughing at the dagger-eyed look Jules shot him. "Better get to it. Daylight is burning," Cade added quietly.

Jules was acutely aware of that fact. And he still had to tell his bride that her wedding night wasn't going to be what she most likely imagined. And it sure as hell wasn't going to be what *he'd* imagined either.

"This has to do with keeping Dorrie safe and catching Connor."

Dorrie straightened her back and looked at her new husband. "How do you plan on doing that, Jules?"

He smiled back at her. "It will take some cooperation from you." He nodded when her mouth dropped open. "I've hired two guards. One will be visible, staying by your side. The other will be out of sight, following both of you."

Ian frowned. "You're thinking Connor will only notice the one guard and show himself to the second man?"

Jules nodded. "I think it will fool him enough that we'll be able to grab him before he realizes it."

"That's brilliant, Jules." Dorrie beamed at him. "And I

know it will work." She turned and faced her father. "You should do the same thing with Mam."

"Except for it to work, you wouldn't be able to tell Maggie about the second guard," Cade said quietly.

All three watched as Ian rubbed his chin for several long moments. "You mean if this man is her brother, Maggie might give him a warning." Ian nodded. "I'm not sure she could help herself. She's always spoken fondly of Connor." The carpenter looked at his daughter with a sad smile. "So I'd be using a trick on your mam. I've never done that to her, or kept a secret from her. And I'm not sure I can do it now." He glanced over at Jules. "It's a good plan, but I'll have to think on it."

Understanding Ian's predicament, Jules turned a serious look on Dorrie. "Can you contain your curiosity enough to keep close to the one guard without constantly looking around for the other?"

Dorrie nodded, her caramel curls dancing around her shoulders. "Of course I can. I want Connor caught so he'll stop bothering Mam and Anna."

"And you," Jules reminded her. He glanced out the window and frowned before turning back to Ian. "There's something I need to talk to Dorrie about privately."

Both Ian and Cade immediately set their glasses on the desk. Cade turned and left the room, followed by Ian after he'd stopped and kissed his daughter on the cheek.

"Remember you're a wife now, and you need to support your husband."

Dorrie stared after her father before giving Jules a puzzled look. "What is Da talking about?"

Jules sighed and ran a hand through his hair. He'd been dreading this moment all morning, but here it was, and he couldn't get out of it. "I don't know a good way to say this,

Dorrie, so I'm just going to come right out with it." He paused while she continued to stare at him in silence. "I need to leave."

"Leave?" Dorrie blinked several times as if she didn't quite understand the word. "Leave when?"

He gave another glance out the window. "Right now. I'm already going to be late meeting Ethan."

"You're leaving to meet Ethan? Why?"

"We'd already arranged it, remember? I have no way of getting word to him, except to show up." He gave her an apologetic smile. "I'd send someone else, but we might have to do some tracking, depending on what Ethan's found, and I need to be there." When she remained silent, he thought she might need a bit more reassurance. "Cade will be here. He'll look after you."

"I didn't marry Cade, Jules." Dorrie rubbed a hand across her brow and then sighed. She turned her gaze up to his. "This has to do with that Green Gang?"

Jules nodded. "Ethan's been trying to pick up their tracks, and I agreed to meet him at the crooked pine that's about halfway to Robbie's ranch."

"I know it," Dorrie said softly, not taking her eyes off his. "And I realize your work is important, Jules."

He ran a finger down her cheek. "So are you. And I'll make it up to you. I swear it." He took her hand in his and fingered the ring he'd put on her third finger just a few hours ago. He lifted her hand to his lips and gave her finger a soft kiss. "This was my mother's wedding ring. I don't think I've had a chance to tell you that."

Dorrie's eyes widened and her gaze grew soft. "It was?" She looked at it with wonder before smiling at him. "I'll treasure it." Dorrie glanced over at the door before slipping a hand into his. "And I'll walk out to the stable with you."

He gave her hand a gentle squeeze and together they left the study and turned toward the front door. Jules didn't want to take the short route through the kitchen where he'd have to give up part of his time with Dorrie to answer a lot of questions from the women. He wanted every second he could have even if it was only for a short walk to the stable.

Hafen was already saddled and waiting for him. Jules took the rifle he'd left leaning against the outside of the stall and slipped it into the casing on the saddle. After checking the cinches, he knew he'd stayed as long as he could. Turning back to his bride he grinned as he pulled on leather gloves and settled his broad-brimmed hat more firmly in place. "I'll be gone for a few days, maybe a week depending on what Ethan's found. I'll send you word if I can."

"Jules?"

He wasn't prepared when she reached up and swept his hat off his head before she threw her arms around his neck and pressed her whole body to his. He caught her closer, feeling every one of her curves against the hard muscles of his chest. He'd barely managed to open his mouth, but didn't get a word out before she rose on her toes, sliding up his body as her mouth settled on his. In a flash, heat flooded his blood and raced through him as she moved her tongue against his and her body strained to get closer. His arms tightened until she was crushed against him. Even the restless movements of Hafen behind him didn't register until his horse's head gave him a hard bump on his back, almost knocking them both to the ground.

Jules did a quick step to keep his balance then turned and glared at the big animal while Dorrie raised a hand to her mouth in an attempt to smother her laughter. She took a step back and Jules reluctantly let her go.

"You come home as soon as you can, Jules."

Letting out a frustrated sigh, Jules stepped up into the saddle. He turned Hafen and walked the horse until he was right next to his wife. Leaning over in the saddle, he gave her upturned face a quick kiss on the forehead.

"You can count on that, honey."

20

The late afternoon sun was sinking in the sky as Jules walked his horse up to the crooked tree in the middle of the open range. The tall, dry grass crackled and split as Hafen stepped through it, the noise easily carrying across the flat expanse of land leading up to the coastal hills not too far in the distance. The tall light-colored chestnut that Ethan favored for his mount was grazing in the shade of the tree, but his friend was nowhere in sight. Jules pulled his own stallion up a good twenty feet away from Ethan's horse and sat quietly in the saddle. The only sound in the air was the soft creak of leather as Hafen shifted his weight into a more comfortable stance.

A good thirty seconds passed before the low whistle sounded. Jules smiled. He and Ethan had been using that signal for more than a decade. Nudging Hafen in his sides, Jules continued to walk his mount forward until they were next to Ethan's horse. Throwing one leg over Hafen's broad back, Jules dismounted and turned to loosen the saddle cinch and retrieve his sack of supplies and his rifle.

"You'd think a US Marshal would know better than to turn his back on someone he couldn't see."

Jules grinned but didn't turn around. "Don't have to see you, Ethan. I can smell you a mile away. You could use a bath."

Ethan snorted and rose up from the tall grass. "I've been busy." He strode over to a boulder and leaned his rifle against the rock before pointing at a pile of broken branches. "I got the wood. You can make the fire, and I'm hoping some coffee. I ran out a few days ago."

Jules tossed the bag of supplies across the fifteen feet separating them, smiling when Ethan easily caught it with one hand. "You dig the coffee tin out, and I'll make it."

The two spent the next thirty minutes working in companionable silence as Jules built the fire and Ethan retrieved one of his canteens. He filled a small pot with water. Once the coffee was boiling, Jules poured out the strong brew into a tin cup and handed it to his friend before readying a cup for himself. He settled his back against the old tree trunk and took a long sip as he studied Ethan.

"Can't say that scruff on your face improves your looks much."

Ethan shrugged. "Wasn't going to waste my water on shaving. Didn't bring a razor with me anyway."

"How's Robbie?"

"As irritating as ever," Ethan grunted. "He says they haven't seen any strangers around, but he put up the guards. I doubt if he'll keep the hands guarding the place long. He thinks those men have headed back to the Northern territories. He figures they heard you were looking for them and don't want to tangle with a US Marshal."

Jules frowned. A distant bell went off in the back of his

mind, but he couldn't place it before Ethan's next words distracted him.

"Found the tracks north of here, just like Robbie said."

"Which way were they headed?"

"North." Ethan smiled. "Just like Robbie said."

"Got a visit from Ben Hanson. He has a ranch about a day's ride from yours."

Jules' friend nodded. "I know it."

"It seems the Green Gang paid him a visit. Put a good scare into his wife and kids, took some supplies, then headed out. Hanson's wife said they were headed southwest." Jules paused and considered it for a moment. "Hanson thinks they may have been trying to avoid him and the hands since they were working in the north pastures."

"Maybe. Could be they needed supplies for their trip north."

The marshal grinned at his friend. "Just like Robbie said."

"Don't tell him that. His head's already too big for that hat he wears." Ethan's dry tone had Jules chuckling.

The tracker picked up a short stick and drew a circle in the dirt next to the fire, then drew a smaller oval inside of it. "This is Robbie's place." Ethan drew a line through one third of the circle. "This is the ground I've covered. Didn't see any tracks with two crooked hooves except for over here."

Jules leaned forward and studied the crude map Ethan had drawn. There was still a lot of ground to cover to the south of Robbie's ranch, but the tracks Ethan had discovered were definitely to the north. "Where did you lose them?"

Ethan placed his stick at a point along the road that led from San Francisco to the border of Oregon. "If they left the road, I couldn't find the track, but didn't have a chance to look much. And I couldn't tell which way they headed once they crossed that road. Too many recent tracks to sort them out. Might have searched a bit more if I'd known you were going to be late."

"Only a couple of hours, Ethan. I thought you might like the peace and quiet the way you've been avoiding company the last few years."

"And I thought you'd be early, the way you like gabbing with people."

"You must have been out in the sun too long. You're mixing me up with Robbie."

His friend reached up and scratched at the beard sprouting from his chin. "That man does like to talk. I went to the bunkhouse to sleep just to get away from him."

Jules laughed and reached over to pour more coffee into his tin as Ethan gave his chin another hard scratch.

"If that hair on your face is bothering you, you can use my razor."

When his friend gave him an astonished look, Jules wished he'd kept his mouth shut.

"You brought a razor? What for?"

The marshal shrugged. "The usual reason." Jules raised his cup to his mouth and took a long sip, ignoring the speculative gleam in Ethan's eyes.

"You've never brought one before."

"Sure I have."

It didn't surprise Jules when Ethan ignored that and continued to study him.

"It seems there's something going on here that I don't know about. You're late meeting up, you bring a razor with you. And now that I've got coffee in me, I'm noticing that you're dressed fancier than a man who's looking to spend time on the trail."

"Because I have a clean shirt on? You might try it some time."

Ethan grinned. "You might as well tell me what's got you so wound up, or I'll just have to ride back into town right now and ask around."

When he made a motion to get up, Jules waved at him to stay where he was. "I was late because I had to deal with the man who's been following Dorrie, Anna, and Maggie around. Dorrie caught him talking to Anna."

His friend's grin instantly faded. "He got Dorrie and her sister alone?"

Jules nodded. "He did. Then Dorrie and Amelia got this hairbrained idea to follow him, and that's when Dorrie went missing."

Ethan shot to his feet. "Is Ammie missing too?"

The marshal looked up at his friend towering over him. "No. Just Dorrie, but I found her." Jules waited as Ethan sat again and his breathing evened out. "The bastard had tied her up and left her to choke on the filthy rag he'd stuffed into her mouth." Jules' finger's tightened so hard that small dents appeared in the side of the cup he was holding.

"What kind of protection have you put around her?" Ethan's practical tone had Jules' shoulders relaxing again.

"Guards and my name."

Ethan nodded. "That's good. How many..." His eyes went wide, and his jaw dropped to his chest. "Did you say your name?"

Not quite sure how his friend would take the news, Jules gave a stoic nod. "I did."

"You married Dorrie?"

At a loss for words, Jules stuck with the same answer. "I did."

"When?"

"This morning."

Ethan was on his feet and hauling Jules up to his before the marshal could blink. His oldest friend gave him a bear hug and then a hard slap on the back. "Congratulations! I can't believe she agreed to marry you. Or Ian and Maggie let her."

Jules grinned. "They might have had a few reservations about it."

"More than a few, I'd bet," Ethan laughed. "Why didn't you send Cade to meet me and stay with your bride?" Suddenly his mouth dropped open again. "Did you say this morning?" Ethan barely waited for Jules' nod before he burst into laughter. "So you're spending your wedding night with me and your horse rather than your bride?"

He'd barely managed to choke the words out before he had another laughing fit, while Jules stood, glaring at him.

"Cade has to leave in a couple of days to escort that federal judge back to Sacramento, so he couldn't come. And Dorrie understood."

That set Ethan's laughter off again. "I'll bet she did. I'm thinking every one of our aunts will be standing on your doorstep when you get home, with their shotguns in their hands."

"Shut up, Ethan."

"Not a chance, Jules." Ethan continued to grin as he looked up at the sky. "We still have daylight left. Why don't we head out to where I found those tracks and take the road south to see if we can find them going off the road? We can see if they're heading south after all and get you home in a couple of days. Plenty of time for you to use that razor of yours to make yourself presentable while you come up with the proper way to grovel while you apologize to your bride for leaving her alone on her wedding night."

"Sounds good. And you still need to shut up, Ethan."

His friend laughed. "I'll give it a try, but no promises." He picked up his coffee mug and threw the last of the contents onto the fire. "Let's ride."

FROM A HILLSIDE, the man with green eyes snapped his spyglass shut. He'd been watching the tracker for several hours and then waited uneasily as the other man had joined him. Through his lens he'd seen the badge on the man's chest. He'd been nervous when the two men started to break camp and ready their horses, and then astonished when they'd ridden off in the opposite direction.

Letting out a breath of relief, he waited until their silhouettes had faded into the distance before he shut his telescope with a snap and crawled to the opposite side of the hill where he'd left his horse. Once he was settled in the worn leather saddle, he took a firm grip on the reins and turned south.

21

"I'm tellin' you, Patrick. It was that tracker the whore you took up with in town told you about, and a marshal. He's probably the same one you saw going into Maggie's shop. And the marshal and that tracker were cozy with each other. Friends. Just like that whore said."

"I heard you the first time you blathered on about it, Connor." The oldest of the O'Hearn brothers didn't look up from where he was squatting next to the small fire. The flame was reflected in his green eyes, and the scarf he'd taken from Dorrie was twined around his neck.

"We're not deaf." Liam, the third brother, was sitting with his back against a log, a bottle of whiskey stuck in the grass by his side. Only a year younger than Patrick, and two years older than Connor, Liam tended to side with whichever of his brothers he favored at that moment. And lately that had been Patrick, since the oldest had been willing to keep him supplied with whiskey.

"It's a wonder you aren't deaf with all the drink you've poured down your throat." Connor's voice was filled with disgust as he turned his back when Liam raised the bottle in a mock salute.

"And I'm still waitin' to hear which way this marshal and his tracker friend were headed." Patrick rose to his feet and stretched his back.

Except for a slight variation in their hair color, the three men bore a striking resemblance to each other, with sharp features and green eyes. And each of them was a version of their father, right down to his narrow shoulders and slighter build.

Connor pursed his lips in annoyance. "North. They went north."

His oldest brother grinned, showing a row of teeth in different shades of brown. "Then is seems this expert tracker has them chasin' their tails."

His youngest brother crossed his arms over his chest. "That isn't meanin' they won't be comin' back this way."

Liam let out a snort. "We'll be gone by then, won't we, Patrick?"

The other two O'Hearn brothers ignored him and continued to stare at each other. Patrick finally shrugged. "If you've somethin' to say, Connor, then get it done."

"You've turned us into killers, Patrick," Connor stated flatly. "And abusers of women. Da and Mam would turn over in their graves if they knew it."

Patrick shook his head. "Not killers, little brother. The man drew a gun on us, and he had it aimed at you. What I did was keep you from gettin' shot."

"You should be grateful," Liam called out.

Connor stuck his chin out and braced his legs apart. "We were robbin' the man, Patrick."

"It wasn't his money we took. It belonged to that bank," Patrick countered. "Is that all that's botherin' you then?"

"That woman at the ranch almost fainted from the scare we gave her, and you shot at a child." Connor's eyes narrowed as he glared at the man standing on the other side of the fire. "A child, Patrick."

"Only to scare him. He rode off without a scratch."

"And what about the woman you left tied up in that warehouse you told us about? How do you know if anyone ever found her? She might be dead, too, and she's Maggie's daughter."

Patrick leaned over and spit into the fire. "She's not blood. Blood wouldn't have kept me from talkin' to me sister or me niece. And she has the look of English about her. So does that husband of Maggie's, and he's put guards around our sister to keep her away from us."

"Maybe because he doesn't know we're her brothers?" Connor's insolent tone had Patrick's fists clenching at his side. "Maybe we should stop this nonsense and simply introduce ourselves? Make our apologies to Maggie for not comin' back for her like we promised." Connor turned his head and looked off into the distance, past the trees surrounding the small river where they'd made their latest camp. "We could take up a piece of land and get back to farmin'. Build a life close enough and we could be part of Maggie's again."

"Farmin'? Like we did before?" Patrick's mouth twisted into a sneer. "So some man with more guns than we have can come along and take it away again? What good did those years of work do us? Here we are, right back where we started from and nothin' to show for the time in between."

"Da lost our farm in a card game."

"There's no justice in winning a hand or two from an old man who had too much drink in him." Patrick's eyes began to glitter with emotion. "And our da never got over havin' our land taken from us. It killed him." He pinned his youngest brother with his stare. "Is that what you want? No justice for our own blood? They take from us. We take from them. That's the fairness of it."

"Then we've had our revenge already, Patrick," Connor said quietly. "We've taken money, food, and if we claim another piece of land, we've come full circle and that should be the end of it. That marshal never needs to know it's us he's been chasin'."

"It won't be the end of it until we have our sister back with us, and her child as well. The last words our da said to us was to go find Maggie so all the O'Hearn blood would be under one roof again. That's what Da wanted."

Connor shook his head. "Da may have wanted that, but what about what Maggie wants? Maybe she loves this husband of hers and wants to stay in her own house. What would you say to her then, Patrick?"

His older brother laughed. "That she's daft. But she isn't going to say that, Connor. You know she only married the man to put a roof over her head and food in her belly after we left. It's the way of women when they have to see to themselves. And now she has her own shop. Her daughter told me that Maggie owns it. Our sister's done well and she owes somethin' to the family."

"I don't know what happened to Maggie after we left, and neither do you. And she doesn't owe us anythin', Patrick. We left her here. Why would she come with us and bring her money with her? And if you try to force her, you might be bringin' more lawmen down on our heads."

Patrick grinned. "All I'm seein' is one lawman, and we can take care of him easily enough."

Liam stirred, drawing one leg up to rest an arm on top of his knee. "Connor's right. Somethin' happens to that marshal, and we'll have a whole posse of them chasin' us down. Shootin' a marshal will bring us bad luck."

"Luck is it?" Patrick crossed his arms and shook his head at Liam. "I say the heavens are smilin' on us because our luck's been good. We have money, and pretty soon we'll be together with Maggie again and have even more of it."

"Luck runs out," Connor said quietly.

"Does it now? I haven't been noticin' that lately." Patrick squatted back down by the fire and held out his hands to warm them. "But we'll leave it to the marshal's luck and what fate has in store for him. If he doesn't come around, then he'll live a long life. Otherwise..." Patrick trailed off and shrugged.

Connor drew in a long slow breath. Sometimes there was no reasoning with his oldest brother. But as Patrick had said, blood was blood, and he couldn't go against his own kin. The youngest O'Hearn nodded and strode off to unsaddle his horse.

22

D orrie absently ran the dishrag over the plate she was holding. Once it was dry, she carefully placed it back onto the shelf, centering it on top of the rest of the dinnerware stored there. With that chore done, she looked around the neat and tidy kitchen to be sure she hadn't left anything unfinished for Dina to do in the morning.

With the children off for a week at Shannon and Luke's ranch, the house was quiet without their constant noise and laughter. Cade had left that morning on business in Sacramento, and Abby had been called out to see a patient. With no one else to cook for, Dina had gone home to her husband at Dorrie's insistence. She'd assured the residence's longtime housekeeper that she was more than capable of putting together a supper just for herself.

But when the sun had disappeared behind the horizon, Dorrie wasn't hungry enough for anything more than a piece of bread and honey, which she had consumed with a decided lack of enthusiasm. The silence in the house only made Jules' absence that much more noticeable, especially when she had little to do in a household already kept well in hand by Dina and Abby. She'd always been busy at her mam's shop, or with chores at home. Having so much leisure time seemed more of a burden than a luxury, especially as the hours dragged by.

With a sigh at her lack of gratitude for the warm welcome she'd received into the McKenzie home, she took her cup of water and crossed the kitchen and took a seat at the table. She reached over and ran a finger along the spine of the leather-bound journal resting on the table. Shannon had brought it with her when she and Luke had come to town to fetch the children. When it had been placed in her hands, Dorrie had been in awe that her aunt would entrust her with something so valuable.

"Since you're the first of the children to marry, I think we should start a new tradition," Shannon had said as she'd handed the journal to Dorrie. "A week with the journal as a wedding present for joining our large family." Then the blond-haired, blue-eyed Shannon had winked at her. "Although you were already part of it, but still. You might find the family history interesting. And now we'll be adding your courtship and marriage to Jules."

Thinking it hadn't been much of a courtship, unless you counted the part where she'd been tied up and left in the dark, Dorrie had still been thrilled with the gift, and enthusiastically agreed it was a grand tradition for them to start. But looking at the journal now, a niggling strand of doubt wove its way into her thoughts. It was Connor's words that started it. She loved her family with all her being, but she wasn't blood. Something he obviously put a great deal of store by. And if he was indeed Mam's brother, did that mean deep inside that her mam felt the same way? In her heart,

Dorrie didn't think so, but still, now there was that small well of doubt.

And what about Jules? He knew where he came from. She couldn't help but wonder how he felt about having a wife who didn't have any idea who her people were. Dorrie had a vague memory of a mother and a father, but it was more of an impression or feeling than once having known them. The fact was, she couldn't recall a face to go with the feeling. And she'd never thought much about it. She was hardly the only child to end up at Lillian's Orphan ranch. Robbie had too.

No, she'd never wasted a moment on such doubts. Until Connor's words, along with Shannon placing the journal in her hands.

Tired of the whole argument going on in her head, Dorrie picked up the journal and wandered out of the kitchen. Thinking she'd start a fire in the parlor and settle in to read a few of Shannon's stories, she paused when she came to the door to Jules' study. It was wide open and she could imagine him sitting behind his desk, reading his correspondence.

She switched directions and walked into the study. Taking a long matchstick sitting in a pot next to a bookshelf, she lit both of the lamps in the room before settling into one of the over-sized leather chairs placed in front of the desk. She opened the journal, not surprised that it started with Lillian being abandoned in San Francisco, long before gold was discovered by Mr. Sutter.

Wiggling into a more comfortable position, Dorrie yawned as she focused on the words. But before she'd barely read a paragraph, her eyelids started to drift down.

～

Jules walked into the kitchen, surprised it was dark except for the slight glow coming from the banked fire in the stove. He went to the sink and pumped water into a basin, using the dishrag hanging on a peg to wash the dust from his face, neck, and hands. Even though it was still early in the evening, the house was completely silent. He wondered where the family was, although at the moment he was only interested in one.

During the ride home he'd hoped that Dorrie hadn't gone back to her parents' rather than stay in a house she wasn't yet used to. But if she had, he was going to go straight to the Dolan home and fetch his wife. Fortunately, once he'd led Hafen into the stable he'd run into Frank Brown, his deputy who was now tasked with keeping an eye on Dorrie. The quiet man with the thick beard and steady eyes had assured him that Dorrie was there.

He stopped in the back hallway and listened, still not hearing any movement in the house. Thinking his bride must have retired to bed early, Jules continued down the hall. He was halfway to the front foyer when he noticed the light coming from his study. When he saw Dorrie, curled up in one of the big chairs, he smiled and shook his head. She was sound asleep.

Moving quietly, he set his hat on the desk and unbuckled his gun belt, laying it carefully next to his hat. Turning, he knelt in front of Dorrie, bracing his arms on the sides of the chair as he studied her. Long lashes brushed against her cheek. A thick strand of her hair, that had taken on a mysterious fire in the lamplight, had come loose from the ribbon in back and trailed down the front of her shoulder. Leaning over, he brushed his lips softly against hers, then watched as her eyes slowly came open to stare into his.

She lifted a hand and touched the side of his face. "It's a wonderful dream."

"I can make it better." Jules dropped his head again and fit his mouth against hers, moving his tongue over her lips until she opened for him. When her arms twined about his neck he shifted so he could hold her close as he continued to kiss her, unwilling to let go of a moment he'd been dreaming about for days.

When he finally lifted his head, she slowly opened her eyes and smiled at him. "You're right. You made it better than my dreams."

He gave her another quick kiss before rolling back on his heels. "I know Cade's escorting that judge back to Sacramento. Where are Abby and the kids?"

"Abby's out with a patient, and the children went to stay with Shannon and Luke. I'm the only one here."

Jules flashed a huge grin. "Is that a fact?"

Dorrie laughed and leaned forward until her mouth was barely an inch away from his. "Yes, it is, Marshal McKenzie."

He reached down and removed the large book from her lap, twisting around to set it on the desk. Then taking her hand in his, he rose to his feet, drawing her up with him. Without a word, he swept her up in his arms, smiling when she gave a sharp gasp and threw her arms around his neck.

"You stay just like that, honey."

"Jules! What are you doing?"

He exited the study and headed for the front stairway. "What every good husband does in the evening. Taking his wife to bed."

Jules wasn't surprised when she went suddenly still in his arms, but almost stopped dead in his tracks when he felt her soft lips slide up the side of his neck.

Her breath wafted across his cheek and ear. "That sounds like a fine idea, Marshal."

His grin back in place, Jules held her closer to his chest and took the stairs two at a time, reaching the second floor within seconds and striding down the narrow hallway toward his bed chamber. Once inside, he slammed the door shut with the back of his boot heel and headed straight for the large bed set in the center of the back wall.

He put her on her feet then froze in place when she started to undo the button of his shirt. He kept still as she gently pushed the sides away and ran her hands up his bare chest and then over his broad shoulders, taking the shirt down his arms until they were free. She dropped the garment to the floor.

They stared at each other, their gazes remaining locked as she reached for the top button of his britches. Jules had to touch her, so he ran his hands gently along her arms as she continued to slowly undress him. When he stood before her with nothing but his bare skin, she wound her arms around his neck and kissed him with a passion that had his mind reeling and his breath catching in the back of his throat.

His hands went to her waist and within seconds he had her skirt dropping to the floor. When she gasped and stepped back, he immediately had her blouse undone. When she wore nothing but her chemise and pantaloons, he picked her up and laid her on the bed, following her down until his whole length was pressed against her. Dorrie stared up at him, her eyes wide as he placed soft kisses along her cheek.

"Don't be scared, honey. We'll take it slow."

He smiled when he felt her nod. Leaving her cheek, Jules trailed his lips the length of her neck and then over the gentle swell of a breast. One hand peeled the chemise to her waist in a single fluid motion as his mouth sought the pebbled peak of her breast. Taking it in gently, he continued his assault on her senses, returning to kiss her until she was moaning softly into his mouth as he slowly removed her pantaloons and let his hand wander up and down her body, touching and caressing until she was writhing next to him, trying to press herself closer. He hoped she was ready for him because he doubted if he could wait another second to make her completely his.

She opened for him as their mouths fused together. It was a mixture of agony and pure ecstasy as he entered her slowly, murmuring words of encouragement as he continued his assault on her mouth. When she pulled him even closer, he thought he might explode but clamped down an iron control, moving in a slow rhythm until he felt her tense beneath him. When her back suddenly bowed up, he let himself go, following her into an overwhelming wave of pleasure.

It took Jules several minutes before he realized he had his full weight on his bride and was most likely crushing her. Reluctantly moving to one side, he wrapped an arm around her and kept her close, smiling when she snuggled in against him.

After several moments of silence, he tipped his chin lower to look at her. "Are you all right?"

Dorrie nodded, her hair sliding over his chest. He closed his eyes to savor the sensation.

"Are you?"

Jules grinned at the innocent question. "I'm better than fine, honey. It isn't often a man has a dream come true."

She stacked her hands on his chest and lifted her head and rested her chin on them. "You dreamed about this? With me?"

He laughed. "Most men dream of 'this', honey. And yes, with you. Who else would I be dreaming about?" He deliberately schooled his features into a serious look. "Haven't you been dreaming about me?"

Jules suppressed a grin as Dorrie blinked up at him.

"Well, yes. But not like this exactly."

"Like what exactly?" Jules grinned. The room was dark so he could barely see her face, but he was certain she was blushing all the way to her toes.

Dorrie tapped a finger against his chest. "Us being together in a bed with no clothes on, Jules McKenzie. And I know when you're teasing me."

"Is that a fact?"

When she made a motion to leave the bed, he tightened his hold on her to keep her in place. "Oh no, honey. I'm too tired to go chasing you around the house. We're just going to stay right here and get some sleep."

"Is that a fact?"

He laughed at Dorrie's dry tone and the clever way she'd turned his words on him, as he settled in more deeply against the pillows.

"Please spend the night with me, Mrs. McKenzie."

"Well since you've asked so nicely, I'd be happy to, Marshal."

23

J ules opened his eyes to rays of sunlight beaming into the room through the large window. Taking a glance outside, he judged that they'd slept later than he was used to, but still had most of the morning to start in on his work. Or to enjoy. When Dorrie made a sleepy sound and moved closer to his warmth, he smiled. Maybe enjoy more than work. After all, he was newly married. That surely entitled him to a day or two off.

He carefully adjusted Dorrie's weight against his shoulder, not wanting to wake her. Like he had only a few hours ago. He knew he should have been more of a gentleman and left his bride alone and let her sleep. But he'd still been half asleep himself when he'd reached for her in the dark. When she'd responded eagerly to his touch, it would have been easier to stop breathing then to keep from making love to her.

He yawned then automatically tightened his hold on his wife when the bedroom door opened. He frowned as Dina walked into his room as if she was used to doing that any time she pleased. The fact was, he couldn't remember her ever having done that since he was out of short pants, and especially if he was supposed to be sleeping.

Of course his cousin would have had no way of knowing he'd come home last night since he'd left his hat and gun in his study rather than the front hallway. So she'd probably thought Dorrie was alone in the bedchamber. His bride stirred beside him as he pulled the covers up higher over her shoulders.

"Good morning."

Dina's cheerful greeting had Dorrie's eyes popping open. She immediately slid further under the heavy quilt until only her eyes showed over its edge. Jules chuckled at her modesty. Especially since it hadn't been on display at all the night before. He sent up a quick prayer of thanks for that piece of good fortune.

"I've prepared a bath for you in the next chamber" Dina wrinkled her nose at Jules. "And you make sure your bride uses it first. It's nice and hot, so don't dawdle too long." She crossed the room and laid a robe on the end of the bed before walking over to open the connecting door to the smaller chamber with the tub. With those tasks complete, she quietly left the couple to themselves.

Jules could see the steam rising from the large copper tub next door. Sighing as his idea of spending the rest of the morning in bed with Dorrie faded away, he tilted his chin down and smiled at his bride when she looked up at him. "She might be small, but no one in this house disobeys Dina, and that includes Cade. So we'd better get to that bath and then downstairs to enjoy the breakfast she'll have waiting for us."

"All right." Dorrie looked around at the bright sunshine pouring into the room. "I guess we forgot to draw the curtains last night."

He grinned at the sudden shyness in her voice. He would never have believed that Dorrie had a shy bone in her body. "We were in too much of a hurry to get our hands on each other." He'd made the bald statement just to tease her a bit, and then chuckled when she let out a loud gasp and moved away from him.

Stacking his hands behind his head he looked up at the ceiling. "Well, you heard what Dina said. You're supposed to use the bath first, so go right ahead, honey."

Dorrie wiggled over to the far edge of the bed then shot him a suspicious look. "You are going to close your eyes, aren't you?

"Why? I've seen you without clothes." Jules was enjoying himself. Teasing her had been fun when they'd been growing up, but teasing his wife was a pure pleasure.

"It was dark last night, Jules."

"Not that dark, honey." When it looked as if her whole face was on fire, Jules relented and squeezed his eyes shut. "Fine. They're closed."

He waited until he felt her weight leave the bed before he opened his eyes just a crack and enjoyed the sight of his naked wife scrambling to get her arms through the sleeves of the long robe Dina had left for her. When she suddenly turned her head and shot him a suspicious look, he quickly shut his eyes again.

"You aren't fooling anyone, Jules McKenzie. And that wasn't a very gentlemanly thing to do, taking peeks like that."

Jules opened his eyes and grinned at her. "Outside that bedroom door, I promise to be the perfect gentleman." His grin grew wider. "But inside our bed chamber, I'm going to be all husband. And your husband enjoys looking at you the way nature intended."

Dorrie moved to the end of the bed and glared back at him, with her hands on her hips and one foot tapping on the floor. "I think some things are best left to the imagination."

"Not when it comes to you, honey. You're perfect."

He wasn't disappointed when she smiled at his compliment. "You're impossible, Jules."

"And you're beautiful, Dorrie." He tilted his head in the direction of the waiting tub. "You'd better make use of that before I decide I have a better idea." He wiggled his eyebrows up and down, then laughed when she fled the room, closing the adjoining door behind her.

IT WAS over an hour later before they made their appearance in the kitchen. Dina wanted to serve them a proper wedding breakfast in the dining room, but gave in to Dorrie's insistence she'd much rather stay in the cozy kitchen, and didn't issue a word of protest when the younger woman helped her dish out the food and put it on the table. Jules smiled proudly when Dorrie refused to have one bite until Dina sat with them, declaring that family should be at the table together.

Once they were all comfortable and enjoying their eggs and thick slices of ham, Dorrie glanced over at the closed kitchen door.

"Shouldn't we wait for Abby?"

Dina shook her head. "Oh, she left several hours ago, dear. She was expecting a few early patients today, then intends to spend the afternoon and evening with your mam and Lillian, planning your wedding party for the family."

She picked up her coffee cup and smiled over the rim. "It seems you'll have the house to yourselves tonight."

"Is that a fact?" Jules grinned at the stain of red splashing across his bride's cheeks.

She shot him a warning glance. "I haven't asked yet how you and Ethan fared searching for the Green Gang?"

Accepting her change of subject with a wink, Jules bit down on a piece of ham and chewed silently for a long moment. "Not so well. We went back to the last place Ethan had tracked them to, but they'd taken to the road. We came south looking for any more signs but didn't see any."

"Then you think they went north?" Dorrie frowned.

"I don't know." Jules dabbed at his mouth with a check-ered napkin. "Could be they headed back to Oregon. They came as far south as Ben Hanson's ranch and were only looking for supplies. We're going to head out there in a day or so and see if we can pick up their tracks, although the ones Ethan found further north were fresh."

"How can you be sure which tracks are theirs?" Dina's eyes wrinkled at the corners.

"One of the horses has two crooked shoes and there're always three sets running together."

"Oh. There's three members in the gang?" Dorrie set her elbows on the table and rested her chin in her hands. "I know you said they killed that poor Wells Fargo guard, but they didn't hurt anyone on Mr. Hanson's ranch, did they?"

Jules' eyebrow shot up in surprise. "Do you know Ben Hanson?"

Dorrie shook her head. "Not really. But I met his wife at Katherine's Tea Shop once, along with her oldest daughter. She's a very sweet little girl."

"They had a good scare, but they weren't hurt. When Mrs.

Hanson saw the men ride up, she sent the children out the back window to hide in the fields. The oldest boy decided to go for help and had shots taken at him as he rode out of the barn."

The two women gasped, and Dina's hand flew to her mouth. "Lord have mercy!"

The marshal gave her a reassuring smile. "Lucky for the boy, no one in the gang is a very good shot. All he got were a couple of scratches from the chips flying off the rock they did manage to hit."

Dorrie let out the breath she was holding. "But they shot at a child! How could they do that?"

"I don't know," Jules said quietly. "Hanson's wife didn't get a good look at their faces since they kept them pretty well covered. But she said they all had green eyes and weren't very big men. She also said there was something funny about the way they talked. As if they had some kind of accent. And their boy heard the name Patrick."

His wife sat up straighter in her chair, her eyes bright with interest. "What kind of accent?"

Jules shrugged. "She didn't know. All she was sure of was there was something different in the way they talked."

"They're from the north, can't shoot well, and they talk funny." Dorrie tapped one finger against her lower lip. "Maybe they used to be trappers?"

"Trappers?" Jules' brow furrowed as he considered it. "Trappers are usually pretty fair shots."

"With long rifles," Dorrie agreed. "But maybe not with handguns?"

She had a good point there. Jules said he'd put it to Ethan to see what he thought of the idea, which had Dorrie beaming and Dina reaching over to pat his hand.

"That's a good idea your wife has, and you're a good husband to give it some thought." The older woman stood up and gathered up her plate, smiling when Dorrie also stood. "Now I won't hear any of your nonsense about helping with the dishes, dear. The two of you are newly married. Go out and enjoy the day together. You're both entitled to that."

Since that fit right in with his own plans, Jules rose and put an arm around his wife's shoulders, pulling her into his side. "I need to see to that correspondence Cade left piled on the desk and pay Sheriff Adams a visit to give him a report on our progress, but both of those can wait until the afternoon." He smiled at Dorrie. "I thought we might spend a few hours looking at houses."

"I'd like that very much, Jules."

The soft smile on Dorrie's face was enough to have Jules bending his head and stealing a kiss.

Dina gave an exaggerated sigh. "I see you two are going to be as bad as your brother at keeping your hands to yourself." She waved a wooden spoon at the pair. "While the marshal was running about with Ethan and neglecting his lovely bride, I took the liberty of asking Cook to find several houses that might be suitable for you." Dina smiled when she mentioned her husband. "I left the list on the table in the foyer. And just so we have a clear understanding, I'll be stopping by your new home every day to help until we can find you a suitable housekeeper."

Dorrie gave a small jerk against his side.

"But Dina. I don't need any help to keep a house. We don't need to spend any money on that."

"I'm sure you're very capable of running a household, dear. But you'll need a hand at home when your start your own venture, and certainly after the children come." Dina smiled when Dorrie's eyes popped open.

"My own venture?"

"Of course, of course." Dina gave one quick bob of her head. "All the women in the family have a venture dear, and I'm sure you'll be no exception. Lillian helps run The Crimson Rose. The gambling hall is so large and busy that Charles can't do it by himself. Abby is a doctor and your mam has her dress shop. Shannon writes stories for the penny press back East, and even Ammie has started her own inquiries business, though I still think that's not entirely proper for a young woman, but she's always had a mind of her own."

Dorrie laughed as she held up a hand. "I hadn't considered it, but you're absolutely right. And there is something I've had on my mind for a while." She gave Dina a wink. "But I'll need to talk to Cook about it first and hear what he thinks."

Jules wasn't sure what Dorrie had in mind, but if it involved working with Cook in The Crimson Rose, he wasn't entirely sure he liked the idea. His hand moved over her slim waist. Kids sounded like a great idea, and the sooner the better. But first he needed to find them their own house, and their own bed. That he purchased for them. He appreciated the comforts of Cade and Abby's home, but a man should be able to take his wife to a house and bed he provided for her himself.

He nodded at his cousin. "We'd better get started on that search."

～

It was late afternoon when Jules pulled a laughing Dorrie into Katherine's Tea Shop. He'd enjoyed the day because he'd spent it with Dorrie. It had warmed his heart to watch her walk through the houses, opening cupboards and carefully examining floors. He'd had one he was partial to, but hadn't heard her preference yet. But that could wait until they got home. Right now he wanted to sit in a public room and show off his wife. He'd always thought she was pretty, with her richly colored hair, deep-brown eyes, and slim figure. But the more time he'd spent with her, the more he'd become convinced she was the most beautiful woman in the city. And he was a lucky man to be able to claim her as his wife. He'd also be lying if he said it didn't give him a burst of warmth every time she smiled just for him, or called him "husband". He liked the sound of it.

He didn't care how much ribbing he'd take from Ethan and Robbie over it. The fact was, he liked being married. It fit him like a glove. As long as it was to Dorrie. While he helped her into a chair at one of the small round tables in Katherine's shop, he started to mentally plot how he intended to get her to admit she liked being married to him too. All of his ideas required the privacy of their bed chamber.

Smiling to himself, he nodded politely as Katherine bustled over to their table.

"I've heard the most wonderful rumor about you both." She made a pointed glance at Dorrie's left hand. "And I see that it's true. You're married?"

"We are," Dorrie beamed back at the woman, holding her left hand out so Katherine had a chance to admire her ring.

"It's lovely," the hostess declared in a voice loud enough to carry across the shop.

Feminine heads gathered together as furtive looks were sent toward their table and low whispers rose up around them.

Showing no reaction to the gossip mill she'd started,

Katherine smiled at the young couple. "What can I get for you, and it will be my treat."

Knowing better than to argue with a woman who looked as satisfied as their hostess did, Jules murmured his thanks and took Dorrie's hand in his. "What do you want, honey?"

Dorrie squeezed his hand before looking up at Katherine. "Just tea, please. We've spent the day looking at houses and I'm parched."

"You've been looking at houses? Isn't that wonderful!"

Katherine hadn't lowered her voice one bit, which had Jules rolling his eyes and the whispers across the shop start up again.

"I'll have the same," Jules said. Katherine smiled and nodded before hurrying off.

His wife leaned forward and kept her voice low so it didn't carry past the two of them. "Let's drink it quickly and go home before we have a parade of gossips stopping by our table."

"I couldn't agree with you more, honey." Jules had already had enough of showing off his wife and now wanted her to himself.

They were rising from the table fifteen minutes after Katherine had delivered their tea. Jules wanted to leave when Katherine was busy in the kitchen, so they wouldn't have to listen to her protests. But Dorrie insisted on thanking the proprietress for her generosity, which had them delaying another five minutes. He breathed a sigh of relief once they were again in their buggy and on their way.

It only took them ten minutes to reach home. Since Frank, Dorrie's guard, offered to unhitch the wagon, the newlyweds walked into the house hand in hand. There was a note propped on the kitchen table from Abby, letting them know she intended to spend the night at Lillian's house, and that Dina had left for her own little cottage. Jules read the note out loud, set it back onto the table, and swept Dorrie into his arms. He gave her a long, thorough kiss, lifting her against his chest until her toes barely touched the ground. When he finally lifted his head, he smiled into her upturned face.

"That will have to hold you for a while, Mrs. McKenzie. I need to take a look through the correspondence before I take you to bed."

Dorrie pushed away from him. "Jules! It's not even dark yet, much less time for sleeping."

"Wasn't intending on sleeping."

"Jules!"

"What?" He leaned over and gave her another quick kiss then grinned at her. "I really do need to go through the correspondence."

"Don't you have to pay a call on Sheriff Adams too?"

He shook his head. "I'll do that in the morning. Ethan won't be by until ten or so."

"Then I'll fetch my book and take it into the parlor to read." Dorrie smiled at Jules.

They walked together toward Jules' study. When he saw the tall stack of mail in the center of the desk, he ran a hand through his hair and sighed. "Cade doesn't much care for paperwork."

His wife eyed the stack right along with him. "I can see that." She walked over and picked up the journal from the edge of the desk. "It's a good thing my book has a lot of stories to read," she teased, giggling and dancing away when he made a grab for her.

She jumped just out of his reach, clutching the journal to her chest. "I'll go along now to the parlor and leave you to it, Marshal."

"Uh huh." Jules watched her until she disappeared into the hallway, then sighed as he took a seat at the desk and picked up the letter on top of the stack.

DORRIE HUMMED SOFTLY to herself as she sat on the divan in front of the fireplace and curled her legs up onto the cushion. Settling her back against the high arm of the divan, she opened the journal, skipping over the first story which was from Lillian, and starting on the page that was titled "Maggie O'Hearn Dolan"

"There was a great famine in Ireland, so we had no choice but to leave our homeland and find a new life in America," Dorrie read out loud, smiling. She continued on silently. Barely five minutes into her mam's story her eyes grew wide, and all the color drained from her face. She reread the words twice, hoping she'd misunderstood. But on the third time around she had no choice but to accept what the words were screaming at her.

Dorrie slowly closed the journal and rested it on her lap, laying one hand on top of the leather cover.

"Oh, Mam. What are we going to do?"

24

The next morning, Jules stood in the foyer and frowned at his wife. Dorrie was being uncharacteristically quiet, with her head bowed as she stared at the floor.

Something was wrong.

The thought had taken root after they'd made love the night before. She'd touched him with a desperation he'd sensed more than felt. And sometime during the night, she'd rolled away from him, clinging to the far edge of the bed. This morning she'd barely said a word. Now she was standing there, her head down and her eyes averted. And even though she was only a foot or two away, Jules felt it was miles. There was an unseen barrier between them, one he'd never felt from her before.

He didn't like it.

Jules uneasily shifted his weight from one foot to the other as he strapped on his gun belt then picked up his hat, settling it firmly on his head as he continued to watch his wife. When she still said nothing, he put a finger under her chin and lifted her face to his.

"What's wrong, honey?"

Her gaze shifted to his as her lips barely turned up at the corners. "Nothing is wrong, Jules." Her smile grew a pinch wider. "I'm going to miss you today."

Not even for one second did he think that was all of it, but he'd have to wait until later to get to the bottom of whatever was bothering Dorrie.

"It's only a courtesy call, so I won't be gone long." He locked his eyes with hers. "We'll talk when I get back."

She drew in a quick breath. "All right." She looked over her shoulder. "I need to go help Dina in the kitchen."

He brushed his lips across her mouth. "I'll see you later."

Dorrie nodded and backed away before turning and heading down the hall. Jules watched until she'd passed beyond the door to the kitchen. He shook his head as he walked onto the porch where Frank had Hafen waiting for him. Jules took the reins and stepped up into the saddle, leaning back slightly as he stared at the deputy.

"Make sure you keep a close eye on my wife today."

The tall bearded man looked over at the house and then back at the marshal. "Is there something I need to know?"

Jules shrugged. "I'm not sure, but something's bothering her, and she isn't sharing."

Frank smiled. "New wives can be a bit skittish. It takes time for them to settle down. At least mine did."

The marshal nodded his agreement and set Hafen into motion. He appreciated Frank's words, but he'd known Dorrie most of her life. And right now she wasn't acting skittish. If he had to put a word to it, she almost seemed scared.

DORRIE WIPED off the table and counters as Dina started

peeling carrots for the evening meal. She half-listened to a story Dina was telling about her husband overseeing the kitchen at the Crimson Rose, and slowly counted off the seconds. When a good ten minutes had gone by, she neatly folded her dishrag and set it by the sink.

"I need to go to see Mam this morning." She turned around and gave Dina a bright smile. "She wants to do some measurements for a fancy dress for the party."

Dina stopped her steady scraping of a paring knife across the skin of a carrot to look over at Dorrie. "Oh? I thought Abby said at breakfast that Maggie already had the dress well in hand."

"She needs to do a little more measuring," Dorrie repeated since she had no other excuse to give. She walked over to a peg by the kitchen door and retrieved the shawl she'd hung there yesterday. "I want to catch her before she goes into the shop for the day."

"Does Jules know you're going out? I thought he was going to spend the day with you when he got back from his call on the sheriff?"

"I'm taking Frank with me." Dorrie hoped that round-about answer would satisfy the older woman. "And Ethan will be by at ten to talk their plans over with Jules. I should be back by then." She injected a cheery note into her voice. "I'm looking forward to seeing Ethan."

"Of course, of course. We haven't seen him very often in the last few years, have we?" Dina picked up her paring knife and continued to scrape the carrots. "Don't be long, dear."

Relieved at not having to answer any more questions, Dorrie scurried out the door in search of Frank. She found him sitting on a hay bale in the stable, cleaning his gun. He quickly agreed to hitch up the buggy and take her to her mam's, but not until she'd declared that she needed to be measured for her wedding dress. He seemed satisfied with that explanation and set to work. Dorrie wandered outside and impatiently waited for the carriage to be ready. She really wished she could have gone to her mam's by herself, but that would only have had Frank ordering her back into the house and probably sending word to Jules. Not wanting that kind of attention at the moment, she settled for him accompanying her, sure she could convince him to wait for her in the carriage.

Since she deliberately chattered all about the fitting during the entire ride to her parents' home, her friendly guard was more than happy to agree to stay outside with the horse and carriage, rather than sit through what Dorrie was sure he perceived as the ordeal of a dress fitting. So she was alone when she walked into her family home and called out a greeting.

Maggie walked out from the kitchen, drying her hands on a dishrag. She smiled warmly at her oldest daughter.

"Well then. I wasn't expectin' to see you today, but glad I am that you're here."

She walked over and gave Dorrie a kiss on the cheek then stepped back and studied her daughter's face. "I'd expected you to have a happier look about you. Isn't that husband of yours home yet?"

"He is, Mam." Dorrie unwound the shawl from her shoulders and draped it over the back of a nearby chair. "And he makes me very happy. But there's something I need to talk to you about."

"That's fine then. Let's go into the kitchen and have a cuppa and a cozy chat just like we always do." Maggie reached out and took her daughter's hand, pulling Dorrie into the large kitchen at the back of the house. "Your da's gone to make some furniture, and your sister is with him this mornin'. He's going to teach her how to do the ledgers."

While Dorrie fetched the tin of tea and two cups, Maggie lifted up the steaming pot of water she always kept on the stove and brought it over to the large table in the center of the kitchen. The two women worked side by side, preparing their cups of tea, neither speaking until they were both seated with a warm cup of the fragrant brew sitting in front of them.

"Now then, daughter. What is it that's brought you here so early in the mornin'?"

Dorrie smiled. "Not so early, Mam. I know you've been up for hours."

Her mam chuckled. "I always get out of me bed at dawn with your da. It's a good habit for a wife."

Nodding her agreement, Dorrie looked cautiously around. "You're sure no one else is here?"

"Who else would be here? And what's gotten into you, I'm wantin' to know?"

Not sure where to start, Dorrie leaned back in her chair and sighed. "I've been reading Shannon's journal. The one she writes all the family stories in."

Maggie's eyes grew wide. "Have you now? I didn't think Shannon ever let it out of her sight."

"Shannon's going to let the new brides in the family read as a wedding gift."

Her mam took a sip of tea, her green eyes bright with amusement. "It's a lovely gift." She wagged a finger at Dorrie. "But don't be thinkin' you can question me about any of it. What's done is done, and that's all there is to it."

"Yes, Mam. What's done is done."

Maggie frowned at her daughter. "What's gotten into you then? You're actin' very strangely."

Deciding she might as well get it over with, Dorrie took a quick sip of her tea then set the cup onto its saucer with a loud click. "Jules was telling me about the Green Gang. Do you know that's the name he's given to the men he and Ethan are hunting for?"

Her mam nodded. "Your da mentioned it. He said they beat an army payroll master and killed a bank guard on a train."

Dorrie slowly nodded. "That's right. They also paid a visit to the Hanson ranch not too long ago."

"They did?" Maggie gasped. "Is everyone all right?"

"They're fine, Mam. Mrs. Hanson had her children hide in a field while she dealt with the men by herself. But not before they took a shot at her oldest son when he went for help."

"But he's not hurt?"

"No. He's fine."

Maggie snorted, and her mouth pulled into a frown. "May the fates do the same to them for committin' such a cowardly act, shootin' at a child like that."

"The fates." Dorrie had heard her mother say that from time to time when she'd been growing up. But it wasn't until now that she heard it again echoing in her head. Only this time in a much deeper voice. "Connor said that to me when he tied me up."

Her mam reached over and gave her arm a gentle pat. "Did he, now? It's still hard for me to believe that Connor would do such a thing." Her gaze turned sad. "I would never have thought it."

"Mam, Mrs. Hanson didn't get a real good look at the men, but she did notice all three of them had green eyes."

"There're three of them?" Maggie's hand holding her tea cup froze in midair as Dorrie nodded back at her.

"Yes, three. And they're all on the smaller side, like their da."

"Now how would you be knowin' if those men took after their da?"

Dorrie ignored her parent's question and doggedly continued on. "And Mrs. Hanson said they talked funny. With some kind of accent she didn't recognize."

Maggie didn't say a word, but visibly tensed as she looked at her daughter.

"Their son heard one of them call out a name. It was Patrick."

"Pat..." All the color drained from Maggie's face as she dropped her tea cup onto the table. It rolled over, spilling the tea across the hard wooden surface and sending it over the side to drip onto the floor. Both women ignored it as they stared at each other.

"Green eyes, smaller builds, an accent, and there're three of them, Mam," Dorrie said softly. "Do you think the other two are named Connor and Liam?"

"Patrick." Maggie blinked several times before a glimmer of anger crept into her gaze. "It wasn't Connor. It was Patrick. If I had thought for a moment it was him..."

Dorrie frowned in confusion. "Who was Patrick, Mam?"

"The man who tied you up and tried to lure Anna away. I'm sure of it. It would be just like Patrick to go on about you not being blood, as if your da or I would care about that. And I kept tellin' your da that Connor would never say such a thing, or leave you tied up and helpless in the dark. But Patrick would. He always did have a mean streak about him."

When her mam seemed to retreat into a past that Dorrie knew nothing about, she took one of Maggie's cold limp hands into hers and started to rub some heat into it.

"Listen to me, Mam. Those men Jules and Ethan are chasing, they're your brothers, aren't they? I read the story you told Shannon, about how they left you and never came back. Do you think that's why they're here? They've come to get you?"

Maggie turned her head and looked at Dorrie. She blinked several times as if she were trying to bring her daughter into focus. "If Mrs. Hanson's description of them is true, then they're me brothers." She sighed and looked at her hands that were clasped together on the table in front of her. "So much time has passed, and I've not had a word since they left the gold fields all those years ago."

"I didn't know you had three brothers, Mam. I've only heard you mention Connor. And Da has never talked about them."

Tears were in Maggie's eyes when she looked over at her daughter. "Connor was me favorite, and the only one of me brothers who wrote after they left. I could have never been born for all Patrick and Liam cared, so that's how I came to think of them too. Put them both right out of me mind, I did. And when Connor stopped writing, I was sure he was dead, along with me own da." She managed a tiny smile. "And even though your da has never met any of them, he's never forgiven them for leaving me to the fates in that terrible household."

Dorrie tried to smile back at her mam, but the worry still weighed heavily on her. Mam's brothers were the Green Gang, and they'd killed that bank guard and were now wanted men. Wanted by her husband. The US Marshal.

"What are we going to do?" Dorrie said softly to herself. But not so softly her mam didn't hear her.

"Do?" Maggie pushed herself to her feet and braced her arms on top of the table. "First, we're going to get into that carriage you brought and go to your da's warehouse. I need to tell me husband about this. I've been keeping things from him long enough, and Patrick can be a dangerous man when he's crossed. I'll not have him comin' near you again, or talkin' to Anna." She frowned at her daughter. "What did Jules have to say about all this?"

"I haven't told him."

Maggie straightened to her full height and put her hands on her hips. "You haven't told your husband? What are you thinkin', Dorrie? You should have gone to him with this when you first laid eyes on the words in Shannon's journal, daughter."

"You're my mam. I couldn't have my husband questioning you about men who kill, and maybe accusing you of hiding them."

The Irish woman's mouth dropped open. "Dorrie. Jules is family, even before you took him as a husband. He wouldn't have done that. He'd have asked me about me brothers, and well he should. But I would have told him the truth and that would have been the end of it."

Dorrie raised a skeptical eyebrow. "You didn't tell Da that you thought the man following us was your brother."

Her mam gave a short laugh. "I didn't have to. He suspected it as soon as I did, since he heard the description of the man too. We just didn't speak it out loud until he wouldn't let me leave our bedroom until I did." She sighed. "But I should have talked to him about it, and he's told me as much. I've promised to never keep secrets from him again."

Since it had been eating at her conscience from the second she'd read the journal yesterday, Dorrie knew in her heart that her mam was right. She shouldn't have kept it from Jules. "All I could think to do was to tell you about your brothers. I was afraid for you, Mam." Dorrie's eyes misted over with tears. "I wasn't thinking straight."

Maggie sighed. "You need to trust your husband above all others, daughter." She smiled. "Even over your mam."

Maggie rose and briskly shook out her skirts. "Well then. What's done is done. You've told me. Now you'll be takin' me to your da's workplace and then goin' straight home to talk to your husband." She waved Dorrie toward the front of the house. "Go get your shawl. We need to be on our way."

25

"Where is she?" Jules couldn't keep the sharp note out of his voice and knew he'd have to apologize to Dina for it, but damn it, he wanted to talk to his wife. He'd thought of little else even during his visit to the city's sheriff, and had raced home only to discover that she wasn't there.

"Mind your tone, Jules McKenzie," Dina said without any real heat behind the words. "Dorrie went to pay a visit to her mam, that's all. She said she'd promised to stop by so Maggie could take some measurements for her wedding gown."

"What for? We're already married."

Dina rolled her eyes at the imposing, and clearly annoyed man she'd helped raise. "Fine. The dress she intends to wear to the family party to celebrate your wedding." Dina's brow wrinkled. "Although I don't know why she'd need to see Maggie about measurements."

Feeling completely at sea, Jules ran an agitated hand through his dark hair. "I thought every woman got measured for their clothes."

"Dorrie's full grown, Jules. Maggie should know her own daughter's measurements without having to take them again every time she makes a gown for her."

That gave him one more thing to chew on. Dorrie knew he'd wanted to talk to her, he'd told her so before he'd left. But she hadn't said a word about going to visit her mam. And now Dina had him thinking the reason for the visit was more of an excuse to leave than anything else.

Completely at a loss as to what his wife was up to, Jules decided he'd corral her the minute she walked into the house, and wasn't going to let her out of his sight until she told him what had changed so suddenly between them. He didn't like it, and he meant to fix it. But he couldn't do that until she came home.

"I'll be in my study." Jules gave Dina a lopsided grin. "I'm sorry I growled at you. If you'd let me know when Dorrie gets home, I'd appreciate it."

Dina smiled. "Of course, of course."

Since he couldn't do much more than that, Jules nodded his thanks and turned toward his study. Finishing looking through the correspondence and getting out the maps he would need to go over with Ethan should help take his mind off his wife. And right now, he needed to think about something else besides Dorrie.

He'd managed to pass an hour and was studying a notice from the US Marshals' station in Chicago, when Ethan appeared in the doorway, a steaming mug of coffee in his hand. He raised it in Jules' direction.

"Came in through the kitchen hoping Dina would have coffee on the stove."

"She usually does," Jules acknowledged. "Did you get some rest?"

Ethan shrugged. "Enough." He walked into the room

and set his mug on the edge of the desk as he eyed the letters scattered in front of Jules. "You ready to talk over our plans?"

Jules nodded and moved the correspondence to one side before picking up the map he'd found earlier and slapping it down on the hard surface of the desk.

Ethan looked at the map and then back up at his friend. "Something bothering you?"

"Not finding any trace of the Green Gang, and my wife."

The dark-haired tracker grinned. "I'm guessing that isn't the correct order of it." He stroked his chin. "You've only been with your wife a couple of days. Are you saying that you're already having a fight?"

"We aren't fighting," Jules grumbled. "I wanted to talk to her this morning, and she isn't here."

His friend's grin grew even wider. "You mean after only two days you've misplaced her?"

Jules glared at the man who looked as if he was going to burst out laughing at any moment. "I haven't misplaced her. She went to see her mam."

"You're mad at your wife because she went to visit her parent?" Ethan shook his head. "You might be holding the reins too tight, Jules."

The marshal let out an exasperated snort. "That isn't it. She's been acting strange. Yesterday, everything was fine. Hell, it was better than fine. Then today she's treating me as if we barely know each other. And when I tell her I want to talk to her, she runs off to see her mam without saying a word to me about it."

"She's a new bride, Jules. Even if you have known each other for years, it's going to take her time to settle in."

"That's what Frank said."

"Who's Frank?"

Jules unrolled the map and anchored the corners to the desk with some small stones he'd set to the side. "The deputy I have keeping a watch over her when I'm not around."

"Is Frank married?"

"Yes."

Ethan nodded. "Then he's giving you sound advice."

Maybe I am making too much of this, Jules thought as he smoothed out the map's surface. Forcing the whole puzzle of Dorrie aside, he pointed to a section of the map north of the city. "Here's where you last found the tracks, and we searched the road from there back to the city and didn't find anything."

Leaning over, Ethan studied the route Jules had traced with his finger. "So you want us to start at the same point and head north?"

"It's a thought. We could also go out to the Hanson ranch and see if we can pick up a trail from there. Mrs. Hanson saw which way they headed."

The two men discussed their choices for a good thirty minutes before Jules caught a movement in the doorway from the corner of his eye. Turning his head, he straightened up when he saw Dorrie standing there, her eyes wide and her hands clasped together in front of her.

Ethan looked up and then followed the direction of Jules' gaze. When Dorrie broke her staring match with her husband to look at him, the tracker smiled.

"Hello, Dorrie. I haven't had a chance to congratulate you yet."

"Thank you, Ethan."

The quiet response had him glancing over at Jules, whose eyes were still locked on his wife.

Clearing his throat, Ethan picked up his empty mug. "I'll

see if I can scare up another cup of coffee." He paused next to Dorrie and gave her a gentle pat on the shoulder before heading down the hallway toward the kitchen.

"I need to talk to you, Jules, if you have a minute."

Not sure what was going on in her mind, Jules gestured for her to come in and waited silently until she'd taken Ethan's place across the desk. When several moments passed, and she still remained silent, he let out the breath he'd been holding. Whatever it was, he'd rather know it than not.

"What do you need to say, honey? Whatever's been bothering you, it can't be all that bad." At least he hoped it wasn't.

"It might be."

Jules' heart sank a little and his stomach did a flip. He could tell by her face that she was unhappy about something. And whatever it was, she clearly thought he wouldn't want to hear it.

"Just spit it out, honey, and I'll find a way to fix it."

"Not this time, Jules." Dorrie gave a sigh and finally lowered herself into the leather chair. "You're a US Marshal, and you can't be anything else. And they are who they are. This can't be fixed."

"They?" Jules' eyes narrowed. "Who are you talking about?"

Dorrie flinched but raised her gaze to meet his. "I went to see Mam."

"Dina told me. To get measured for a gown."

His wife was shaking her head before he'd even gotten all the words out.

"No. I went to see her because of the journal."

Jules' eyebrows snapped together. "Journal? What journal?"

"Shannon's. The one she keeps the family history in. Including the story about how Mam came to San Francisco."

When his wife briefly closed her eyes, he slowly sat in the chair behind the desk. "I'm listening."

Dorrie opened her eyes but kept her gaze on her hands folded in her lap. "I didn't read very far. Only to the part where her family abandoned her." She finally looked up at him again. "When her da and brothers left her on her own."

He sat up straighter in his chair. "Brothers? So she did have more than one?"

"She did." Dorrie nodded. "And she described them to Shannon. They took after their da, so they weren't big men. They all had green eyes and what Mam said was the sound of Ireland in their voices."

An icy finger of dread settled into the pit of Jules' stomach.

"She said their names were Connor and Liam." Dorrie stopped and drew in a ragged breath. "And Patrick."

Jules shot to his feet and leaned his arms against the desk. "Three of them? With green eyes, an Irish accent, and one of them was named Patrick?"

He ignored the visible tremble in his wife's shoulders as he stared at her in disbelief. She'd just given the perfect description of the Green Gang.

The cold continued to spread, making Jules' features go hard and his voice harsh. "Did your mam say the story in Shannon's journal was true?" His heart closed a little more when his wife slowly nodded.

"She did," Dorrie said softly. She looked up at Jules with pleading eyes. "Connor was her favorite. When she thought it was a brother following her, she only thought of him. She didn't know about Patrick until I asked her about him and told her what Mrs. Hanson had said. Mam said to tell you that Patrick had a mean streak even back then, and it was most likely him who killed that guard and tied me up." She looked back down at her hands. "She's telling Da about it now."

"Just like you're telling me now." Jules' spine went rigid. "It was Maggie who told you to talk to me, wasn't it?"

"Yes," Dorrie admitted in a small voice. "But I would have, anyway."

Jules thought it over for a moment. "How did you get hold of Shannon's journal?"

Dorrie braced herself as if she was expecting a blow. "She left it for me to read while you were gone with Ethan."

"And that's what you were reading yesterday in the parlor, while I was going through the correspondence?"

"Yes."

"So you knew about the three brothers yesterday and didn't tell me."

"I wanted to, and was going to." Her eyes were soft and pleading. "Really I was."

"But not before you went to your mam first." Jules didn't like what that meant, but he wanted to know. He had to know. "Did you think I would haul your mam over here and question her? Accuse her of hiding those men?"

"I don't know what I thought, Jules. I just wanted to talk to Mam."

"You didn't trust me," Jules said flatly, holding up one hand when Dorrie made a sound of protest. "You didn't trust me to treat your mam kindly and with respect."

He didn't wait for her response but strode over to the door and yelled down the hallway. "Ethan. Get in here."

Jules had barely stepped back behind his desk when

Ethan appeared in the doorway. He looked at Dorrie's bent head and frowned. "Why are you yelling?"

"Dorrie has something she needs to tell you." Jules sent a pointed look to his wife. "Tell Ethan what you told me about Maggie's brothers."

"Brothers?" Ethan switched his gaze to the woman sitting quietly across from Jules.

"She has three of them," Jules cut in before Dorrie could say a word. "Connor, Liam, and Patrick. All on the shorter side, all with green eyes and an Irish accent that's likely the same as Maggie's." He narrowed his eyes on Dorrie. "Did I leave anything out?"

"Only that Mam said Patrick had a mean streak."

"What about her father?" Jules suddenly asked. "Didn't he abandon his daughter in San Francisco as well?"

"Mam didn't mention him except to say she thought he was dead, and I didn't ask her anything more about him."

"Well, I guess I'll just have to go over there and demand an answer."

Ethan shot a surprised look at Jules, who ignored his friend as he continued to stare at his wife.

Dorrie's back stiffened and her chin came up. "I know how you feel about me, Jules, and I don't blame you. And I can't tell you how sorry I am. But now you're just being insulting, and I won't sit here and listen to it." She turned away from her husband and walked out the door without a backward glance.

For a full minute the only sound in the study was Jules' hard breathing and the clock ticking away on a shelf.

"You were hard on her," Ethan finally said.

"She was hard on me," Jules shot back. "She didn't trust me enough to come to me first with what she read in your sister's journal."

The tracker whistled softly as he perched on the edge of the desk. "That's how she found out? From Shannon's family journal? When did she read it?"

Jules scowled. "Shannon dropped it off when she came to pick up Emily and Sam."

Now Ethan frowned. "So Dorrie's known about the three brothers all this time and hasn't said a word? That doesn't sound like her."

"She didn't get around to reading the journal until late yesterday," Jules admitted. "But she still had plenty of time to tell me before she went off to warn her mam of what she *thought* I might do."

Ethan raised an eyebrow at that, but changed the direction of the conversation. "What do you think this means?"

Jules sighed and sat down, leaning back in the chair as he considered the possibilities. "I think they've come to get Maggie, and they aren't going to leave without her."

"Agreed," Ethan nodded. "Which means they'd be close enough to come into town." He glanced at the map. "So somewhere in this area." He drew a circle just to the north of the city.

"Which includes Luke and your sister's ranch, the Hanson ranch, and Robbie's, as well as several others in that same area." Jules studied the map. "Mrs. Hanson said they went southwest."

"So away from our place." Ethan bent over and studied the map as well. "I'm betting they're closer to Robbie's. Fewer people take that route across open country. Most take the longer way around on the road."

The marshal nodded. "Which is why I'll leave in the morning to give him a warning and make sure he doubles up on those guards." He looked over at Ethan. "Cade will be back the day after tomorrow. You wait and get more rest and let him know about the brothers, then head on out to the Hanson place and track them back from there." He pointed to a spot on the map. "I'll meet you here, in that grove of trees by the river."

Ethan watched as Jules carefully rolled up the map. "You might give your wife a little more benefit of the doubt, Jules. She's only been your wife for a few weeks, and most of that time, you were gone. She was Maggie's daughter for a lot longer than that." He waited until his friend looked up from the map. "Dorrie would have told you."

Still numb from believing his wife hadn't trusted him to be fair to her mam, Jules only shrugged. He'd deal with his wife after he had the Green Gang in custody.

This wasn't going to end well for the O'Hearn brothers, and that was a fact, which only fueled his sour mood. He knew it would hurt Dorrie's mam to see her family arrested by her son-in-law, and the last thing he wanted was to hurt anyone in his family. But he was a US Marshal with a job to do.

And both he and Dorrie would have to decide how they were going to deal with that too.

26

"Maybe I should have told her I was leaving and where I was going, instead of just writing a note."

Other than pricking up his ears, Hafen showed no reaction to his rider's conversation. But that didn't bother Jules. He was used to having one-sided conversations with his horse, no matter how much Cade made fun of him for it. Jules would bet that his older brother did the same thing after he'd spent days on the trail with only his mount for company.

And Cade wasn't there now anyway.

"But she should have trusted me. What did she think I would do? Arrest her mother?"

She's only been your wife for a few weeks. Ethan's voice echoed in his mind and had Jules frowning. He knew they hadn't been married long. He didn't need his friend to remind him of that. Especially when Ethan wasn't anywhere in sight.

Hafen's breathing grew louder as they climbed a small

rise. At the top, Jules pulled the horse up and took a look around. Off in the distance was the stand of trees that lined the bank of a small river that ran through the rolling hills. And in between was a long section of flat grassland. Jules glanced up at the sun.

He'd been riding for six hours and figured he was still a good ten miles from Robbie's place. The sun had already passed the midpoint in the sky and started its descent toward the western horizon. Judging by its current position, Jules figured he'd be at Robbie's around suppertime. There would still be enough daylight for them to ride the perimeter of the ranch and tighten up the nightly patrols the hands were making. Once Robbie was properly warned that the Green Gang was most likely in the area, Jules would take off at first light to meet Ethan, and hopefully Cade, at the crossroads. From there, the hunt would be on.

Setting Hafen back into motion, Jules' thoughts immediately drifted back to Dorrie. He blew out a breath and ran a hand through his hair. The fact was, he was feeling a little guilty when it came to his wife. He'd told himself he was being considerate by not waking her to let her know he was leaving, but he knew it was really because he hadn't wanted to talk to her.

He'd been angry last night as he'd worked late, writing out his plan and leaving it for Cade to find. And still angry when he'd finally gone to bed in the guest chamber rather than his own. And his mood hadn't changed much when he'd left just after sunup. But hours in the saddle, most of it spent thinking about Dorrie, had given him a chance to look at the whole situation a bit differently.

He was still angry, but had to admit to himself that much of that came from the sudden shock of realizing he'd have to hunt down the brothers of an honorary aunt he'd adored most of his life. And having no idea how she would feel about him after he did.

And now he was mostly uncomfortable with the way he'd treated his bride. She'd been right to tell him he'd been insulting, because he had been. And downright mean.

Jules felt the heat creep up his neck. In a million years he'd never meant to be mean to Dorrie. The look of shock and then sadness on her face would stay with him for a long time. He was right to be angry with her. She should have come to him first after she'd read Shannon's journal. But she was right too. And so was Ethan. Dorrie had been Maggie Dolan's daughter a lot longer than she'd been his wife. He shouldn't have needed his friend to remind him of that.

Jules wished he'd kept quiet and given more thought to what came out of his mouth. And most of all, he shouldn't have taken to a bed separate from his wife. He'd spent what little was left of the previous night tossing and turning, not only about their argument, but because she wasn't there next to him. He'd gotten used to her being in his bed that quickly and knew down into his bones that he would never get another good night's sleep unless they were together.

Dorrie had already apologized, but he'd been too caught up in his anger to listen. The first thing he would do when he got home was to tell her he appreciated her telling him how sorry she was. And then do some apologizing of his own. He hoped that would be enough, although he still planned on finding a way to make it up to her — the argument, his anger, his behavior... all of it.

Feeling as if a weight had slid away from his chest, Jules reached down and gave Hafen's muscular neck a firm pat. As he did, his gaze fell to the ground. Quickly pulling Hafen to a stop, Jules backed the big horse up a few steps, his eyes glued to the bare patch of ground below Hafen's hooves. There must have been a good rain a few days before because the ground was still muddy. Especially in those spots that had been churned up by several horses.

Jules slid off the saddle and crouched next to a set of tracks. He reached out and traced one with his forefinger. One horse that had recently passed this way had two crooked shoes. He studied the ground around them. It looked like that horse wasn't alone since there were two more distinct sets of tracks.

Rising to his feet, Jules walked along, following the tracks until they disappeared into the tall grass. He looked up and frowned. The horses were making a direct line toward the stand of trees.

CONNOR SLID down from his perch high up in an old oak with its thick gnarled branches. His feet were barely on the ground when a firm hand landed on his shoulder.

Patrick whirled his brother around. "What did you see, Connor? Is that tracker followin' us?"

The younger man scowled and pushed Patrick's hand off his shoulder. "It's not the tracker. It's that marshal we saw ridin' with the tracker when they went north. The one you said was likely the same one hanging around Maggie's girl."

Patrick's brow lifted as he looked past his brother, as if he could see the marshal through the cover of the trees. "Is it now?"

"He stopped and was looking at the ground. I think he's picked up our trail."

"Did you see which way he's headed?"

Connor shut the spyglass in his hand with a loud snap. "He's comin' right at us, Patrick."

Liam quickly turned to look in the direction of the unseen intruder. "Maybe we should be goin' then?"

"Goin'?" Patrick scoffed. "Where? If you don't mind me askin'."

"Well I don't want to wait for him to get here and arrest us. I don't want to spend the rest of me life in no stinkin' jail." Liam spat on the ground before glaring at his oldest brother.

The eldest O'Hearn brother only shrugged. "If goin' off somewhere is what you want, I say we leave the horses tied up at the edge of the trees and go to that small knoll just to the west of us. He won't be seein' us there."

"He'll find the horses," Liam complained.

"We won't let him do that."

Liam grinned. "Are you suggestin' we ambush the man?"

Patrick shrugged, ignoring the heated glare from Connor. "I'm suggestin' he might be a horse thief, and we can't have any of that now, can we?"

As he and Liam picked up their rifles, Connor braced his legs apart and didn't move an inch to join them. "He's a US Marshal, is what he is, Patrick." He switched his glare to Liam. "You shoot a US Marshal and it won't be a jail you'll be seein' but the end of a rope."

"He was alone, wasn't he?" Patrick asked, smiling when Connor gave a reluctant nod. "Then who's to tell that we're the ones who shot him?"

Liam stepped over to stand beside Patrick. "That's right."

Connor shifted his weight when Patrick bent over and picked up a second rifle. He held it out to his youngest brother. "We're blood, Connor, so you'll be comin' with us. When I was complainin' about the marshal before, we agreed to let fate decide." Patrick jerked his head to the side. "Well it seems fate has decided to hand us a gift, and it would be bad luck not to take it."

27

J ules had approached the lone group of trees slowly, stopping beyond what he deemed was the range of a rifle. He sat, studying the area as Hafen lowered his head and munched peacefully on the grass. He could barely hear the rush of water from the small river, and the trees and undergrowth were thick enough that he could only see a few feet beyond their edge. He waited several minutes, finally recognizing the faint sound of a hoof stomping hard onto the ground. Hafen raised his head, his ears perked forward, before lowering it again to continue his grazing.

The marshal looked at the ground, his eyes following the set of tracks that led into the trees. His gut told him that the brothers were nearby, but they should have raised an alarm by now. Unless they weren't aware of his presence. Jules considered it for a moment. It would have been foolish not to have posted a lookout, but then if Hanson was to be believed, they didn't seem to be very adept with a gun. And men who couldn't shoot, might not know to post a guard. Or maybe they felt they didn't need one. It was isolated enough out here that they probably weren't expecting any company.

When another few minutes had passed and there were no signs of life among the trees, Jules was about to dismount and quietly approach the small oasis on foot when suddenly a shot rang out, thudding into the ground a few feet in front of Hafen. The big horse instantly jumped to the side and danced away as a second and then a third shot rang out. A sharp blow to Jules' side spun his upper body around. Only the instinctive clamping of his knees and a desperate grab for Hafen's mane kept him from tumbling to the ground. With a supreme effort, Jules gave a hard yank to the reins, pulling the big stallion around before setting a sharp heel to its sides. He heard the yells behind him as another volley of shots rang out and then stopped. Jules didn't think they'd given up. It was more likely they were getting on their horses. He tightened his grip on Hafen's mane as the big animal leaped forward, running as soon as his feet hit the ground. Less than a minute later, Jules heard the pounding of more hooves.

He didn't have to look around to know the O'Hearn brothers were coming after him.

More shots rang out as Jules did his best to keep Hafen out in the open, away from any possible ambush points among the small knolls dotting the grassland. Hafen ran as if the devil were on his heels, opening a wider gap between them and their pursuers, while Jules used every ounce of his strength to stay on the horse's back. But he could feel the warmth of his blood soaking into his pants and knew he wouldn't be able to hang on much longer.

His strength was spent.

They were skirting past a small hill when Jules grunted

as he pulled Hafen around and sent him partway up the hill, stopping next to a row of boulders embedded in the ground. Breathing as heavily as his horse, Jules slid his rifle out of his saddle holster and tossed it, along with his saddlebags and blanket, over on the other side of the boulders. Gritting his teeth, he slid out of the saddle, grunting at the jarring force when his feet landed on the ground. He hung onto the stirrup as he tried to keep his balance.

When he felt as steady as he could, he leaned on the boulder and shuffled forward until he was standing by Hafen's head. He could still hear the hoof beats in the distance, but they were definitely coming closer, and he hoped like hell this trick would work. If it didn't, this might be the last day he'd draw breath.

Standing so Hafen could see him, Jules carefully repeated the hand gesture Rayne had taught him, then managed to croak out the word "barn". Still breathing heavily, the stallion backed up a few feet and then stopped.

Jules took several short shallow breaths, the sound of the hoof beats behind him matching the rapid beat of his heart. He drew his gun and held it by his side in one hand as he used the other to repeat the hand gesture again, and concentrated on putting more force into his voice.

"Barn." When the stallion still hesitated, Jules pointed his gun away from his leg. He repeated the hand gesture then let off a single shot as he loudly said, "barn."

He closed his eyes when Hafen wheeled around and took off down the hill, heading back out onto the open grassland. With the fading light, he was counting on the brothers not noticing they were chasing a riderless horse. And without carrying his weight, Jules knew Hafen would outrun anything the O'Hearn brothers were riding.

He crawled over the top of the boulders, barely feeling the sharp edges jabbing into his chest. Jules fell to the ground on the other side, landing on his back. He lay there, not moving, his eyes closed as he listened to the trio of horses coming closer. He held his breath until they thundered by without stopping.

Jules lifted himself enough to peer through a crack in the rocks. He saw all three horses chasing after Hafen. By the time they gave up and came back this way, he hoped the light would be faded enough that the brothers wouldn't notice anything unusual up on the hillside.

Jules forced himself up into a sitting position and reached for the blanket that was a foot or so away. Taking the knife out of his belt, he cut it into ragged strips and wound them around his middle, making the binding as tight as he could. The effort sapped the last of his strength and he barely managed to tuck the edge of the blanket away before he slipped back into a prone position.

He lay quietly, waiting for the pain to subside enough so he could reach for his rifle and the saddlebag with his extra bullets. With that small task finally accomplished, he flopped back down again, pulling his rifle to rest on his chest. He knew he'd lost a fair amount of blood, and wondered if his little trick had only put off the inevitable.

A wave of remorse mingled with the pain radiating from his side. Dorrie. He might never see Dorrie again. He'd never have that chance to tell her he was sorry and would make it up to her. He'd never again feel her warmth snuggled against his side. And he'd never be able to tell her what he should have when he'd talked her into marrying him.

He closed his eyes and instantly saw her deep-brown eyes. He could see the smile in them. Jules lifted a hand and then dropped it back to the ground as he stopped fighting the gray crowding at the edges of his vision. He let the image of his wife gently lead him into the darkness crashing all around him as the first heavy drop of rain hit his face.

"I love you, Dorrie."

28

"I've never seen him that angry."

"It's Jules, Dorrie." Ammie wrinkled her nose as she sniffed at the fragrant cup of tea in her hands. "He may be a US Marshal now, but he's still Jules. He won't stay mad long."

Dorrie wished she could believe that. She really did. But, in the blink of an eye, it seemed as if the man she'd thought she knew so well had turned into someone she'd never seen before. She sighed and looked into the darkness outside the kitchen window.

The house was quiet with Cade and the children gone. Abby had already retired to her bedchamber after a long day of seeing patients, and Dina had left a few hours ago to settle in for the night in the homey cottage she shared with her husband. Ammie had come to spend the night at Dorrie's request. Dorrie was sure her new in-laws sensed something had gone terribly wrong between her and Jules. And while she loved and appreciated their calming presence, right now she needed her best friend to talk to.

"He was almost mean." Dorrie's voice was soft, and she had to blink rapidly to keep the tears from escaping.

Ammie reached over and gave her friend's hand a reassuring squeeze. "Almost?"

"Well, he was more insulting," Dorrie admitted. She raised her gaze to Ammie's. "But that's mean, isn't it?"

"It certainly is," Ammie declared. "He should have been more understanding. After all, we are talking about your mam here. It's only right that you heard her side of the story first. You wouldn't want your husband to rush to any judgments." She gave a quick nod. "I would have done the same thing."

Since Ammie hadn't seen her mother in twenty years, Dorrie rather doubted that, but her friend's staunch defense made her smile.

"I'm sure Jules will realize it, too," Ammie continued. "He can't be that mad at you."

"He slept in the spare bedchamber last night."

"Maybe he was just being considerate?" When Dorrie rolled her eyes, Ammie slumped back against her chair. "All right. He's mad."

"And he didn't bother to let me know when he was leaving. He left a note."

"All right," Ammie conceded. "He's really, really mad. But he'll have the whole ride out to Robbie's ranch to think things over, and he'll come around."

"I hope so." *And that's all I can do*, Dorrie silently added. *Wait and hope.*

They both turned in their chairs at the sound of the kitchen door squeaking on its hinges. Frank Brown stood in the opening, his gaze immediately going to Dorrie.

"Excuse me, Mrs. McKenzie. There's something you

need to see." He didn't wait for a response but turned and walked away.

Dorrie and Ammie exchanged a quick, puzzled look but didn't waste any time in following the deputy. When Dorrie stepped inside the stable, she stopped dead. Beside her, Ammie let out a soft gasp.

Frank stood in the middle of the stable, holding onto Hafen's halter as he ran a soothing hand up and down the stallion's neck. Dorrie's gaze shot around the enclosure, looking for Jules. But her husband was nowhere in sight.

"Hafen came in alone."

The deputy's stark words left Dorrie frozen in place.

"Oh, surely not." Ammie shook her head. "Jules probably went through the front door and just sent Hafen to the stable. He's one of Rayne's horses, so I'm sure he's very well trained."

Dorrie didn't say a word as she walked forward, her gaze fixed on the stallion who turned his head and stared back at her. She reached out and ran a hand down the length of a muscular shoulder. She could feel the matted coat and dried sweat as well as smell it. Along with something else. Pulling her hand away, she studied the dark flecks covering her palm. Blood. It looked like dried blood.

"Mr. Brown? Pull Hafen around so this side is closer to the lantern. I need to see if he's injured himself."

The deputy did as she asked, then came around to bend his head next to hers. He straightened up, a frown on his face. "I don't see that he's cut anywhere."

"No, it doesn't look like it." Dorrie pointed at the thin, dark streak running down Hafen's shoulder. "But that's blood."

Frank reached his hand out and swiped it along the

horse's side. He examined his hand for a brief moment before he nodded his agreement. "Yes, it is."

"Oh no."

The quiet sound of dismay in Ammie's voice had Dorrie closing her eyes. She took in several deep breaths, willing herself to stay on her feet.

"I can get together a search party at first light. There isn't much we can do in the dark." The deputy gave Dorrie a sympathetic look. "I'm sorry to say this, Mrs. McKenzie, but there's no telling how far this horse came on his own, or where he came from. But we'll do our best to find the marshal, I promise you that."

Dorrie stiffened her spine and took a step back. She gave the deputy a polite smile. "Thank you, Mr. Brown. And I'll need you to do that. But I'm leaving tonight to find my husband."

"But Mrs. McKenzie…"

She cut him off by turning toward Ammie. "I'm leaving tonight. What I need is a tracker. Ethan's in town. He's waiting for Cade."

"Which is what we should do, Mrs. McKenzie." Frank's voice came from behind her.

"And what *you* should do if you feel that's the right thing," Dorrie countered over her shoulder. "But Cade might have something delay him." She returned her gaze to Ammie.

"I'm leaving tonight," she repeated. "And I need Ethan. But I don't know where he stays in town. Can you find him? He'll come if you ask him to."

Ammie stepped forward and took both of Dorrie's hands into her own. "I know where he stays. You go change and get together whatever you'll need to take with you. I'll be back with your tracker within the hour."

As Ammie lifted her skirts and ran out of the stable, Dorrie turned back and pointed at the stallion. "Get Hafen some water but leave him the way he is until Ethan gets here. He'll want to have a look at him."

"HE'S BEEN RUN HARD." Ethan kept up his slow walk around the stallion, sliding his hand over the coat that was prickly with dried sweat and what was most likely Jules' blood.

"What do you think happened?" Ammie asked.

Ethan looked over at her before shifting his gaze to Dorrie. "Could be lots of things."

"He isn't dead, Ethan," Dorrie said quietly. "I would know it."

Abby, who Dorrie had awakened to tell her about Jules, put an arm around her young sister-in-law's shoulders. "I don't think so either. That's not a lot of blood."

Ethan only grunted as he finished a complete circle around Hafen.

Dorrie was dressed in her boy's garb, her rifle in her hand and two saddlebags at her feet. "I've got food and extra bullets."

"I'll need them."

She closed her eyes on a wave of relief. Ethan was going to help her. And if anyone could find Jules, it was Ethan Mayes. But first there was an argument she needed to win.

"We, Ethan. We will need them." She waited patiently for the expected negative shake of his head. "I'm going with you. I can ride all night, and I can shoot. I'll keep up."

The dark-haired man she'd always considered a brother moved his gaze from her face to her gun and then to the saddlebags at her feet.

"She's a good shot," Ammie put in. "I practice with her. I'm sure she's as good as most of the men Mr. Brown will be organizing for the search."

"We aren't waiting for them." Ethan frowned, keeping silent for a full minute. "Can you ride at night?"

"Of course," Dorrie said. She'd never actually done such a thing, but she'd stay on her horse no matter what.

"You can't read signs in the dark, Ethan," Frank said. "Not even you are that good."

Ethan shrugged. "I won't have to. I know when the marshal left, and when Hafen showed up here. It's a sure thing that the horse came back a lot faster than Jules went out, so I figure he's five or six hours out. It's midnight now. We'll wait a few hours before heading out. By the time we need to pick up his tracks, we'll have enough light."

Frank Brown scratched his beard. "You're sure you know where to look for him?"

"Jules, Robbie, and I have made that ride out to The Orphan Ranch so many times since we were kids that I've lost count. And we always go the same way. I know the direction he took. I'll find him."

The deputy didn't look convinced. "But how are you going to pick up his tracks out there in the open country?"

"The men in the family have their ways, Mr. Brown." Abby smiled at the deputy. "Why don't we leave Ethan and Dorrie to their preparations. I'll put some coffee on, and you can make a list of the men you want to gather here by the time Cade arrives." The doctor latched onto the deputy's arm, looking over her shoulder at Ethan as she nudged Frank toward the stable door. "Make sure you come back with the marshal, Ethan."

Ethan nodded back at her and motioned to Dorrie, who

hurried to stand beside him. Ammie walked over and gave her friend a hug. "You'll find him. I know you will."

Dorrie hugged her back. "Yes." She glanced at Ethan. "We both will."

Ammie stepped in front of the tracker and put her arms around his waist, giving him a hug as well that lasted barely more than a moment. When she stepped back, she gave him a trembling smile. "Make sure you bring both of them back, and yourself as well."

He abruptly nodded and turned around, grabbing Hafen's halter and leading the stallion into his stall.

Ammie sighed and shook her head at Dorrie's questioning look. "You be careful. I'm going to go wake up Dina and Cook and ask them to come over and stay with Abby, at least until Cade comes home."

Nodding her gratitude, Dorrie waved her friend off. "Go. Then get some sleep. I'll send you word as soon as we're home with Jules."

29

D orrie stretched her back, wincing at the pain but not uttering so much as a sound. She didn't want to give Ethan any reason to wish he'd left her at home. They'd been riding for hours, Ethan setting a brisk pace, but taking care to ease off for periods of time so as not to tire the horses. As the sun peeked over the horizon, and the night gave way to the morning light, Dorrie became more anxious. Ethan had started to shift from one side of his saddle to the other as he scanned the ground. But so far, he hadn't found Hafen's tracks.

"What did Abby mean about having your ways?"

Ethan turned his head and lifted one dark eyebrow. "What?"

"About how to find a certain set of tracks out in the open country. She said the men in the family have their ways."

He smiled. "Well, since you're now Jules' wife and all, I guess you're entitled to be let in on our secret."

Since he was staring at the ground and not at her, Dorrie shifted in her saddle to help ease the ache in her lower back. "What secret?"

Ethan smiled as he continued to keep his gaze down-
ward. "When Robbie was sixteen or so, he managed to get
himself lost in the hills. It took us a while to find him
because there were so many horses that had passed that
way, we didn't know which set of tracks belonged to his. So
we decided to have a mark put into each of our horse's
shoes."

"A mark?" Dorrie's brow furrowed in thought. She'd
never heard of such a thing.

"Yep," Ethan nodded. "Hafen has a small 'J' on his left
front hoof, and Biscuit here as an 'E'."

"Then Robbie's horse has an 'R'?" Dorrie was impressed.
That was very clever.

"He does." Ethan pulled up on the reins. He frowned at
the ground as Biscuit ambled to a stop. Setting the animal
into a slow walk, Ethan rode along for another few minutes
before he stopped and turned in his saddle to look back and
grin at Dorrie. "Found Hafen's track." He nodded. "I thought
Jules would follow this old trail." Ethan pointed off in the
direction they'd been going. "He headed that way."

Dorrie stood in her stirrups and eagerly scanned the
grassland in front of them, looking for any sign of her
husband. "Do you think we're close to him?"

"Calm down, Dorrie. These are Jules' tracks going out to
Robbie's place. I figure we're still a good hour, maybe more,
from where Hafen was sent home."

She bit her lower lip. Her nerves were already stretched
tight, and the ball in the pit of her stomach grew with every
passing minute. Jules was in trouble. She knew it. And they
needed to find him right now.

As if he'd read her mind, Ethan set Biscuit into a quick
trot, never taking his eyes off the ground as he followed
Hafen's trail. Dorrie kept her mare close behind and her

eyes constantly moving over the countryside. Another twenty minutes passed when Ethan suddenly stopped, lifting one arm to let Dorrie know to do the same. She pulled her mount up and watched as Ethan began to move back and forth across the grass, finally stopping a good fifty feet to her right. He quickly dismounted and knelt, running a hand over the ground. He finally stood and motioned for her to join him.

"What do you see?" Dorrie asked once she drew close to where Ethan was waiting for her.

"Another set of Hafen's tracks. Only these are headed in the opposite direction." Ethan stared back to the faint trail they had been following. "And he doesn't have a rider."

Dorrie frowned. "How can you tell that?"

"It must have rained last night because the ground is soft, and these tracks are shallower than the first set we found. That tells me Hafen didn't have as much weight on him."

"Oh." The ball in Dorrie's stomach grew another notch.

Ethan remounted. "We're going to follow these. Hafen would have taken the most direct line for home, so they'll show us the fastest way to Jules."

It was another half hour when Ethan stopped again. Used to the routine by now, Dorrie pulled up behind him and waited while he dismounted and studied the ground. He abruptly straightened up and stared off into the distance while Dorrie waited silently. Ethan walked along for a good five minutes, traversing back and forth as he studied the ground. He finally stopped and slowly turned to look at her.

"There're other tracks crisscrossing over Hafen's." He paused and rubbed his chin before looking off to his left and pointing to a small stand of trees. "We need to head over there and cut some branches to take with us."

"Branches?" Dorrie swiveled around in her saddle and raised one hand to shade her eyes as she stared at the trees. "Why?"

"The blood on his saddle tells me Jules was hurt." Ethan pointed at the ground. "These new tracks have a horse with two crooked shoes."

Dorrie drew in a quick sharp breath. "Mam's brothers were chasing Jules?"

He nodded. "The Green Gang. But they weren't chasing Jules. Hafen's tracks still aren't deep enough to be carrying a rider. It looks like this is where the gang gave up running after a horse they couldn't catch."

"But..." Dorrie frowned as she tried to figure out what Ethan was saying. "Why would they chase Hafen?"

"I'm guessing they didn't know Jules and his horse had parted company."

Dorrie's hand shot up and covered her mouth. "You think Jules fell off his horse?" Before Ethan had a chance to respond, Dorrie shook her head. "No. That can't be right." She shook her head again. "Jules told me he had to say 'barn', and give a hand signal, for Hafen to come home. How could he do that if he fell off his horse while he was being chased?"

For the first time in hours, Ethan grinned. "Which is why we need those branches."

Dorrie was too tired to unravel the riddle Ethan was giving her. "What does that have to do with finding Jules?"

"Because, Mrs. McKenzie, it's just like you said. Your husband must have sent his horse home as a decoy, so the Green Gang would follow Hafen and not be looking around for his rider."

Hope sizzled along Dorrie's arms. A decoy? That meant Jules was likely hiding somewhere, waiting for help. She wanted to start yelling for him right then, but Ethan stopped her before she opened her mouth.

"We need to be quiet. If that gang is still around, we don't want to give them any warning we're headed their way." Ethan mounted his horse and did a slow scan around them.

"What are the branches for?" Dorrie leaned forward to whisper her question.

"In case we need to carry him back to town. I'd just as soon make a hammock we can lash to the back of one of our horses rather than drape him over my saddle."

"Oh." Dorrie turned her mount toward the trees. "Then we'd better get to it." She closed her eyes when she heard the soft scrape of metal against leather.

Ethan rode up beside her. "Get your rifle out, Dorrie. And keep it out from here on."

THE SUN WAS WELL PAST the horizon as the two riders, each with two long branches settled across their laps along with a rifle, came up on a small hill. Dorrie shifted in her saddle. She was suddenly feeling restless. Her gaze left Ethan's broad back and shoulders to wander over to the hill they were heading straight for. She passed right over the clump of rocks about a third of the way up before her attention was drawn right back to them. As they came closer, she studied them more intently. There wasn't a sound or movement from anywhere around them, but she couldn't take her eyes off the small line of boulders, or ignore the growing tingle running down her spine.

Ethan made another abrupt stop, studying the ground. "I've lost Hafen's tracks. They've been washed out in the rain." He circled around a second time before dismounting.

He continued to mutter under his breath as Dorrie once again stared at the boulders. The tingle got stronger, and she could feel herself being pulled up that hill. And she knew why.

"Ethan," she said quietly. "Jules is up there. Behind those rocks."

Dorrie turned her horse and steadily climbed the hill, not stopping until she'd reached the boulders. She was barely off her horse when Ethan pulled Biscuit up beside her. He dismounted while she scrambled over the boulders, almost tumbling headfirst to the other side. She caught herself just before she landed on top of her husband.

"Jules!" She scrambled to the ground, kneeling beside him as she placed a hand along his cheek. "Jules? Can you hear me?" When he remained motionless and his eyes stayed shut, Dorrie leaned over and placed her ear gently against his chest. She held her breath, praying. When she heard the faint but steady heartbeat and felt the shallow rise and fall of his chest against her cheek, she threw her arms around his shoulders and gave out a single sob.

Ethan gently drew her up. "Here. Let me have a look at him."

Dorrie's eyes fell on the ragged strip of blanket wrapped around her husband's middle. She lifted one of Jules' limp hands in her own as Ethan gently prodded around his friend's side. Jules gave a sudden jerk and let out a deep moan. It was the sweetest sound Dorrie had ever heard. She bent over until she could speak gently into his ear.

"It's all right, Jules. We're here. Just lie still now."

"Dorrie?"

It was barely a whisper, but she heard him. Squeezing

his hand, she brushed a kiss along the stubble on his cheek. "I'm here. We're going to get you home."

The grip on her hand grew firmer. "Stay with me, Dorrie."

She smiled through the tears dripping down her face and onto his. "Always, Jules."

30

"Escaped? What do you mean they escaped?"

Jules ran an agitated hand through his hair. It had been close to three weeks since he'd made the harrowing trip home. He didn't remember much about it, except for the pain. And Dorrie. Every time he'd cracked open his eyes, she'd been there right beside him. And when he didn't have the strength to do more than grit his teeth against every jolt from the uneven ground, he'd felt her hand holding his, her words of encouragement, and at times her tears on his face. She was the reason he'd held on. He wanted to stay with her. His whole being had fought for it, through every hard mile of the trek back to San Francisco.

But now that he was almost completely healed, and had gained the better part of his strength back thanks to Dorrie's constant vigilance and the skill of Doctor Abby, he hardly ever saw his wife. She was making herself scarce, and he knew why. Their last fight still hung between them. He needed to make it right, but how was he going to do that unless she stayed around him long enough for him to apologize? But he'd have to put that aside for the moment while he dealt with his brother and this new problem. Jules moved restlessly against the pillows propped up behind his back as he stared at Cade.

"It took you ten days to track Maggie's brothers down and bring them back to San Francisco. And in barely ten more days you lose them again?" He glared at the man who was sitting in a chair pulled up next to Jules' bed.

"I didn't lose them. The city sheriff did."

"And how did Sheriff Adams come to do that?" Jules demanded.

Cade gave a casual shrug that had Jules' eyes narrowing in suspicion. His brother didn't look distressed at all over the escape of the Green Gang.

"The sheriff didn't like the idea of them occupying one of his cells, so he decided to move them to that prison out on the point. They escaped during the move. Got a report this morning they were spotted heading south. I've sent a telegram to the marshal in Los Angeles, but I'm thinking they're going to Mexico."

Jules wished he could be sure of that. "Why would Sheriff Adams do a fool thing like moving them?"

His brother gave him an amused look. "It's his jail, his decision."

"But *our* prisoners," Jules flatly stated. "Why did the sheriff's men move them?"

"I was busy. Couldn't get around to it fast enough to suit the sheriff."

"Busy?" Jules' eyes narrowed even more. "Doing what?"

"Federal business." Cade stared blandly back at him. "We're short a man who's been lounging about since he was shot. I've had to pick up the slack."

When Jules stared at him, the disbelief clear on his face, Cade leaned back and rubbed a hand against the scar on his face. "Sometimes things aren't don't fall into absolutely right or wrong, Jules, and a man has to balance what's important in his life." He paused for a moment as he stared back at this brother. "You took an oath to uphold justice. So did I. But justice can be served in different ways. That gang fled to Mexico and won't be back. You have my word on that."

"What's important in life," Jules slowly repeated. "Like family, maybe?"

"Family's always important," Cade said. There was a long moment when the two brothers stared at each other before Jules finally nodded. He wasn't sure what had happened to Maggie O'Hearn's brothers, but he was sure of two things: Cade would never allow any man to be killed in cold blood, and if he said that justice had been served, then Jules believed him.

"Family's always important." Jules settled more comfortably against the pillows at his back. "So what have you been doing the last few weeks while I've been laid up?"

"Like I said, federal business."

Irritated, Jules let out a snort. "I'll be back tomorrow going through all that correspondence you've probably let pile up. I also need to look in on Hafen. I expect he's not too happy with me." At Cade's puzzled glance, Jules smiled. "I had to fire off a shot near his hooves to get him to head back home."

The older marshal rolled his eyes as he got to his feet. "You can talk to your horse another time. You need to talk to your wife first. Abby's upset with you, and that doesn't sit well with me."

Jules frowned. Abby? What had he done to upset Abby, besides getting shot?

"*Your* wife is unhappy, and that's making *my* wife upset," Cade supplied. "You need to do something about that. Abby says Dorrie will be getting sick herself if she keeps working so hard to keep her mind off you."

"What?" A spurt of alarm shot through Jules. "Dorrie's sick?" He swung his legs out from under the coverlet and over the edge of the bed.

Cade reached out and put a hand on top of his brother's head and held him in place. "Hang on there. I said she *might* get sick unless you straighten things out between you."

Jules' shoulders slumped. "Hard to do when she's barely talking to me." He stared at a point on the far wall. "I think maybe she's changed her mind about being married."

"Is that why you've been sticking to your bed? Because you're afraid to talk to your wife?" Cade shook his head. "You're acting like the back end of a mule. Which is how you got her mad at you in the first place."

"I'm not afraid to talk to my wife," Jules grumbled. But Cade had hit close to the truth. What would he do if Dorrie told him she didn't think their marriage was a good idea after all?

"You aren't thinking straight, Jules," Cade said quietly. "A woman who walks most of the way back to town, just so she can stay beside her husband and hold his hand, has some powerful feelings for the man."

"I know she did." Jules said. "Ethan told me. And I can smell that soap she likes to use when I wake up every morning, so I know she's been sitting with me during the night."

Cade rolled his shoulders then grinned at the man sitting on the side of the bed. "Abby thinks Dorrie's avoiding you because it's *you* who doesn't want to be married anymore, and that's what's making your wife miserable." He nodded at Jules' astonished expression. "What are you going to do about that, little brother?"

Jules shoved the last of the coverlet away and got to his

feet. "I'm going to fix it." He looked around the tidy room before he pointed to the wardrobe in the corner. "I'd appreciate it if you'd get me my pants."

"YOU CAN'T FORCE us onto that ship."

Dina's husband, Cook, didn't bother to answer as he finished tightening the rope binding Patrick's hands tightly together. Ian glanced over at the brother-in-law he'd only met a few hours ago when he and Cook, along with a few other trusted men, had liberated Patrick and his brothers from Sheriff Adam's escort.

"You'd prefer prison and then the rope?" Ian asked.

Patrick's lips drew back over his rotting teeth and formed into a jaunty-looking smile. He stared at the woman standing quietly to one side. "You won't let them do that, will you Maggie, girl? We're your blood."

Her brother's smile reminded Maggie so much of her own da that her heart began to ache. But not soften. These men might be her blood, but they weren't family. She felt Ian come up behind her. Maggie leaned back against her husband's chest, comforted when his arms came around her.

She'd loved this man for more than twenty years, and would love him even beyond the time she took her last breath. She only wished her brothers had known a life as happy as hers had been. She was sorry, but not surprised, to hear about their da, but what was done was done. And that's all there was to that.

"We share blood, Patrick, and sorry I am for it, but we aren't family, and you hurt mine. I can't have that."

"He just put a scare into that whelp you adopted,

Maggie," Liam's voice had a whine in it that grated on Maggie's nerves.

"She's me daughter whether you like it or not, Liam. And the lot of you went along with putting a bullet into her husband. And that's after you killed that poor bank guard and took shots at a child."

"Patrick," Liam said quickly. "Patrick did all those things."

"Shut your mouth, Liam," his older brother growled.

"We didn't know that marshal was married to your daughter," Connor said quietly.

Maggie's eyes softened as she looked at the only brother who had ever truly cared about her. She wished Connor had made other choices in his life. But he hadn't.

"That makes no difference, Connor. And I'm doubtin' if it would have changed anythin' even if you had known it."

Connor sighed. When he looked back at her, there were tears in his eyes. "We should have come back for you all those years ago, Maggie. I've always been sorry for that."

Ian's chest muscles tensed against his wife's back. "But you didn't. And in all the years since then you never once tried to come back for her, did you? She could have died here, and almost did, because her family had no more use for her." He turned his head and spat on the floor.

Maggie ran a soothing hand up and down the muscular arm crossed in front of her. "Ian is right. You stopped bein' me family long ago."

"Then why are you here now?" Patrick demanded. "Come to enjoy seein' us trussed up and tossed on a ship back to Ireland?"

"Trussed up, yes. Going to Ireland? No," Cook said calmly. He crossed his long spindly arms over his chest as he stared at the three men. "Where you're going, you won't have any way to come back. And whether you survive there or not will be up to you. That's the only chance you gave your sister all those years ago, so that's all you'll be getting now."

"And you should be grateful for that." Ian's voice was low and quiet. "The only reason you're being given that much is because I love my wife enough to spare her the pain of seeing her brothers swinging from the end of the rope."

"And I'm grateful for his love," Maggie added. She gave a long slow look to each of her brothers.

"Goodbye. May the fates be kinder to you than you've been to others."

31

Two days later, Jules walked into the kitchen and searched for his wife among all the feminine bodies milling about the crowded space. The room was alive with colorful skirts and happy chatter as the food preparation was well underway for the delayed wedding celebration being held that afternoon.

Finally spotting Dorrie standing in front of the open pantry, Jules loudly cleared his throat. "Excuse me, ladies, but I need to talk to my wife."

Dorrie turned around, a large bowl of apples in her hands. "Oh, Jules. Can it wait for a bit? I need to help get the food ready."

He didn't answer her directly, instead choosing to wade through the women in their large extended family until he was standing right in front of her. Leaning over the bowl his wife was holding, he captured her chin in one hand and placed his lips on hers, giving her a thorough kiss right there in the middle of the packed kitchen.

He lifted his head and smiled when Dorrie had the same

dazed look in her eyes that she'd had the first time he'd kissed her. He took that as a good sign.

Behind him, Dina made a clucking noise. He imagined she was shaking a finger at his back. "That boy is just like his brother."

"Then Dorrie is a very lucky woman," Abby laughed. She tapped her brother-in-law on the shoulder. "Perhaps you should, um, speak to your wife outside?"

Jules looked over his shoulder and grinned at the doctor. "An excellent idea." He plucked the bowl out of Dorrie's unresisting hands and passed it along to Abby before he bent at the waist and lifted his wife into his arms.

"Jules!" Dorrie gasped and clamped an arm around his shoulders. "Put me down. You'll hurt yourself."

He grinned at her. "I will, Mrs. McKenzie. Outside. Just like the doctor ordered." He nodded his head at the women around him. Every single one of them were wide-eyed with their mouths open. "Ladies. We'll be back before the party."

As Dorrie made a strangled sound of protest, he carried her down the hallway and past the open parlor doors, where the sound of Ian and Cade's conversation came to an abrupt stop. Jules kept right on walking until he was on the hard-packed street in front of the house. He finally set his wife on her feet, then quickly took the precaution of taking one of her hands in his. He didn't want to have to chase her down if she decided to march back into the house.

"Whatever has gotten into you?" Dorrie demanded.

"I wanted to talk to you. And show you something."

Dorrie looked around. "Show me what?"

"You'll have to wait and see." Jules started to walk, swinging their joined hands between them.

He adjusted his longer stride to her much shorter one, and even whistled a little, ignoring the strange look from

Dorrie that he caught with the corner of his eye. They walked along, holding hands, for a good fifteen minutes before Jules finally stopped.

"This is it."

Dorrie looked around before shaking her head. "It's an empty space. This is what you wanted me to see?"

Jules nodded and put an arm around her shoulder. "It's a good piece of land." He urged her forward until they were standing in the center of the wide plot. "And no one would ever get tired of looking at that." He swept his free arm forward, pointing at the sparkling bay in the distance.

"It's beautiful," Dorrie agreed.

"I bought it."

She wiggled out from under his arm and turned to face him. "You bought this land?"

"For us." Jules smiled at the stunned look on her face. "You didn't seem to take to any of the houses we looked at, so I thought we might build our own. I've already talked to your da about it, and he's going to come up tomorrow and have a look."

"A house?" Dorrie glanced around, wonder in her voice. "You want to build a house for us?"

"There's a lot I want us to do together, Dorrie. But there are some things I need to say to you first." He captured one of her hands with his and drew her over to a flat-topped rock. He picked up the single red rose he'd placed there earlier that morning and took a long, deep breath.

His nerves were kicking up until he stared into her deep-brown eyes. Just like he had ever since he'd known her, he could see the smile in them, and suddenly the whole world became a perfect place. Jules felt the familiar warmth from whenever his wife was near spread through him.

"I'm sorry. That's what I need to say first. I treated you

badly, and I…" His words were cut off when Dorrie put a hand over his mouth.

"You don't have to say any more, Jules. I'm sorry too. I should have come to you first about Mam's brothers." She paused as moisture gathered in her eyes. "I do trust you. With all my heart. I need you to believe that."

Jules kissed her palm before gently removing her hand. "I never stopped believing it, honey. My mouth got away from me because I was afraid I'd have to hang your mam's brothers, and that she would hate me for that." He blew out a short breath. "And you would too."

Dorrie rose on her toes and placed a soft kiss on his lips. "It would have been sad, but not your fault. Mam's brothers did this to themselves. You had no hand in it. Mam knows that. And so do I." She looked around again before smiling at him. "If building me a house is your way of apologizing, I should tell you that single rose you're holding would have been fine."

He chuckled and leaned down to steal another kiss. Straightening up, his smile faded into a serious look. "I'll never be mean to you again, Dorrie. That's a promise. And I'll never sleep apart from you if we're in the same house." He grinned. "Or the same city, or within a day's riding distance of each other."

She laughed. "Is that also a promise, Marshal?"

"It is." He cupped a large hand around her cheek. "And there's one more thing."

He sank to one knee as Dorrie gasped, holding the rose out to her. Jules smiled when she tugged on his hand, unsuccessfully trying to get him to stand up again.

"Charles once told me he named his gaming hall after his wife, because she was a prefect crimson rose, beautiful and full of the deep color for all the love that makes a woman special. I love you, Dorrie McKenzie. I've loved you for a very long time, and will love you until time stops for me." When she went perfectly still, he lifted her hand and kissed his mother's wedding ring that his wife now wore on her finger. "I should have told you that and given you a proper proposal the first time. So I'm asking you now. Will you marry me?"

Dorrie surprised him when she sank down and knelt right along with him.

"I'm already your wife, Jules McKenzie, and I wouldn't change that for all the proper proposals in the middle of the town square. I've loved you for most of my life, and I always will."

Jules closed his eyes a moment and savored the joy humming all through him. When he opened them again, it was to stare into the eyes of the most beautiful woman in the world. He got to his feet, drawing Dorrie up with him, then ran a gentle finger down her soft cheek.

"Is that a fact?"

His wife was laughing when he pulled her into his arms and pressed his lips to hers.

AUTHOR'S NOTE:

To My Readers ~

I hope you enjoyed Dorrie and Jules' story. There's something about a romance novel that will never go out of style. Whether its set in the past or contemporary, racy or sweet, it's hard to pass up a good love story.

I want to take this opportunity to thank you, the reader. Time is precious, and I so appreciate you spending some of yours to read my books. I enjoy writing, and am very lucky to be able to do just that. And even luckier to have someone read my stories.

Thank you, and happy reading!

Cathryn Chandler

You can pick-up the any of my other romance novels on Amazon, or read for free with your Kindle Unlimited membership!

Be the first to receive notification of the release of the next novel in the Crimson Rose series. **Sign up** today at:

http://eepurl.com/bLBOtX

If you'd like to know what my latest projects are, and how they're coming along, drop by my website at:
www.CathrynChandler.com

Follow Cathryn Chandler on your favorite media:

Facebook:
https://www.facebook.com/cathrynchandlerauthor/?fref=ts

Twitter: @catcauthor

Website/blog: www.cathrynchandler.com

All authors strive to deliver the highest quality work to their readers. If you found a spelling or typographical error in this book, please let me know so I can correct it immediately. Please use the contact form on my website at: www.cathrynchandler.com Thank you!

And finally: If you like mysteries, I also write those under the pen name: Cat Chandler, and they are also available on Amazon.

Made in the USA
Monee, IL
20 January 2022